T0367225

THE
MONTEVIDEO
BRIEF

J. H. GELERNTER

THE
MONTEVIDEO
BRIEF

A Thomas Grey Novel

W. W. NORTON & COMPANY
Celebrating a Century of Independent Publishing

Copyright © 2023 by J. H. Gelernter

For information about permission to reproduce selections from this book, write to Permissions, W. W. Norton & Company, Inc., 500 Fifth Avenue, New York, NY 10110

For information about special discounts for bulk purchases, please contact W. W. Norton Special Sales at specialsales@wwnorton.com or 800-233-4830

Manufacturing by Lake Book Manufacturing
Production manager: Anna Oler

ISBN 978-1-324-02036-3

W. W. Norton & Company, Inc., 500 Fifth Avenue, New York, N.Y. 10110
www.wwnorton.com

W. W. Norton & Company Ltd., 15 Carlisle Street, London W1D 3BS

1 2 3 4 5 6 7 8 9 0

This book is dedicated to my beloved New Jersey Devils.
When are you bums going to retire Sergei Brylin's number?

THE
MONTEVIDEO
BRIEF

Prologue

AFTER WINNING HER REVOLUTION, the United States had lost the protection of the Royal Navy, and her merchant fleet quickly became a plaything for pirates. In deference to a public desire not to have any sort of standing military, the American navy was kept small and used infrequently. Then, in November of 1803, Barbary pirates seized one of America's few warships, USS *Philadelphia*, and turned her into a floating battery in Tripoli harbor. The United States might have followed the European powers—all of whom had lost ships and crews to the Barbary pirates—and either paid the pasha's tribute or abandoned *Philadelphia*'s men to slavery. Instead, the humiliating seizure of *Philadelphia* became the blow which spurred the US to stop turning the other cheek.

From the start of the nineteenth century, American naval power was, in the main, confined to just six American-built heavy frigates. With so small a navy, the United States decided to deal with the Tripolitans by playing their strong suit, irregular warfare. The job of attending to Tripoli was left to the retinue of the third of the six frigates, USS *Constitution*. To defeat the Tripolitans, *Constitution* landed eight marines on the shores of Tripoli, east of the city proper, and then dispatched a single ketch into Tripoli's harbor. The marines' job was to orchestrate a surprise attack from the rear. The job of the ketch—named *Intrepid* and commanded by Stephen Decatur—was to blow up *Philadelphia*, opening the city to a naval bombardment from the front.

As *Intrepid* passed the mole and entered Tripoli's inner harbor, Decatur gave the helm to his Maltese pilot. With only a single reef shaken out of the small mainsail, their way was slow. Decatur waited till *Intrepid* was just a few dozen yards from *Philadelphia*'s mainchains, then signaled for the Maltese pilot to make his hail:

"Ahoy the frigate," said the pilot, in Arabic. "We have just sailed through a terrible great blow"—this was true, in fact; the weather in the southern Mediterranean had been filthy—"and we've lost our bowers. Can we make fast to you till daybreak?"

Dim sounds of discussion floated down from *Philadelphia*'s quarterdeck. From an American intelligence man inside Tripoli, Decatur knew that *Philadelphia*'s magazine was stocked and her guns manned and ready to be run out. If her crew conceived the slightest notion of what *Intrepid* was up to, the little ketch would instantly be reduced to splinters and driftwood.

But after a few moments' talk, word came down from the quarterdeck granting permission for *Intrepid* to seize herself to *Philadelphia*. As she sailed closer, Decatur could see that *Philadelphia*'s gunports were open.

Philadelphia threw *Intrepid* a line so she could pull herself alongside. At the same time, a voice began to shout in Arabic. Decatur spoke no Arabic, but was able to pick out the word "Americanos."

In a calm and steady voice, Decatur gave the order "Hold fast, men; wait on my word." Ten very long seconds followed, with the Tripolitans beginning to run out the guns, and the Americans heaving *Intrepid* closer and closer to *Philadelphia*'s hull. There was the low peel of wood hitting wood, and Decatur shouted, "Now, boys! Let's take her!"

He was the first man to leap from *Intrepid* onto *Philadelphia*'s side, grabbing hold of her mainchains and pulling himself upward—

Philadelphia's main deck was twelve feet higher than *Intrepid*'s, but Decatur's crew, with the skill of able seamen, rushed up her side like so many monkeys. Some went in through the gunports; others over the gunwales, and in seconds the ship was a frenzied battlefield. To keep the affair quiet as possible, the Americans carried no guns. The fighting was hand to hand and saber to scimitar, and brutal. In a desperate, bloody battle that lasted less than five minutes, the Americans killed twenty Tripolitans and took one prisoner; the rest went over the side, swimming for shore, shouting for help and a counterattack. Decatur could see a boat at quayside loading with palace guards, pushing off, pulling towards them. Soon they would have to repel boarders. Behind him lanterns were handed up from *Intrepid*; eight in all. They were handed out and Decatur gave the order, "Go the fire teams."

Eight two-man teams spilled down the hatchways; each man had studied drawings of the ship and knew just where he was headed. Five to storerooms, one to the gunroom, one to the berth deck, and one to the cockpit. Each fire team had its fire—its lantern—carried by one man, while the other carried turpentine-soaked rags and a three-inch spermaceti candle. The rags were placed and the candles readied; Decatur checked each room and then shouted for all to hear:

"Fire!"

The candles were lit from the lanterns and dropped on the rags. The firemen beat a hasty retreat to the main deck; Decatur followed them up. As expected, *Philadelphia*'s harbor-bound, dry timbers lit explosively. Decatur barely escaped the columns of fire pouring up the hatches.

"Back to *Intrepid*!" shouted Decatur over the roaring fire, and all hands began to climb and jump back to the ketch, which was already spreading sail. Decatur was last aboard, dropping down onto *Intrepid*'s deck and giving the order to cast off *Philadelphia*'s line. The line caught and Decatur cut it free with his saber. Men seized oars and pushed off the burning hulk—but the fire created a powerful backdraft, and even rowing for their lives, *Intrepid*'s crew couldn't escape the pull. Decatur grabbed the tiller and turned *Intrepid*'s bow back towards *Philadelphia*—filling her sails—and then tacked away just short of the fire. And then she was sailing large and flying up the harbor channel towards the waiting *Constitution*. Not a single American had been killed or wounded.

ONSHORE, an American intelligence man named Philo Parker watched the inferno and stroked his beard. The beard was an unaccustomed addition to the mustache he wore normally; it was part of his disguise as a Moroccan Jew on pilgrimage to Jerusalem. Behind his beard and robes, Parker had gathered all the information *Constitution* and Decatur could require regarding the harbor, the currents and prevailing winds, the gunboats and batteries and the manning of the captured frigate. These data were written in lime juice over a prefabricated Arabic letter and delivered to *Constitution* by way of the Danish consul in Tripoli, Nicholas Nissen.

As Parker watched, the *Philadelphia*'s magazine exploded. The blast nearly knocked him off his feet. A few hundred yards to his right, every pane of glass in the pasha's palace shattered.

In the morning—with *Constitution* looming at the harbor mouth, and no *Philadelphia* to stop her—the Pasha of Tripoli sued for peace. Parker took charge of redeeming the *Philadelphia* crewmen who'd already been sold as slaves; he was also obliged to inform the eight commando marines that, with Tripoli already capitulated, they were obliged to disband the small army they'd raised, and give back the pirate city they'd captured. ("Derna," it was called—the marines hadn't intended to capture it, but when they'd requested innocent passage, its potentate responded with the challenge, "My head or yours.")

A month later, Parker would read in a Gibraltar newspaper that Horatio Nelson had called the destruction of *Philadelphia* "the most bold and daring act of the age." Then at breakfast, Parker glanced over the paper's summary of the event, chuckled to himself, and buttered a scone.

I

June 9th, 1804
Vienna

THE GRAND FESTIVAL HALL—so called—of the Palais Lobkowitz had been filled with about two hundred chairs, all facing the east end of the room, where an orchestra were tuning their instruments. Thomas Grey was seated in the last row, watching a tempestuous conductor walking among his musicians, stopping here and there to make some remark to one of them, once grabbing an oboe from a frightened-looking member of the woodwinds and proceeding to tune it himself before handing it back with undisguised contempt.

He looked to be about Grey's age; actually he was a decade older. Though Grey had never before seen him in the flesh, he knew the man well by reputation. He was shorter than Grey had imagined—quite short, if he'd been an Englishman, still somewhat short for a European, at about five foot three. His close-cropped, forward-combed hair made him look something like a Roman consul who'd accidentally been dressed in a high-collared coat, over an even higher-collared shirt, brown breeches, and high black jackboots.

The conductor's height notwithstanding, there exuded from him an aura of command that put Grey in mind of Grey's chief, the head of the British secret service, Sir Edward Banks. Though perhaps that had something to do with both men wearing their own hair. Even Grey, who preferred to follow Sir Edward's example in eschewing wigs, was wearing one this evening, so as not to stand out among a crowd of Vienna's elite.

These particular elite were friends and friends-of-friends of the seventh Prince Lobkowitz, Joseph Franz Maximilian. Grey's invitation had been obtained by—or, it would be more accurate to say, purloined from—Vienna's British consul, who parted with it reluctantly and with considerable irritation. Prince Lobkowitz was Europe's most famous patron of music, and the evening was to be the private debut of the newest composition of his most famous protégé, Ludwig van Beethoven. Apparently, the symphony—Beethoven's third— had been named, by Beethoven himself, the *Sinfonia Bonaparte*. In a city where Napoleon was, as a rule, either disliked or hated, it was a bold statement. But Beethoven had the stature to do as he liked. And Grey assumed he didn't know Napoleon's work the way Grey did.

This thought brought Grey back to his purpose in attending the concert. He was here to take possession of an extremely expensive article, purchased—half in advance, half on delivery—from the Spanish ambassador to the Kingdom of Prussia, who—well known in German circles for his love of modern music—was a frequent guest at the private concerts of Prince Lobkowitz. Prior to his elevation to ambassador, he had been one of the secretaries of the "Prince of Peace," Manuel Godoy. From serving as a trusted adviser of Spanish king Charles IV, Godoy had effectively taken complete control of Spain and its government. His title "Prince of Peace" came from his frequent involvement in the negotiations of peace treaties among the European powers; in 1802, he had negotiated the Treaty of Amiens, a brief peace between France and Britain. After the negotiations concluded, Napoleon sent a disgusted letter to Charles IV calling Godoy the true king of Spain and informing the oblivious Charles that his wife, Queen María Luisa, was Godoy's mistress. So strong was Godoy's grip on Spain that, when his bodyguard intercepted the letter in the king's mail, Godoy not only allowed it to be delivered, but allowed it to become an article of court gossip.

Shortly after Amiens, Godoy had negotiated a secret treaty between Spain and France. At the time, the two countries had an outstanding peace agreement under which Spain agreed to remain neutral in exchange for an assurance from Napoleon that he would not cross the Pyrenees. In the two years since Amiens, it had taken British intelligence enormous effort to confirm that there *was* a secret treaty, to learn then the names of the small group of Spaniards and Frenchmen who were privy to its contents, and then to identify one of these who would be amenable to unveiling the treaty in exchange for a great deal of money.

One of Grey's colleagues in Spain had, at great length, identified as the best candidate Fernandino María Basco y Anda. Among his other duties as one of Godoy's private secretaries, Basco had been a courier of drafts between the negotiating parties when they met, in early 1803, in San Ildefonso. And he had been chosen to write fair a copy of the final document. Tonight, Basco y Anda—who, like most Spaniards, found the almost fantastic arrogance of Godoy highly objectionable—would accept the second half of his bribe, and disclose the secret compact. At the ambassador's unwavering insistence that nothing be put in writing, Grey would receive the information by word of mouth.

Grey felt mild guilt at having been chosen for this most pleasant of assignments. Colleagues of his in Iberia and the Holy Roman Empire had spent years working towards the elucidation of the secret treaty, but here Grey was, the man at the command performance, where the maestro of the orchestra was the maestro himself. Grey had been chosen for the job for no more complex a reason than his facility with language; he spoke German better than his colleagues in Spain, and Spanish better than his colleagues in Germany.

"There's an extra horn," said an elderly, ill-looking man now seated beside Grey.

He'd been escorted into the hall by several attendants, one of whom supported him while the rest cleared the way for him to process to the front of the room. The man, conducting them with his cane, made it clear he would go no farther than the last row, where Grey rose and helped the unfamiliar man into a seat. The attendants, some of whom must have been in the man's employ, and others of whom wore the livery of the House of Lobkowitz, had hovered momentarily, like hummingbirds at a hyacinth, looking anxious. With a gracious smile and a polite but expressly firm tone, the man had said to them, "*Raus, bitter,*" and then to their hurt faces, "*Danke schön, meine Kinder.*"

"There's an extra horn," he'd said, in English.

Grey wondered what anglicism had given him away. Though, with the British consul's invitation in hand, he was not incognito.

"I'm afraid I don't know enough of music to see it," said Grey, in German.

The man answered again in English.

"Do you mind if we speak in English? I haven't in some while, and I like to stretch the old muscles."

"Of course, sir."

"But I am prevented; they are beginning, see."

The man pointed with an uncomfortable, swollen finger towards the front of the room. Beethoven was centered before the orchestra, facing the audience. At English concerts, Grey had seen modern orchestras conducted in the new style of Haydn, using a baton rather than a staff. Here in Haydn's city it was unsurprising to see Beethoven doing the same; facing the audience with the long baton in his hand, he looked like an assassin holding a long dagger, prepared to cut, without passion, someone's throat. With a slightly slow stroke left to right, he silenced the audience. His voice was deep, particularly for a man of his height, and it commanded the complete attention of everyone in the room. He spoke in German.

"No doubt over the course of the evening, you have had, or will have, a chance to thank His Serene Highness, the Prince Lobkowitz, for his grace in creating this evening."

Grey could see the prince, seated at the center of the first, hemicircular row, in a throne of modest extravagance.

"I must add my own deep thanks; to you he is prince; to me he is something even greater, a patron. He does me great honor in his patronage; I hope it will prove some honor in return that I dedicate to him my *Sinfonia Bonaparte*."

Dedicating a piece to one man while naming it after another struck Grey as mildly absurd, but he wasn't familiar with the professional conventions of music. In any case, the audience—Grey included—stood to applaud the prince for having won this dedication. This went on for about a quarter minute before the prince waved for everyone to resume his seat, and extended an open hand towards Beethoven, telling him he might begin.

Beethoven nodded and turned to face the orchestra. He raised his baton over his head—it was pointed directly upward—then brought it down violently, and the orchestra struck the first chord. From the first instant, the music threw everyone in the room off-balance. After a very short pause, the same giant chord was struck again—the audience waited for the second repetition, the natural feeling (Grey's, in any case) was for a natural set of three. But instead, the theme began. An exceptionally simple theme, so simple that Grey—as he was, no student of music—recognized it as a seesaw back and forth through a simple major triad. It sounded almost pastoral, but as it ended, the theme crashed into a C-sharp. In his chest, Grey felt the building of a sense of unease . . . as if the entire emotion built up by an opera, by a *Don Giovanni*—the tension of the statue of the commendatore dragging Giovanni to hell—had been squeezed into a dozen notes. And then the music was back to its harmless, pastoral major triad. Grey cocked his head to one side, an unconscious movement of confusion that bordered on concern. He felt the tension of the audience around him. The theme built up, from the almost-thin sound of a horn to the whole orchestra, and exploded again. And now the theme was broken up, and strung over individual blasts of music, with concussive pauses between them. And then the flutes, harmlessly playing the pastoral again—only to be beaten back by the angry horns asserting a furious rushing recapitulation, sliding through a second theme into a third, this one soft and smooth and comforting. The music danced from deep

bass to high treble, was quiet and then built up again to the booming reworking of the original theme mixed with the new ones—and
more stabs of the orchestra with abrupt pauses. And then another new
theme? Or just the descent back towards the original. Now the stabs
had no pauses between them, and a repetition of the theme was played
by the full orchestra—with the jarring sharp note now omitted. This
time it was triumphant, as if Haydn or Mozart had written it. Fiery
and energetic, but familiar. The tension in Grey's chest eased somewhat. The music pulled him along like an eight-in-hand team of wild
horses, but now they were running over ground he recognized. The
strings danced to the forefront of the music, playfully, then building
to another giant but natural restating of the theme.

The tempo began to slow dramatically, like a boat coasting slowly
up to a pier. And then the original theme burst back in, in a low
register . . . not overfast, but full of some powder waiting to deto-
nate. And now the playful strings sounded less playful, dancing on
top of the deep theme . . . the trivial but very deep original theme,
now passing through different chords, different triads. Colors flashed
through Grey's head with each variation. Stabs now, again, fragments
of the alternate themes, dueling with the principal.

And then, from nowhere, a key change—or so Grey thought—
and a new wandering, scale-ish theme. Grey didn't know; couldn't
find the correct words with which to describe it to himself. The deep
strings and the high horns were fighting, not with each other, but
beside each other, like two men shoulder to shoulder on a barricade.

The horns pulled back, and strings began to play a sort of vamp,
and very quietly.

A horn player entered too early, playing the original theme—a
mistake? And then a moment later the whole orchestra was playing
the theme again.

Was there another key change? Grey couldn't follow it. The music
bombarded the room like a broadside from HMS *Victory*. A rolling
broadside, actually. And with *Victory* fighting both sides, as she had
at St. Vincent.

Then peace. Flutes. Quiet. And then building, speeding back towards some theme. The same chord, over and over. Then back to the theme.

Another new key? Or just a new chord? And the strings were playing their own playful reordering of the pastoral. New and flighty. Noncommittal. And then another buildup—all the cannon firing at once, and a new version of the theme—doubling the second to the last note, excluding the last. Stabbing, giant chords.

DUNN.

DUNN.

Doooooon.

The first movement ended, and Grey felt as if he'd been punched in the face. He'd never heard anything like this before. But he had no time to consider it before the second movement began.

It was slow; quiet and mournful. A dirge. A wailing from the horns. The theme from the first movement went unstated, but lingered at the edges. There was an echo of it. It was a ghost and this was its funeral music. The music built up—in Grey's mind—along those lines; as if it were a choir of mourners gradually swelled by new arrivals. There was a moment of flickering anxiety. The mourners were standing on the edge of a cliff, looking down into a chasm, wondering if they'd fall headlong into it; backing away, choosing to absent themselves from felicity a while. And then they were reassembling—a brigade of mourners—or, as Grey saw it now, a brigade in mourning, which had now to put grief behind it and begin to think of the next battle. And now, to march towards it. Was this the French army or the Austrian? Perhaps both.

Flickers of optimism broke through. Sun through clouds. But the clouds were still there. A new, march tempo. Was the pastoral theme back? Something was wrong with it, it felt upside down. It was quiet, very quiet. The army was disappearing over the horizon. And then it was gone.

And then the third movement rushed in. Water through a flood-gate. Boys running alongside a triumphant army as it marched home, falling in step with the soldiers, holding sticks like swords and muskets. It was joyous. Triumphal . . . With small hints of menace lurking beneath, quickly stamped away by the joy of the revelers. Wives rushing to greet their husbands. The slowing of the pace, greeting friends, accepting drinks . . . and then building up again to triumph, as the men went into their own homes, with their own families; with their wives, and then shut their doors behind them. As quickly as it had flooded in, the third movement was over.

And a dizzying descent down a new theme into the fourth movement. A low plucking of the music, a farmer's dancing echo of the symphony's theme, a cheerful, expressive recapitulation—though again, with hints of occasional, minor menace—and then outright menace, like one of those Slavic sword dances. (From where had the Slavs come?) But still there was considerable joy in the music. Maybe these were the sounds of the festival in the town square to celebrate the army's return . . . The music was spreading out into thick, broad harmonies. And then stabs—painful stabs of dissonance. And a new tempo, rapid, a rapid walking pace. Ready to break into a run, but holding itself back. And the joy was peeling away, a sort of grim sangfroid was setting in. It was neither happy nor sad, just forceful.

And then it finally did break into its run—and the triumph returned, with the music running, bounding over obstacles, its sword raised high in the air, leading troops of music behind it.

And then it was over.

Grey felt slightly intoxicated. He let out the breath he'd been holding and shook his head. He looked over at the elderly man sitting beside him. The man's face was a curious mix of wonderment and unsurprise.

"I've never heard anything like that before," said Grey.

"No," said the man. "No one has."

THE APPLAUSE WAS MUTED AND BRIEF. And yet as the crowd rose to its feet—allowing footmen to clear the chairs and quickly return the auditorium to a festival hall—a dense pack began to form around Beethoven, everyone wanting a word or a shake of the hand of the famous composer. Beethoven nodded politely, though unsmilingly, to several people, but spoke only to Prince Lobkowitz. Then he turned and walked through the orchestra and disappeared into some private side room. The prince said something to those who'd been anxious for Beethoven's attention, then followed after Beethoven, with a simply dressed man of about twenty beside him. Grey turned away from the fuss, to help the old man beside him to his feet—but saw the man's attendants had already returned. One of them—more or less inadvertently—elbowed Grey as he rushed to take the old man's arm. On a normal evening Grey might have made a point of this, but feeling as he did, he simply backed away and removed a cigarillo case from his pocket.

The young man who'd accompanied the Prince Lobkowitz towards Beethoven's withdrawal now appeared again and spoke something into the ear of the old man, who nodded and—waving his attendants away; using only his cane—began to walk forward, with the young man beside him—presumably towards the prince and Beethoven. Grey wondered who the man was, but didn't have time to dwell on the question. He had a rendezvous to effect.

One side of the hall was studded with French doors that opened onto a low terrace. Grey opened one and stepped out into the warm night, leaving the bustle of the party behind. Footmen had started to appear with trays of champagne. Grey lit a cigarillo and waited.

A few minutes later, he heard one of the doors open behind him—releasing a flood of party sounds onto the terrace. Grey turned; it was the young man who had escorted the old man, and the prince. Could he possibly be the Spanish ambassador to Prussia? Grey very much doubted it, but all the same, gave the passphrase, to make certain.

"May I offer you a cigarillo, sir?" he said, in German.

"Oh—why yes, thank you. Very kind," said the man, in German.

This was not the correct countersign—had he been Grey's rendezvous, he should have said, "No, I am not in the smoking vein." So who was this man? Grey held out his case for the man to take one of the long, thin cigars.

"I enjoy trying different blends," he said, as Grey ignited a match for him. "It's a sort of proxy for seeing the world."

He smiled. "Thank you, Mr. . . .?"

"Blake. Thomas Blake." Grey used his pseudonym of the night, and offered his hand. The young man shook it.

"Ferdinand Ries."

Grey nodded, and for a moment they smoked in silence, both looking back towards the party.

"I couldn't help but notice you speaking to the prince," said Grey after a moment.

"Yes," said Ries. "Well, not speaking perhaps—delivering a message. I am Herr van Beethoven's secretary."

"Ah," said Grey. "That must be a most fascinating employment."

"It is, sir. I am also one of his pupils."

"I didn't realize he taught."

"Yes," said Ries, "though not regularly. In fact, I am his only student at the moment, which is how I was pressed into secretarial duty, ha ha. Herr van Beethoven was briefly a student of my father's in Bonn, and Beethoven does not forget favors."

Grey nodded.

"Do you mind if I ask you who the elderly gentleman was whom I sat beside during the concert? I saw that you escorted him off as well."

Ries looked slightly surprised, only for a moment, and then—after taking a pull on the cigarillo—said, "That was the composer Herr Haydn."

"Haydn?" said Grey. "Well, I'll be goddamned. Pardon me. I wish I had known."

"I gather you're not a German," said Ries.

"I'm English," said Grey.

Ries nodded. "Of course Haydn was in your country for many visits. But, of course, I should not make the vulgar mistake of assuming anyone has had the unearned luck that I have had, in making the acquaintance of some of these great men."

Grey nodded. Sensible fellow.

"If I may ask—without intruding on the confidence of your employer—was Haydn Beethoven's teacher?"

"According to Haydn, yes," said Ries, with a laugh. "According to Beethoven—well—it depends on the hour of the day. They have a somewhat uneasy, yet very close, friendship. Though I should not say more."

Grey nodded, and for another moment they smoked in silence.

"I've never heard anything like the Symphony *Bonaparte*," said Grey, finally.

"No," said Ries. "Nor had I. Perhaps you have read that Herr van Beethoven has been ill. Quite ill. I have hoped that this is an excision of the passions which caused the illness, and which it has caused."

Grey nodded. Another man was stepping out onto the terrace now. Grey had not wanted to force a quick end to the Ries conversation, for fear of its seeming suspicious—but he suspected this new man was his Spanish ambassador. It was time to move on.

"I hadn't read of his illness; I'm sorry to hear of it—one of Herr Haydn's men is looking for someone," said Grey, gesturing inside at an imaginary footman. "You, perhaps?"

"Yes, possibly—if he is not, I should in any case return before I am missed."

Ries smiled again, dropped the cigarillo butt and stepped on it. "My thanks to you, Mr. Blake, for the smoke."

"And to you, Mr. Ries, for the company."

They shook hands and Ries walked back into the party, and Grey turned to a man who had, for the last few minutes, been lingering at the edge of the terrace, looking out into the night.

"May I offer you a cigarillo?" said Grey, approaching him.

"No, thank you; I am not in the smoking vein tonight."

"They are very good, though," said Grey, opening his cigarillo case; opening, this time, the false bottom, revealing a letter of credit in the amount of twenty-five thousand pounds sterling, issued by an agreed-upon Geneva bank, notarized with a signature recognizable to the ambassador.

The ambassador nodded; then shook his head as if he'd changed his mind. "No, thank you, I must decline; my health, you know."

Grey nodded and closed the case, palming, as he did, the now-approved letter of credit.

Speaking in the same quiet but conversational tone of voice, the ambassador said:

"The Treaty of San Ildefonso says this: In recognition of France's policy of peace towards the Spanish Crown and empire, Spain commits to declare war on Great Britain, to close its ports to all British ships, martial or merchant, and to put all its harbors, in Iberia and the empire, at the disposal of France. The reason for the treaty's secrecy is that it provides that these terms will not come into effect until the arrival in Madrid of a final Armada shipment of Spanish gold and silver from our mines in South America, without which Spain would not be able to prosecute a war, and whose shipment during a war would be to risk its seizure by the British navy. The shipment will consist, in its full extent, of no less than of five hundred and fifty bars of iron, one thousand six hundred of tin, one hundred and fifty thousand of gold, along with five million minted gold and silver dollars."

Grey resisted the impulse to whistle. "When will the treasure fleet leave South America?"

"I don't know. No one in Europe does. To protect and secure this shipment, the details are delegated in their entirety to the governor of the River Plate. All that can be said with certainty is that it must arrive before the end of this year, or else Spain must declare war on Britain without it, or else be invaded by France. The treaty allows only for these three possibilities. These are the data I have, in their entirety. Let us shake hands and go our separate ways back to the party."

"How many ships of treasure, and how many of them men-o'-war?"

"As I said, Mr. Blake, no one in Europe knows anything more than I have already said. This is all. And I must go."

He stuck out his hand. Grey shook it, and slid discreetly from his palm to the Spaniard's the letter of credit.

Basco y Anda was already walking back towards the hall, back inside where Grey could hear a mix of argument and laughter. Grey was sorely tempted to follow him . . . Having now the introduction to Ries, having exchanged a few words with Haydn, perhaps he might have a chance to speak to one of the great men before the evening was through. But he knew the news he carried could not wait. Not an hour. Not a minute. In no more than six months, Britain would be at war with one of the richest and most powerful empires in the world. But now, for the moment, it was Britain that had the initiative. And there was not a moment to lose.

Grey walked quickly along the party's edge and out into the streets of Vienna.

2

TWO WEEKS LATER AND BACK IN LONDON, Grey was seated in his office in the old Admiralty House on Whitehall, the quarters of British naval intelligence. Having expended what he considered to be an adequate quantity of time wading through a month's missed correspondence, he had turned—along with a piece of hard cheese and a fractional loaf of bread—to new and detailed drawings of the entablature of the Parthenon, newly published by Britain's ambassador to the Sublime Porte, Lord Elgin. They were extraordinary. Magnificent. Sculpture with the complexity and naturalism of a Renaissance painting, but two thousand years older. Grey could imagine that seeing them in person, they would have the same concussive power of that *Sinfonia Bonaparte*, which he couldn't get out of his head.

"At luncheon?"

Grey looked up. For some time he'd been expecting a messenger summoning him to Sir Edward Banks's office, but standing in his open doorway was, instead, his colleague George Fairbanks, one of the men with whom Grey shared a secretary.

"Breakfast, I think," said Grey. "What time is it?"

"Where's the Breguet?" said Fairbanks, pulling his watch from his waistcoat.

"Being resprung," said Grey.

"Half past one. As it is breakfast, though, can I give you lunch at my club?"

"I'm not sure when I'll be through here," said Grey.

"Neither am I," said Fairbanks, "but shall we say five, tentatively? If you arrive before I do, have them give you a drink for me."

"As you like," said Grey. "With my thanks."

"Arrived from the continent this morning?"

Grey nodded. "And where are you arriving from, at half past one?"

"Lord's," said Fairbanks.

"Playing or watching?"

"What a fellow you are, Grey. Playing. Old Harrovians."

"Cricket's not really my game," said Grey. "Happy and Glorious, were you?"

"I don't know; I imagine they're still playing. One of the company youngsters arrived at the grounds just a few hours ago and told me Sir Edward wanted a word. Fortunately the boys were able to find a substitute for me—though to find a true substitute, I'm afraid, would be something impossible"—a chuckle from Grey—"but I'm afraid when I left, we were much more batted against than batting."

Grey laughed.

"Have you seen him yet? Sir Edward."

Fairbanks nodded. "But he told me wait."

"Pardon me, gentlemen," said a junior member of Sir Edward's staff, standing behind George Fairbanks and looking embarrassed at having intruded on the conversation. "Mr. Grey, Sir Edward wonders if he could have a word."

"Thank you, Blakeney," said Grey, standing. "If you'll excuse me, George."

"Until five," said Fairbanks.

ENTERING SIR EDWARD BANKS'S OUTER OFFICE, Grey nodded to the two secretaries on duty, in turn, as he passed them and approached the ebony door that guarded Sir Edward's inner sanctum.

"Please to go in directly," said the second.

"Thank you," said Grey; he opened the door and stepped into his chief's office, approached Sir Edward's desk and stood silently, waiting for Sir Edward to look up from his work.

After about twenty seconds, he did. "Grey," he said. "Please to be seated."

Grey sat down in one of the two well-stuffed wingbacks that faced Sir Edward's desk.

"Before I come to the point, I must ask you, how was the concert?"

"Furious," said Grey. "I'm afraid I don't know enough about music to say much more than that."

Sir Edward nodded thoughtfully. "In any case—coming to the point: This Spanish business is tremendous, but I'm compelled to disappoint you and say that I am not sending you to South America."

Grey leaned forward slightly; his shoulders tightened. "Sir?"

"I'm sending Fairbanks."

Sir Edward had leaned forward and begun to pack his pipe. The delay gave Grey a chance to think of three or four dozen good arguments against his losing the assignment. Even though, in justice, it had not been his to begin with.

"Fairbanks is a good man," said Grey, when the silence of the pipe-packing became too much to bear.

"Yes," said Sir Edward, striking a match and igniting the tobacco. He took a few stout puffs to get it going, then shook out the match and turned back to Grey. "His being a good man is not, however, why I'm giving him the treasure fleet assignment. It is because I cannot in good conscience send you, at this moment, to the South Atlantic. In the last year and half, you have crossed Iberia and France, gone to the Raj and back, then Frankfurt, France, now Vienna. You have been seriously wounded—that is to say, suffered wounds that might have killed you—at least twice, and I cannot say how many less severe injuries you've had. I don't intend to use you up, Grey. Spend you like a cannon that's been fired too much, too quickly, and bursts. Destroying itself, and others."

"Sir," said Grey, interjecting, "I assure you I much prefer the work to inactivity. If you're worried about my health or fitness for the job—I can say only that they're much better preserved through action than inaction."

Sir Edward nodded. "If you didn't feel that way, Tom, you'd be no good to me." He smiled, slightly. "But you are incapable of sound judgment in the matter. Fairbanks worked on the San Ildefonso business in Spain; he is perfectly qualified to resume working on it. Beginning today, you will take sixth months' leave."

"Sir, with respect—"

"That will be all, Grey; I've work to do. Speak to Willys and then draw an advance salary from the paymaster. We'll speak in the new year."

Grey stood. Sir Edward had already resumed reading some memorandum. Grey walked silently out of the room, a sour taste in his mouth.

Closing the ebony door behind him, he turned right and walked through the open door of Aaron Willys's office.

"Aaron, may I ask what in the dear's name is going on? I understood from you—and I think, quite clearly—that this matter was mine to pursue to its conclusion. I would otherwise have declined the assignment to Vienna and undertaken a personal commitment, of the greatest importance, in St. Petersburg. I believe the word 'duty' was used. Rather shabbily, I would say, if it was meant only to keep me on hand to use as a pageboy."

Willys was sitting behind his desk, writing.

"Sit down, Tom, and stop chattering. What stuff."

He put his pen down and shook his head. "Let me begin by reminding you that this is not a social club where you pick and choose which invitations to accept and which to decline. Let me continue by saying—Tom—that despite our long and close association, if you ever again impute to me dishonesty, I will ask you for a meeting."

There was a moment of silence. Willys was stone-faced. Grey teetered between anger and contrition. Contrition won.

"I apologize, Aaron. Without reserve. You are the last man to whom I would ever give the lie." Grey meant this with total sincerity, and Willys knew it.

"Well, let's forget it then. Tom, I understand why you're angry; I'm afraid when I chose you for the Hispano-frog treaty I assumed that the details would relate to troop commitments or port agreements upon a declaration of war, or something of that nature. The field of play I anticipated did not include a journey to the far corners of the Spanish empire."

"You act as if a journey to the Viceroyalty of the River Plate were a trip to the interior of Sumatra. Surely Montevideo is one of the wealthiest ports in the world."

"Montevideo's wealth is not material, Tom—"

"Very droll—"

"When you delivered Bosco y's report this morning, Sir Edward did not ask my opinion on your constitution for travel. He told me he didn't wish to send you off again so far, so soon, and asked if it was Fairbanks or Macaulay who'd discovered the identity of Godoy's corruptible secretary. I told him Fairbanks. And that was an end to it. Unless there's anything else you recall about your meeting with the Spanish ambassador, I must get on. See the paymaster before you leave. Inform me if you intend leaving the country. And be back here, let us say, the first of February of next year."

"Very well, Aaron," said Grey, standing. "Shall I stop a few days at Buttle's so I'm easily found if you or Sir Edward decide you've made a terrible mistake?"

"That won't be necessary, Tom. Go home. Swim, hunt, read— walk Fred. Please to give my best to Mrs. Hubble and Canfield."

Grey nodded, realized there was nothing more to say, and said, "Fare you well, then."

He stood; Willys nodded back to him and said, "You as well, Tom."

Grey walked out of the office and past the secretaries, and once he was alone in the hall, directed a very pointed profanity to no one in particular.

FAIRBANKS'S CLUB was rather different from Grey's. It was called Spears and was nearby Lord's Cricket Grounds. Where Buttle's or

White's had gaming rooms, Spears had courts for tennis, boxing, fencing. There was a rat pit which was alleged to be long disused, though Grey had his doubts. After stopping at Buttle's to arrange to have his things sent on to his home in Sheerness, Grey indulged himself in a long, aimless walk, retrieved his Breguet, and finally arrived at Spears a minute or two before five. Fairbanks was there already, in the lounge, sipping sherry and going over some papers.

A pageboy led Grey over; Grey announced himself.

"George, if this was an invitation born of guilt, you needn't worry. The affair was yours to begin with; I'm glad to have gotten a concert out of it."

"Well, this way you can get a concert and a meal out of it, ey? Shall we go in?"

"To tell you the truth, I'd rather not—I'm heading back to Kent this evening after a few months' absence and my housekeeper will insist on stuffing me like a taxidermist. A drink, though, would set me up perfectly."

"Certainly, Tom. What will you have? This sherry is very good."

Grey shook his head. "Port. Tawny. Perhaps you've noticed the distressing move towards ruby ports of late."

Fairbanks smiled and waved over the wine steward, ordered Grey's port and another sherry for himself.

"Have you spent much time in South America?" said Fairbanks, as Grey tasted the port and nodded his approval.

"No, never more than a few weeks on a trip round the Cape."

"Good Hope?"

"Yes," said Grey. "I've only been around Cape Horn once, I believe, quite early on after joining the diplomatic." The Diplomatic Service being the publicly affected profession of Sir Edward's men.

"Have you spent much time there? Paulette had longed long to visit the interior of Brazil. She coveted a sloth." Paulette was Grey's late wife, who was never very far from his thoughts.

"What on earth is a sloth?"

"It's . . . well, I don't know exactly. I gather it's something between a bear and a monkey, which hangs upside down in trees and moves very slowly. If you happen to see one, do make an account of it for me."

"Certainly. Though I don't expect I'll end up far in the interior."

"No," said Grey, finishing his drink.

"Well, Tom, as we're not going to eat—how about a game of tennis?"

Grey had worried about something like this. Among his other minor eccentricities, Fairbanks was an irrepressible sportsman, and liked to inflict this irritating proclivity on his friends and colleagues.

"Tennis?" said Grey. "Wouldn't it be less exhausting if we beat each other to bloody pulps in one of the rings?"

"Come on, man. Haven't you just been on a comfortable coach trip around the continent? And with your housekeeper's stuffing on the horizon, I should have thought you'd wish to avoid becoming overfat."

Grey smiled sardonically.

"Very well," he said. "Though you'll have to refresh me on the particulars of this asinine game's asinine rules."

"Splendid!" said Fairbanks. "I'll have a steward find you some suitable shoes, put them in the dressing room."

"I'm not changing clothes, George."

"Of that I had no doubt, Thomas. Just put them a little to disquantity; that will be fine."

Grey rolled his eyes.

"But you don't want to play in boots, you'll recall that you need to move your ankles quite a lot. As in fencing."

"I fence in boots," said Grey.

"Perhaps that's why you've been stabbed so many times," said Fairbanks.

Grey laughed in spite of himself.

Ten minutes later, wearing soft, low-cut shoes and having removed his jacket and waistcoat, Grey stood with Fairbanks at the center of one of Spears's tennis courts.

"How much of the game's play *do* you remember?" said Fairbanks.

"I remember not especially liking it," said Grey. "Little more."

"Very well—though I'm sure some of it will come back to you. This," he said, gesturing to the end of the court on his left, "is the service end. And this"—gesturing to his right—"the hazard end. Behind me, the flat wall, represents what would have been the side of a French cathedral; the protruding angular bit halfway up the hazard end is called the *tambour*; it's there more or less to emphasize the fact that buttresses and things protrude from the sides of cathedrals. You see the court is meant to represent a little market square outside a church where people would play handball—the sloping 'roofs' halfway up the other three walls represent the sloped roofs of market stalls. They're called penthouses. Opposite the cathedral wall is the side penthouse. Down there at the service end is the *dedans* penthouse, and at the hazard end, the *grille* penthouse. The small window on the right-hand side of the hazard wall, below the penthouse, is called the *grille*, representing a shopwindow. If you hit the ball in there, from the opposite end, you score the point. Likewise, the large window beneath the *dedans* penthouse is called the *dedans*, and if you hit the ball in there, you score the point. From the service end, you can also score the point by hitting the ball into the furthest opening of the 'shopwindows' underneath the side penthouse; it's called the 'winning gallery.' If you hit the ball into any other gallery, it's not a point but a chase. I'll come back to that in a moment."

"Shouldn't you be home packing for the South Atlantic?" said Grey.

"The sloop they're fitting out shan't be ready till Monday next," said Fairbanks.

"There's nothing ready sooner?"

"Nothing as fast; any time gained would necessarily be lost at sea. Now, try to attend: The game begins when the man at the service end hits the ball onto the side penthouse; it must land in that large box marked on the floor, marking out the left of the hazard end. That's the service court. If you miss it, it's a fault; two faults and the point goes to the receiver. Once the server has served, a volley begins. If the ball hits the net, the point is lost by the man who struck the net-hitting shot. If it bounces twice in the receiving court, or once there and once in the space immediately to the right of the receiving court, it's a point for the server. If it bounces twice at any other place on the court, at either end, it's a chase."

"For the love of the God, man——" said Grey.

"We're nearing the end," said Fairbanks. "Each point is worth fifteen——"

"Fifteen what?"

"——and the scoring starts at zero, which by tradition is called *l'oeuf*. Then fifteen, thirty, forty-five, sixty. Sixty is game; forty-five is generally called forty, for the sake of simplicity."

"Yes," said Grey. "Clearly this is a game which values simplicity."

"When the score reaches forty and a chase has been made, or whenever there are two chases, the chases are played. This is a regular volley, except when the ball bounces twice on one side, or enters a gallery, it is compared to the original chase spot. If it's nearer an end wall than the original chase, the man who struck it wins the point; if not, his opposite wins it.

"Is that clear?"

"Yes," said Grey. "Though I would venture to say I have never hated the French more than I do at this moment."

"Would you like to serve, or shall we spin for it?"

"Spin."

"One side of my racket has a maker's mark on it; that's up. Call."

Fairbanks spun his racket on its head, Grey said "downs," and down it was.

"Your serve, then," said Fairbanks, stepping over the net onto the hazard end. "Whenever you're ready."

"Do I shout *en garde* or something?"

"*Tenez*," said Fairbanks, pronouncing it like an Englishman.

"*Tenez*," said Grey, and struck the ball. It bounced off the side penthouse, but with a little too much force, and missed the receiving court.

"Fault," said Fairbanks. "Come, again."

Grey hit it again, more softly this time; it rolled in a long arc along the penthouse and landed in front of Fairbanks, who returned it hard, aiming for the dedans but instead sending the ball onto the dedans penthouse. Grey waited for it to come down, bounce once, and then sent it flying towards the grille. Instead it struck the tambour and shot back into the court of play parallel to the net. Without waiting for it to touch the ground, Fairbanks hit a rifle shot towards the dedans. And in it went.

"Fifteen–l'oeuf," said Fairbanks, retrieving a new ball from the penthouse gallery and tossing it to Grey.

"*Tenez*," said Grey, and smacked the ball onto the side penthouse; it bounced and fell at the far edge of the receiving court, Fairbanks ran to play it, smashing it off the side wall—the "cathedral" wall—and over the net. Grey returned it on the fly, aiming for the winning gallery, missing it by a few feet:

"Second gallery chase," said Fairbanks, getting another ball. "Still fifteen–l'oeuf."

"*Tenez*," said Grey. It was another good serve, which, this time, Fairbanks was ready for. He sent it towards the dedans; Grey returned it in the air, aiming for the grille, hitting, instead, the net.

"Thirty–l'oeuf," said Fairbanks, tapping the netted ball, sending it rolling towards Grey.

"Can't we just say 'two–nil'?" said Grey.

"Certainly," said Fairbanks, "if you want to destroy a thousand years' tradition. Perhaps we should adopt the Jacobin standards of weights and measures as well. In which case you may proceed to serve from the two-'metre' line."

Grey shook his head.

"*Tenez*," he said; another good serve, and another shot to the dedans, which Grey returned this time, over the net, and on a bounce, into the grille.

"Very nice shot," said Fairbanks, getting a new ball. "Fifteen–thirty."

"*Tenez*," said Grey. A spirited volley ended with Grey again missing the winning gallery by a foot or two.

"Another second gallery chase. Now, with two, we play the chases, and that means switching ends."

"Naturally," said Grey.

"Resist the impulse to jump over the net," said Fairbanks. "It's a siren call."

Grey laughed.

"Remember," said Fairbanks, "you can win the chase points in the usual ways, or by bouncing the ball twice or putting it into a gallery further from the net than the spot where the chase was marked. Both of them, this time, at the second gallery. The second gallery hazard end and the second gallery service end are equals. *Tenez.*"

Grey returned Fairbanks's serve, hitting the back wall, sending the ball bouncing back towards the net. Fairbanks let it bounce; two bounces, and he won the first chase point, with the ball marked at the "door," between the first and second galleries at the service end.

"That's forty–love," said Fairbanks. "Second chase will be the game point. *Tenez.*"

He served, Grey returned it hard, and put it directly into the dedans.

"Sterling shot, Grey. Thirty–forty. *Tenez.*"

Fairbanks served, Grey returned, Fairbanks volleyed towards the winning gallery, missing it long and sending the ball off the receiving court wall. Grey played it off the side wall, and Fairbanks returned it towards the winning gallery, and this time he didn't miss.

"Game," said Fairbanks. "But well played, Grey. Very well played, for a tonsureless novice."

"Well, I hope you're satisfied, George." said Grey. "This will teach me never to refuse a meal."

Fairbanks laughed. "Yes, indeed. But that was just the first game; we play best of five."

Grey hit a ball at him, head-high; Fairbanks twisted away from it, laughing again, as Grey sighed loudly, and melodramatically cast his eyes up towards the ceiling and heaven beyond it.

An hour or so later, Grey was in the club's dressing room and—having accepted a clean shirt from Fairbanks—was replacing his boots. Fairbanks was rambling on about the superiority of tennis to handball when two gentlemen entered and began to remove fencing accoutrements: heavy leather jackets tied at the back and heavy leather gloves of the sort a cavalryman might wear. They were discussing the news from the continent. And the topic on everyone's lips was still the murder by Napoleon of the Duke of Enghien—a leader of the loyalist French who had died to ensure that intelligence vital to defeating Bonaparte's tyranny made it out of France. He had been caught and killed covering Grey's escape from the Château de Vincennes. Grey held him in as high regard as it is possible for one man to hold another.

"Certainly I agree," said one of the disrobing fencers, as their discussion of the duke's death dragged on, "that no man should be executed by his government without trial, but I cannot bring myself to weep for any member of the frog aristocracy. Doubtless this Enghien was a lazy, overfed pederast like the rest of them."

Grey stood, and with an edge to his voice, said, "Sir, you will forgive me intruding on a private conversation, but you are maligning a gentleman of the first order, and, in life, a particular friend of mine. I will vouch, sir, for his being a man whose courage and decency were beyond question."

"You will vouch for him, eh?" said the man, tossing his fencing gloves onto a leather-covered bench. "And who are you, sir?"

"Grey, sir."

"A member, are you, Grey?"

Now Fairbanks was standing. "He is my guest, sir."

"Well—Fairbanks, is it?" said the fencer, a very tall man, well over six feet. "I suggest you remove your guest from the premises before I'm forced to call a ratcatcher."

In a single, smooth motion, Fairbanks picked up one of the man's discarded gloves and, like a backhand at tennis, whipped it across the man's face. Fairbanks was somewhat shorter than Grey, but very strong, and the heavy leather glove knocked the offending fencer almost off his feet. He staggered backward; was caught and steadied by his sparring partner. Fairbanks threw down the glove between them.

"I will await your response," he said. He turned his back on the man and walked towards Grey.

"I appreciate it, George, but it was my quarrel."

"Nonsense," said Fairbanks. "You are my guest; the quarrel was mine. But perhaps you will second me."

The struck fencer picked up the glove and slapped it furiously on his thigh.

"Of course," said Grey.

3

A s the injured party, the offending fencer—the baronet Gresham, as it turned out—had the choice of weapons. Being a fencer, and showing little imagination, he chose *épées de combat*. As the challenged party, Fairbanks chose the ground: the fencing hall at Spears, not only for convenience, but, as a private club, there would be no concern of an indictment for murder, if either of the men lost decisively.

Grey and Gresham's second, a short, blond man named Talbot, agreed the meeting would take place early the next morning, when the club would be least awake. Agreeing to the rules was simple: because the principal offense had been a blow, there was no question of an apology. The dueling code—which, though Irish, was widely published, and much adhered to, in England—was explicit on the subject:

> *Rule V. As a blow is strictly prohibited under any circumstances among gentlemen, no verbal apology can be received for such an insult. . . . If swords are used, the parties engage until one is well blooded, disabled, or disarmed, or until, after receiving a wound and blood being drawn, the aggressor begs pardon.*

With the swords having been measured against one another and found equal, the principals were now standing sword tip to sword tip. Fairbanks had removed his jacket and waistcoat; Gresham had removed nothing but his hat. Grey asked each man if he was ready, received a confident nod from each, and joined Talbot, who was standing about ten yards away, near the door. The fencing hall was more or less the same size and shape as the tennis court, though without any of the unusual protuberances; just (rather brightly polished) wooden walls and a flagstone floor. Grey looked at Talbot, who nodded.

"On your guard," said Grey, to the duelists, and then: "Begin."

Most agents of His Majesty's secret intelligence service had been seconded from the officer corps of the Royal Marines; others were soldiers, and some, naval officers. Fairbanks had been recruited by Sir Edwards shortly after passing from midshipman to lieutenant. Years going up and down the rigging had left him extremely fit. Gresham was less fit, and nearly twenty years older; he was in his late forties. But he was a soldier, and had seen years of service in the American war, rising to the rank of major. Fairbanks had fought with foils and sabers on any number of occasions—but only in boarding actions, occasional duels, and when his intelligence work required it. Compared to Gresham, this was dilettantes' experience.

The duel was short; Gresham allowed Fairbanks to put him back on his heels, let him step forward, a little too aggressively, then disarmed him with a quick forehand slice to the wrist, and ended the fight with a gratuitous backhand slice across the face, cutting both cheeks and, deeply, the bridge of Fairbanks's nose.

Fairbanks would have continued, undaunted, had Gresham not prevented Fairbanks's retrieval of his sword, which the initial slice to the wrist had made him drop. Using the tip of his own sword, Gresham flicked Fairbanks's *épée* off the ground, into the air, and caught it, as if this were as routine to him as sipping tea. He turned and walked towards Grey and Talbot, past them, and out of the hall. Talbot followed him, and Grey went to staunch Fairbanks's bleeding. As he did, he rang for a porter, and asked if any member of the club who was a doctor had come down yet for his breakfast. The porter went to go check, and Fairbanks was left to console Grey, who was disturbed at having been the cause of the whole thing—essentially—by eavesdropping.

Fairbanks assured Grey he would enjoy the *Schläger* scar. The porter returned with a doctor, who insisted Fairbanks come to his surgery for stitching. Grey went ahead of them, out of Spears, to the street, to hail a coach.

4

FAIRBANKS'S FACE WAS OF NO GREAT CONCERN, having been quickly attended to, but the cut to his wrist had partly cut one of the sinews that controlled the motion of his hand. After varying quantities of Sturm und Drang, regret and irritation, Grey was back in Sir Edward's office, standing at his map table, receiving the briefing that Fairbanks had received just three days prior.

"A fast sloop has been outfitted; you'll leave tomorrow on the second tide," said Willys. "You'll follow the southerlies as normal to Brazil, put in for supplies at Janeiro mouth, and then continue south to the River Plate and Montevideo. You'll pass this letter to our consul there, giving you broad authority to assume as much of his plenipotentiary powers as needed. As soon as you determine the date and route of sailing of the treasure fleet—its complement and so forth; what port in Iberia it sails for—you are to send word as quickly as possible to our fleet on the West India station, at Port Royal. But remain yourself in Montevideo, prepared to revise your intelligence to the West Indian fleet as necessary. When the treasure fleet departs the Argentine, shadow it until our fleet brings it to action."

Grey nodded. It was a simple enough briefing—as he had learned from Basco y Anda, there wasn't much more to say; there wasn't much more that was known. The precaution of confining the plans entirely to Montevideo made good sense. Willys tapped the map at Montevideo.

"We've had our best captains, calculators, navigators, and natural scientists—weathermen—debating routes and periods since you brought in your report. The conclusion is this: The treasure fleet can sail no later than the first of September and be certain of arrival before the end of the year. The summer monsoons mean bringing their gold downriver will be impractical any earlier than the first week of July. Later if we're lucky. This means the earliest they could sail would be in the propinquity of July fifteenth. We believe the sloop we've chosen, an American-built clipper, can have you in Montevideo by then. Every day's delay increases the chance of . . . well, of catastrophe. The clipper's commander will have sealed orders for south of Tenerife, putting you in ultimate command."

For a moment Willys looked up and down the map again.

"I think that's all. Sir Edward?" he said, to see if the chief of naval intelligence had anything to add.

Banks was, at that moment, smoking a pipe and looking out his office window towards Whitehall.

"Grey," he said, turning around, "I need hardly tell you how important it is that this gold never reach Spain."

Grey nodded. No more needed to be said. Willys handed Grey the letter for the British consul at Montevideo and the packet of orders for the commander of the sloop. Willys and Grey shook hands.

"You'll fare well, Tom."

And then Sir Edward shook Grey's hand.

"Grey, I don't like sending you off to do this. As a rule, you're oblivious to your own condition. But I've no choice, so God speed you, there and back again."

5

H MS *PERSEUS* WAS A BALTIMORE CLIPPER, captured from an American merchant in the mid-nineties by French privateers near the Canary Islands, and captured again, shortly thereafter, by the English fleet blockading Brest, where *Perseus* tried to reach safe harbor. There was no question, of course, that Britain had the strongest navy in the world, and the skill and discipline of its sailors were the envy of every maritime power. However, they had never had the last word on ship design. In fact, it was the French who had always been considered the master shipwrights, building sloops, brigs, frigates, and even line-of-battle ships that tended to outstrip their English counterparts in speed and grace and how close they could come to the wind. Grey had wondered if this had something to do with the French genius for architecture. National artistic tendency was something Grey had been giving more and more thought to, since concluding that the Germans had a unique skill in music. The British, of course—and Grey included Irishmen in this—outstripped the world in writing; of this there was no question. Or at least, there remained no question, as Grey, in an attempt to be fair, had set himself to reading the great works of the other European nations; being fluent or nearly so in the major European languages other than Hungarian. (His occasional attempts at Hungarian proved Sisyphean; he suspected he would never speak it unless he found himself at length in Budapest, or closely acquainted with a Hungarian maid.) Dante and Petrarch disappointed him—though he admitted to himself this might be because poetry seems comparatively trivial in a language where everything rhymes. *Candide* and the *Liaisons dangereuses* were entertaining but insubstantial. Most of the other French, Italian, German writers were exhausting; Grey wasn't sure fiction had reached Scandinavia yet, nor Russia. He had been unable to discover any Balkan writers. The Greeks had gotten off to a good start with Homer—and, of course, Grey practically salivated to clap eyes on Lord Elgin's Parthenon Marbles, which were stories written in stone—but the Greeks seemed to have retired from the field after Plutarch. Only Cervantes had, in Grey's mind, lived up to his reputation. But he alone could not compete with the combined powers of Chaucer, Milton, Pope, Swift, Richardson, Sterne, Goldsmith, Sheridan, the new poets—the list was inexhaustible. And Cervantes, much as Grey admired him, could not stand even knee high to Shakespeare. No one could.

Grey's mind was wandering as he stood at the lee rail of the sloop *Perseus.* What had he been thinking about? Yes, the Germans were the undisputed masters of music, the English, of writing, Italians and the Dutch shared mastery of painting, but since the Greeks and Romans had retired, the French had dominated architecture, with the only serious competition coming from Brunelleschi and Michelangelo and some of their followers in the Italian Renaissance. And though Grey greatly preferred the relative understatement of British Gothic compared with French, there could be no denying that it was a French style that England could claim only to have refined.

This genius for physical form, perhaps, extended to their ships. But perhaps, Grey thought, with a certain amount of glee, that long preeminence was coming to its close. Of course he would have preferred the French be supplanted by Britain, but if that were not to be, he could not have chosen another county less objectionable than

the United States. In its short span of existence—which had more
or less coincided with Grey's life; Grey having been born a few years
before the American revolution, to an American mother, in Boston
harbor, on one of His Majesty's ships . . . In its short span of existence, the United States was rapidly winning a reputation for the
quality of its shipwrights, who, for the first time, were being put to
work designing ships built not for storeroom and stability, but for
speed and firepower. The Baltimore clipper was, at that moment, the
byword of ships' speed. Here, riding one for the first time in blue
water, Grey was impressed: they were, sailing large on a moderate
wind, making twelve knots, and Grey suspected that if *Perseus* put
her mind to it, she could go a good deal faster.

"Mr. Grey, you'll be pleased to know that we're making splendid
time," said Captain Duckworth.

He and his first lieutenant had just made noon and marked the
distance they'd covered during the preceding day—that is, the preceding twenty-four hours. At sea, with uncertain chronometers and
a constant change of longitude, the only moment a ship could be
objectively certain of the time was when the sun reached its zenith.
Consequently, as a practical matter, naval days went noon-to-noon
rather than midnight-to-midnight.

"About a hundred and twenty sea miles; we shall be south of
Gibraltar by tomorrow, I daresay—if our wind holds out."

Duckworth had a bright, eager smile on his face, which he'd
worn for the last four or five days. Before that he'd been invariably
stern and serious. Duckworth's title "captain" was a courtesy, as a
sloop is the traditional command of a lieutenant, but the commander
of a ship always ranks a captain honorific. His Majesty's sloop *Perseus*
was Duckworth's first command, and a considerable step towards
being posted to the captains' list, the dream of every naval officer.
His early lack of cheer, Grey suspected, was the result of a first time
being wholly responsible for a ship and her crew. Now, with things
going well, he was becoming able to feel the joy of promotion and
success. His full name was Percival Duckworth; Grey wondered if
the new joy was alloyed at all by his more or less sharing a first name

with his first command. Percy of *Perseus*. Though if he did well for himself, ferrying Grey about, having a catchy sobriquet might help him to a reputation.

"Less than a week to Madeira, I should say." He rapped a knuckle on the lee rail. "And not much longer to the Canaries. And then if we can catch the monsoons and miss the doldrums"—he rapped the wood again—"we may sight the coast of Brazil in under six weeks further. But I'm running much too far ahead of myself. I would scratch a backstay but I must maintain some pretense of being less superstitious than the men."

He laughed, and Grey chuckled politely.

For a moment both men looked out at the endless surround of water, every day a lighter shade of blue, before Captain Duckworth turned back to the spread of his sails, which were his near-perpetual focus. Some captains are obsessed with navigation, some with bright-work, some with gunnery—many, of course, are obsessed with several of these, or all of them—Duckworth was one of the sort obsessed with speed and the trim of every sheet and stay. Virtually all of Grey's life at sea, as a royal marine, had been on square-rigged ships, and he found Duckworth's working of a fore-and-aft rig fasci-nating. He had always assumed, with so many fewer yards and much less rigging, the process would be essentially trivial, and indeed, none of his past sloop passages had impressed him particularly with the working of sails, but as he heard Duckworth call out for a reef in the main topmast staysail and two in the fore topsail, adding a flyer to the jib boom and heaving the main-, fore-, and staysail booms ten degrees towards the starboard beam—and felt the already flying *Perseus* fly just a hair faster—now catching the breeze further forward, letting the press fall more on the bow to keep from losing way to a rising sea—he was impressed.

Duckworth turned back to him. "I'm sure, Mr. Grey, you are aware of my sealed orders, to be opened beyond Tenerife. I sup-pose them to be some description of your function here, as my open orders were rather vague on the subject."

Grey said nothing. To speculate on sealed orders—even worse, to try to extract some part of them prematurely from a man who might know their contents—was, in the service, anathema.

Duckworth, realizing his misstep, tried to recover himself by adding, "I mention it only because I would like to provision you at Tenerife with anything you might need that I might not otherwise think to procure. So do please feel at liberty to inform me of anything you might need."

"Thank you, Captain," said Grey. "Most kind. In fact, that reminds me, I wanted to have a word with the company's cook, if I may. If you will excuse me."

"Certainly, Mr. Grey."

Duckworth was a fine seaman, and his indiscretion nothing more than a symptom of youth, thought Grey as he walked forward. He would likely shape up into a fine captain, once he'd gotten more used to the mask of command.

As an idler, *Perseus*'s cook had no watch to stand, and with a relatively small crew to feed, had a more-than-usual quantity of idle time on his hands. At this moment, he was sitting on the forecastle, as out of the way as he could get, one leg crossed under him, the other protruding straight out through a scupper. This leg, his left, was the source of both his name and his employment. Dick Deadleg, the men called him. If the leg he'd lost above the left knee had been wood, they might have called him Dick Pegleg, but Dick had carved his leg himself from whalebone, and rather than a simple peg, like the leg of a table, he had included a calf muscle and a claw-foot that made Grey think of the feet of French bathtubs. Dick had been an able seaman in his youth, and after the conclusion of the American war, a whaler. There he'd lost his leg, and after some years ashore on a modest pension from his employer, had chosen to rejoin the navy in one of the jobs set aside for seamen who could no longer haul or reef.

It was precious rare to find a naval cook who had any skill at cooking. Since, however, the job required little more than boiling salt beef and allocating tack, peas, cheese, and butter, this tended not to matter. Having spent years assisting in the flensing and rendering of blubber, Dick Deadleg could do that well enough. His real skill, though, and the thing that won him the affection of his crewmates, was in carving. Like all whalers, he'd spent years at sea surrounded by whalebone; like many, he'd emerged a more-than-adept scrimshander. As Grey approached, he was carving out the inside of a shark's vertebra, from a shark caught by the gunroom steward, sold by him to the ship's dentist-barber, for the purposes of practicing with a bone saw, in anticipation of someday earning a surgeon's warrant, and who, when he'd thoroughly sliced it up, had sold the rancid flesh for bait, the teeth for good-luck charms, and the bone to anyone trying to wheedle a whittle out of Dick Deadleg. The vertebra had been purchased by the captain's coxswain, who hoped Dick could make it into a whistle.

Standing above the man, Grey realized he didn't know what Dick's actual surname was. After a moment, he said, "Mr. Cook, might I have a word?"

"Certainly, sir," said Deadleg, bringing a knuckle to his forehead and then grabbing the gunwale, beginning to bring himself to his feet. (Such as they were.)

"No, no, please to stay seated. I'll join you, if I may." Grey sat down on the deck beside him, resting his own legs in the scupper. "You'll forgive me, I hope, for not knowing your name."

"Of course, sir—it's Richardson, sir," said Dick Deadleg.

"Thank you," said Grey.

Richard Richardson. Percy of *Perseus*. It was an epidemic. He shrugged.

"I wondered, Mr. Richardson, if I could talk to you about whaling. The father of a close friend had a career quite similar to yours— from the navy to the fisheries. I've often wondered about it but never found the opportunity to learn the actual procedure for fishing a whale."

The friend in question was Grey's indispensable housekeeper Mrs. Hubble. Though, if he were frank with himself, he was thinking more of Mrs. Hubble's younger sister, Mrs. Boothe, a young widow and mother with whom Grey had begun to develop a somewhat cordial friendship. The propriety of this—of possibly placing

Mrs. Hubble in an uncomfortable position—Grey found questionable, and he preferred not to dwell on it.

"Well, sir," said Dick, "it used to be that the fishing fleet hunted right whales up by the ice and Greenland, but sometime before I made my first trip, most of the whaling had moved to the south seas, where you don't have to race against the end of summer and the ice moving down again, maybe trapping you, if you're lucky, or crushing your ship to shivers. It was all chance, you know—an American, name of Hussey, was captaining a whaleboat out of Nantucket and a big eastern blow—what they call nor'easters, in Nantucket—in the story as I heard it, anyhow—filthy weather pushed Hussey far, far out, and south, and when it'd done, he found himself among a school of sperm whales—first time anyone'd ever seen one, though some Norwegians'll tell you they found some on a beach there, though I don't believe it, as they never come north of the rock. In anyways, Hussey set to killing one, and found the spermaceti, and then right suddenly the fleets began to fish the southern fishery, looking for the sperm whales."

Grey nodded along, saying nothing. He pulled his pipe out of a pocket, and after offering his tobacco pouch to Dick Richardson, who accepted it and filled a scrimshaw pipe, Grey lit his own, and the story resumed.

"Right whales is *right* whales not just on account of them being fat and slow, but they're real friendly too. Swim right over to you. You have to be hard to kill 'em, like a lamb butcher—not sure I'd have had the stomach for it myself, and in anyways I was never a lancer. People say sperm whales are as mean as right whales are kind, but it's not so. Sperm whales'll come up to you too, like schoolchildren, stick their giant nose-heads out of the water so they can get their little eyes a look at you. Did you know they can move their eyes in and out, but not around? Got to move their whole bodies to look around. They only get mean when you harpoon 'em, and I'll be damned before I blame 'em for it. Would you like it if some rum foreigner, giving all the impression of friendship, drove a knife into you just as you was looking him over?"

"I should think not," said Grey, who didn't add that this had happened to him on several occasions. That is, rum foreigners driving knives into him.

"No, just as you say. Well, you're already hard up to the whale—wood on the black leather, we say—since you've lowered your boats after the lookout calls 'On deck there' and points and says that there she blows, and you row where he's pointing till you see the spout for yourself, though it can take six bells or a watch getting to him. He's curious so he comes over when he sees you, you warp alongside him, if you see what I mean, and your harpoon man harpoons him; fixes the barb good and strong in his back, and the whale takes off like a stuck pig. Pulls you along at a prodigious great speed—ten times faster than the fastest clipper; I reckon no man alive has traveled as fast as a whaleman—and does this for an hour, two hours, even three, till he tires himself out and can't pull anymore. Then you warp back up to him again and kill him."

"Why does he run along the surface?" said Grey. "Why not dive?"

"Well, sir, you know that he's a breathing fish, that's what his spout is, you know—his prodigious great nose. Doesn't running get *you* breathing hard?"

"It surely does," said Grey.

"He can't breathe anywhere but the surface, so of course he stays there."

Richardson was being politely tolerant of Grey's obvious ignorance of the most basic facts of oil fishing: he spoke as if to a small child.

"Of course he does dive, on a blue moon, but mostly it's your finbacks who choose to dive, which is why we don't hunt them. In anyways, so you come up on him again, warping up to his side, and your harpoon man has switched places with your coxswain, so he can make a killing cut."

Grey was starting to suspect that perhaps he deserved to be talked to like a small child.

"It's not the harpoon and the exhaustion of the chase that kills him?" said Grey.

Dick Richardson shook his head indulgently. "Course it doesn't, sir. A harpoon's a hook—does a fishing hook kill a trout? Or does reeling him?"

"I suppose not," said Grey, smiling inwardly and drawing on his pipe.

"Course not," said Richardson. "The coxswain comes up to the harpooner's spot in the bow, with a lance—a very long lance, no thicker around than a man's finger, with a shaving-sharp leaf-head on the end. He drives it in a spot behind the left flipper, which we call 'the life,' and cuts his big vein. The whale starts to spout red—that's blood, sir."

Grey nodded.

"And that's when he gets treble mean, the sperm whale. He starts thrashing and slapping with his tail and biting with his giant jaw, twice as long as a man is tall, with teeth the size of guinea hens. Bit right through our whaleboat and bit my leg clean off and swallowed it like a bit of Jonah. Though I reckon it's me with the last laugh, 'cause my dead leg's made from the bone of that same jaw. Well, you try to get clear as far as you can, while he thrashes himself out, spouting blood the while, like a hellish fountain—no Christian man enjoys it, sir, I promise you that—and then he quiets and dies, and you make fast to his tail and tow him back to the ship, which, unless you've got boats out on both sides, has closed with you some, or else the row is hellish long getting back; all of a day, sometimes, so's you end up pulling towards the sidelights."

He took a long drag on his pipe and held it up. "I fashioned this out of the same fish I fashioned my leg from, you know."

"It must have been a prodigious great jaw indeed," said Grey.

"Yes, sir, it certainly was," said Richardson, briefly admiring his pipe before placing it on his lap.

As Richardson had spoken—and smoked—he'd continued whittling at the boatswain's vertebra, only looking up when he'd had to make a point of special emphasis. Now he brought the vertebra up to his mouth and blew through it. It made a loud, hollow, high-pitched whistle, like a tiny conch shell.

"You're a marvelous hand with that, Richardson," said Grey.

"Thank you, sir."

"And thank you for the lesson," said Grey, standing.

"Of course, sir," said Richardson, touching a knuckle again to his forehead.

Grey could see the boatswain walking forward on the starboard gangway, doubtless drawn by the sound of his new whistle. He saluted as Grey passed him. Grey was heading aft again, to the quarterdeck, which the captain had vacated. Not knowing Grey's function, and bound by the implicit, highly conservative etiquette of the navy, none of the subordinate officers felt they ranked high enough to speak to Grey unless spoken to, which meant he could rely on some time to think in peace, without having to contend with the stifling heat of his Lilliputian gunroom cabin.

He should have been thinking, he supposed, about the Spanish treasure fleet—shortly to leave the River Plate with untold riches that would either pay for war to be made on England, or, in capture or destruction, prevent it. For just a moment, he pictured tons of gold bricks sinking slowly through darkening waters to the bottom of the Atlantic Ocean, never to be seen again . . . he saw light sparkling off coins and ingots, and a stove-in Spanish battleship sinking beside them . . . maybe some of the few sailors who could swim desperately grabbing for a few handfuls before they disappeared, trying to swim them back to the surface, only to realize they were much too heavy to carry . . . being forced either to drop them or die . . . Quite a Greek melodrama. What would Perseus have made of it?

Grey rapped a closed fist on her taffrail. The Americans had had the idea of building ships from live oak—that is, evergreen oak that lives through winter. Very hard to work with, but fantastically strong. It was the opinion of most European shipwrights—among them, the English master builders who had worked in Boston and Philadelphia before Parliament decided it was too dangerous to have Americans building their own warships—that live oak was too costly, both in procurement and weight, to be worth using. If this clipper was any indication, they'd have been wrong. But of course the clipper was a small ship; a first-rate ship of the line could have hoisted her clean out of the water with her capstan. The real test would be in battle, between those new ballyhooed American heavy frigates and a competent enemy. The men fighting the French frigates that had encountered one or two of them six or seven years earlier, when they'd first been launched, swore their hulls had deflected French cannon fire as if it were the ships that were made of iron and the shot of wood. But third-hand rumors of French naval actions were not, per se, the most reliable source of information. That granted, it did add another layer of intrigue to the French desire to procure an American lumber monopoly.

Grey turned and looked up the length of the sloop; smaller, of course, than, a whaling ship, but perhaps not by much. He had always admired whaling, especially as a youngster, when whaling ships were the first to explore the half of the globe no man had ever laid eyes on . . . a thousand desert islands in the gigantic expanse of the Pacific, filled with strange and wondrous things. Even now, as Pacific maps began to fill out, there was a tremendous romance to the idea of sailing without orders, to catch the whale but also to see what there was to be seen. He hadn't, of course, ventured the vulgarity of inquiring into Dick Deadleg's whaling income, but it was well known that, unless you captained a whaling ship or owned it— or better yet, both, possibly with interest in the chandler and cooper works that went along with them—you made virtually no money at all whaling; nothing but a tiny piece of the net profit, which, even for a long whale voyage, amounted to less than a good seaman could earn in the merchant fleet in half, even a quarter, of the time, or in fishing the great banks, which meant hearth and home every few months or so. But, not quite illogically, this is what filled whalers with the best seamen in the world (outside of His Majesty's Brave British Tars). Whaling seamen didn't sail the fisheries for money, they sailed for adventure.

Though, being honest with himself, his present preoccupation with whaling had less to do with adventure than with the widowed Mrs. Angela Boothe. Her father was one of the men who *had* made whaling profitable—quite profitable, in fact. He had used his profits to open a seaman's inn on the road to Canterbury, which Mrs. Boothe now managed, she being versed both in housekeeping, by her treasured sister (treasured, that is, by Grey—though no doubt by Mrs. Boothe as well), and in mathematics, by her father, who studied angles, tangents, and spheres for his professional betterment in navigation. He had practiced his studies by teaching what he learned to his younger daughter—his avowed belief being that a man doesn't know something unless he can teach it.

Mrs. Boothe had two children, whom Grey occasionally encountered at his own house, to which Mrs. Hubble's family had a standing invitation, or at her father's inn, which Grey had taken to frequenting on journeys between London and his home, or London and Dover. Grey didn't know what to make of the children, because while they seemed, in and of themselves, inoffensive, they reminded him that he and his wife Paulette had not had children. When she had died, he had been glad that there were no children into the equation to worry about. Now he wished there had been. Not so much for the sentimental notion that a man—or, to particularize it, a woman—lives on through his children, as because it was a joy Grey knew would have surpassed all other joys in Paulette's too-brief life, and it pained him to know it had been denied her.

Of course, he didn't hold this against Mrs. Boothe's children. But it did tend to make him want to keep them at arm's length.

Mrs. Boothe, on the other hand, engendered the opposite emotion. He thought it was, perhaps, strange that this should be the case—that the children should token guilt but not the mother. But Grey, knowing that Paulette was sui generis, never had any concern of her being replaced. So this broadly infantile notion had not affected his growing affection for Mrs. Boothe, planted by an unexpected vocal accompaniment to a hymn Grey and Mr. Hubble had been attempting on piano at last Christmastime. Though some of the effect was owed, no doubt, to Bach, Mrs. Boothe's song had some sort of divine purity in it that seemed to plumb Grey's depths. Becoming actually acquainted with her on subsequent meetings had not dispelled this impression. Grey did not go in much for the so-called lyrical ballads of modern poetry—give him instead Shake-speare or Virgil or Homer; poetry with some bottom—but a line written a year or two earlier by a fellow of rapidly growing reputa-tion, whom Grey knew a little from the London clubs—rather too histrionic for Grey's taste, but not a bad chap; Wordsworth—had seemed to sum up Mrs. Boothe beautifully: *A creature not too bright or good for human nature's daily food—for transient sorrows, simple wiles, praise, blame, love, kisses, tears, and smiles.*

Reciting it to himself, in his head, made Grey blush; he turned away from the other men on the quarterdeck and looked out at *Perseus*'s wake. He tried to turn his thoughts to a more decorous subject. His mind wandered for a moment before settling on *Perseus*'s name-sake. The Andromeda-saving Gorgon-killer. Did Greek sculpture date to the days when, to make a really lifelike statue, all you had to do was have a model pose and then show him the head of Medusa? Grey chuckled to himself. Certainly it would have been a very effi-cient approach to the art. Grey wondered what quality of Medusa's it was that turned men to stone. The only of her particular character-istics that Grey could think of offhand was her hair of snakes. Was it the snakes that petrified people? If one snake is dangerous, no doubt an entire coif of them would prove tremendously discomfiting. Pre-sumably her stony stare was not simply the result of her being hid-eous to behold. After all, the trick to besting her was to look at her reflection in a polished shield. Acting as a mirror, a polished shield would not, presumably, have improved her appearance. So whatever it was that turned a man to stone, it must have been some quality that couldn't be reflected.

This sounded like some silly metaphysical question posed at a debating society at Cambridge. What can be seen directly but can-not be seen in reflection? (Perhaps he should put the question to his scientific Cambridge acquaintance Mr. Atwood.)

Grey leaned on the ship's stern rail. What does reflection do? Well, for one thing, it reverses images. Perhaps Medusa had some-thing written on her forehead that petrified you, and by seeing her in a mirror, you weren't able to read it . . .

Why did mirrors reverse images left to right but not up to down?

Grey grabbed hold of his train of thought and yanked it back to more sensible subjects. He wondered what Mrs. Boothe was doing at that moment. He hadn't seen her now for a month or so, and he had become trapped—by his wandering mind—in repeated reviews of their past meetings, picking apart their walks and conversations with an entomologist's eye for minutiae.

Their last conversation—speaking of Greece—Grey smiled at his own poor, silent wordplay—their last conversation had been about the Rosetta Stone. Grey had been remarking on the world of knowledge that would be opened by the correspondence of the Greek text to the Egyptian and the hieroglyphs. So much of ancient Egypt had survived—so much of their writing—but so far, virtually none of it could be read.

"Perhaps, Mr. Grey, it can't be read because the hieroglyphs are not words," Mrs. Boothe had said.

"Do you mean, Mrs. Boothe, that they may be simple pictures? But they repeat in patterns—the same images appearing again and again."

"No," said Mrs. Boothe, "I don't mean to suggest they are just pictures. Perhaps rather than words, they are notes. Perhaps hieroglyphics are sheet music. Or, written music, that is. Perhaps, Mr. Grey, the walls of those temples, which are covered in drawings of birds and eyes and so forth, are actually giant choir books."

Grey had been so taken aback by this remark that he had actually stopped walking; stopped in his tracks. It seemed to be such a clever thought . . . it had never entered his mind. He smiled.

"I had never considered that, Mrs. Boothe . . . I must certainly put it to someone. Or perhaps you should compose a letter to the Royal Academy."

"Oh, no, Mr. Grey, I'm sure they won't be interested in hearing from a Kentish barmaid."

"Mrs. Boothe, you do yourself a great disservice saying so—that you are a Kentish barmaid. You are a woman of parts."

"You flatter me, Mr. Grey. But I do appreciate it." She smiled, though not at him; she smiled demurely and kept her eyes on the road ahead of them.

Grey, however, was looking at Mrs. Boothe. What a wonderfully unconventional mind she had! And she was so very attractive to him. She was no more than average height; quite slim but not bony. Her dusky hair was parted in the middle and dangled in loose curls on either side of her face; curls that seemed to have escaped the bun-shaped assemblage at the back of her head, skullcap-like. Her cheekbones were prominent without being hard. In fact, her entire face had a sort of gentle softness you might find in the face of a Botticelli.

For a moment they walked in silence.

"Mrs. Boothe, when you were growing up, did you ever have the chance of seeing much painting?"

"On occasion. I was at the St. Martin-in-the-Fields School for Girls for several years, when my father was first establishing The Try Pot and wanted to keep me away from its rougher aspects. Tours were arranged to many of the great houses, when they were empty out of the season. I had the chance of seeing many fine pieces in them."

Grey nodded. "If it is not too personal a question, how did you come to manage your father's inn?"

"Well—if you will forgive me for answering perhaps too personally—after my husband's death, I was disconsolate. Almost bedridden, for some time; only able to rouse myself to take care of my daughters. My father had suggested I might move into The Try Pot, where he lived, at the time. That he would close off part of the inn's upper floor completely and turn it into an apartment for us, for me and my daughters. That way, he said, we might be close enough for him and for my sister to help look after the children. And though he didn't say so, he meant close enough for them to look after me as well. I refused. Mr. Boothe and I had a small house in Portsmouth— Mr. Boothe was an acting lieutenant on *Elephant* when he was killed; had been waiting for the Admiralty to approve the promotion. He felt he could afford to buy a house for us, a small one, near the shore, so that he could see us whenever the channel fleet touched. And that it would be a good fund for me and the children, in case anything were to happen to him."

She sniffed slightly at this last remark, and Grey felt guilty for having introduced the subject.

"In any case, I refused to leave it. My father, gradually acceding to that, prevailed on me at least to let him bring my daughters up for a visit, as the Pot had become quite busy and he wasn't able to get away and see them as much as he liked. To this, I acceded, and after he had had them a few days, he refused to return them—sent word that he was simply too busy to bring them back, and that I would have to call for them myself. So I did—in a fury. But when I arrived, he persuaded me at least to spend the night, as I looked tired from my journey.

"I haven't been back to the house in Dover for near two years now. My father has arranged to let it to the families of young sailors, the income of which he preserves in a fund for me and my children, should I ever need it."

Grey knew he had intruded much too far on Mrs. Boothe's personal affairs—not intentionally, but nevertheless he had. Though he felt also as if it were a story Mrs. Boothe had wanted to tell; never, perhaps, having told it to anyone, and its having—perhaps—weighed on her. But either way, the memory of it brought back his feeling of guilt.

In any case—what was he doing? Standing around like some sort of moonish youth. He resolved to descend to the gunroom to look for any officer who had spent any length of time in Montevideo, in conversation with whom Grey might discover something about the city that he didn't already know. That is, Grey told himself: to work.

6

I N THE EVENT, neither the commissioned nor warrant contin-
gents of the gunroom mess had any particular experience with
Montevideo, but the gunroom steward, begging Mr. Grey's pardon for eavesdropping, told Grey that the captain's cook was in fact
an Argentine, one of the many foreigners who populated the other
ranks of the Royal Navy. Particularly the ranks of cooks hired at foreign ports by captains who developed a taste for something livelier
than English cooking. With Captain Duckworth's permission, Grey
engaged Mr. Gomez—Relicario Gomez—to instruct him in the layout and character of Montevideo and the lower Plate, in between his
duties preparing meals for the captain, which took him little time
because Duckworth was among those English captains who had not
developed a taste for anything livelier than English cooking. He had
merely inherited Gomez from *Perseus*'s former commander.

Thus began an unusually pleasant and—because of good fortune
and Duckworth's preternatural talent for spreading sail—unusually
fast crossing of the doldrums, that tedious, dangerous patch of ocean
between the northeast trade winds off northwest Africa and the
southeast trades off northeast Brazil. They started somewhat north
of the equator and threatened to becalm and desiccate any ship that
passed through them. Virtually all of the explored world had reliable

wind patterns; some of them blowing all year, some changing with the season, all of them more or less dependable. But in the doldrums wind might, on any day of the year, disappear entirely and for weeks on end. Every sailor had heard stories of ghost ships dragging into port with only a half dozen men still able to stand, tongues swollen and black, willing to trade everything they owned for a sip of water.

The passage of the *Perseus*, however, was blessed with a steady southerly wind that compressed to perhaps the shortest time possible the period of the doldrums crossing. So much so, in fact, that the sailors, resolutely superstitious as all sailors are, began to take special precautions to preserve their run of good luck. Of their own volition, they stopped swearing on Sundays, and then stopped swearing entirely. Fishing for seabirds, by hanging fish-baited hooks in the rigging, stopped. Because Grey's Spanish was already near-as-made-no-difference to native fluency, Relicario Gomez helped him improve his Portuguese, a language that—with the empires of Portugal and Spain frequently butting heads along the River Plate—Gomez had spoken from birth. However, in a request relayed through the boatswain to the captain, and then to Grey, the crew wished Grey and Gomez might stop speaking the bizarre-sounding and non-Protestant language, at least on deck. Upon discovering that Gomez was a keen chess player, Grey had commissioned a simple scrimshaw chess set from Dick Deadleg, and—though Gomez was not serious competition for Grey, who had spent all of the previous winter in dogged study of the game—the play was diverting, and a good background to the small talk of the River Plate colony, of which Grey wished to absorb as much as he could.

When *Perseus* sighted Cape St. Roque, her water supply was of no concern, and there would have been no need to send a boat ashore on the bejungled Brazilian coast were it not for another, comparably serious concern. The ship's lime juice supply had proved dyed and diluted—as was sometimes the case, in dealing with excessively profit-minded chandlers, prone to faith that the malfeasance was unlikely to redound to them, with a captain always bearing the ultimate responsibility for the supplies taken aboard his ship. In pleasant keeping with the good fortune the ship had enjoyed sailing by and large, the loose teeth didn't appear until just two days before landfall. Of course, a man who has never been to sea might point out that it was considerable misfortune to have any scurvy aboard at all, but this fails to take into account the attitudes of sailors. No sailor will ever believe a run of bad luck means good luck is around the corner, but every sailor will become increasingly certain, as a string of good luck winds out, that bad luck will inevitably follow. The bad lime juice and hints of opening wounds was enough to relieve the strain of waiting for the blow to fall.

After opening his sealed orders south of Tenerife, Duckworth had discovered that Grey was, in essence, in supervisory command of the ship. Rather than take this as an affront, as some captains would, Duckworth told Grey simply that he and the ship were at Grey's disposal, and that Grey—in private—should feel no obligation to stand on ceremony, but be blunt whenever he felt obliged to give Duckworth instructions. Grey appreciated this, and on several occasions since, he and Duckworth had had lengthy, congenial conversations considering where in the Plate, in this season—accounting for the periodic monsoon rains of these latitudes flooding harbors at river mouths—treasure ships might be discreetly loaded, if the process of loading them was desired to remain out of the public eye. During these conversations, Grey's casual but by no means insubstantial botanical knowledge—built up gradually by reading the works of a botanist acquaintance of his named Kefauver—had emerged. Flora was a topic that could scarcely be avoided in discussing the astonishingly verdant coast of South America. It was for this reason that Duckworth asked Grey if he might lead a small party ashore to gather greenery for the men to eat in substitute for the defective lime juice.

Normally this would be the responsibility of the ship's surgeon, but *Perseus* had sailed with only a dentist (not too costly a decision; most sailors feared tooth extraction considerably more than dismemberment. Marines too; Grey having been no exception. A good tooth-puller put a whole ship at ease). Duckworth said he could, of course, send the dentist-barber if Grey would be inconvenienced by the notion, but that he would feel much more at ease regarding the approach of scurvy if a more plant-inclined gentleman were to take charge. Grey, who had never had a close look at Brazil this far north, eagerly accepted.

A jolly boat pulled ashore with Grey seated in the bow, screwing the buttstock air canister of his Girandoni air rifle to the barrel assembly. The Girandoni was among Grey's most prized possessions—a rare, Austrian-built repeating rifle. He harbored mild hope that the short trip ashore would give him a chance to bring back, in addition to fresh greens, some fresh meat. He didn't especially mind salt beef, but after a month on it, the thought of—say—some roasted venison made the mouth positively water. Now examining the coast he was headed for, Grey wondered if they had deer in north Brazil. He wondered too what latitude marked the northern extent of the sloth (though God forbid he should shoot one).

Perseus had hove to a few hundred yards offshore, at a promising site for herb-gathering—a sandy beach surrounding the mouth of a stream. The air became noticeably sweeter as the boat approached it; the smell of wet growing things gradually overtook the smell of unshowered sailors. After riding through the surf, Grey and the boat crew jumped out, wet-footed, and dragged the gig a safe distance up the beach. Grey told the men to keep a lookout for snakes, and then walked towards the jungle's edge, looking for things edible.

And they weren't hard to find. The stream emerged from the jungle cascading down a step-waterfall of natural pools carved in a rocky, weedy hill that looked as if it had been designed for a Florentine garden; it was surrounded by clusters of hog plum trees, growing the small, sweet, orange fruit only known to grow on Brazil's northeast coast. Above them were long, lanky coconut trees, leaning out over the beach, and a sure sign Grey's party were not its first visitors, as coconuts had followed the Spanish and Portuguese to the new world.

Grey set his six oarsmen to picking plums, a job they attacked zealously, eating and laughing as they plucked the fresh fruit off the low trees. Grey, meanwhile, picked the richest coconut tree and began to climb it, feeling it bow slightly under his weight, feeling the undulating rings of the trunk on his bare shins and feet, reaching the top and shouting "Look out below, boys" as he began to yank coconuts free and drop them onto the sand fifteen or twenty feet below, with soft *pluds* and jokes from the men about what size cannon they'd fit and what sort of women they'd look best on.

Grey pulled off the last coconut and took a moment to look out at the beautiful panorama before him—the bright emerald water deepening to sapphire blue, glittering in the sun; beyond it the *Perseus* at anchor.

. . . And beyond *Perseus*, a brigantine, with the weather gauge and *Perseus* dead ahead. A brigantine flying no colors.

"BACK TO THE BOAT," shouted Grey, dropping from the trunk.

Two of the men had begun to roll a barrel stuffed with hog plums down the beach; Grey shouted to them—"LEAVE IT, LEAVE IT THERE, COME ON—GET THIS DAMNED THING LAUNCHED!"

He began to push the boat back down towards the breaking waves; two men were beside him, then three, then all six, manhandling the boat through the surf. The oarsmen began to climb in and pull away from the beach, fighting the breakers; Grey was last aboard, hauling himself over the gunwales and beginning to repeat "Stroke—stroke—stroke" to get the men pulling together. Against the tide, it would take them five minutes at least to row back to the boat. The brigantine, if she were an enemy, would likely be close enough to fire her small cannon inside of three.

On *Perseus*'s deck, men were at the capstan, hauling in the anchor. Close inshore like this, a brigantine could outmaneuver *Perseus*, but *Perseus* could certainly outrun her, if she could avoid being trapped against a lee shore. As she lay, she was almost helpless; though the two brigs had a roughly equal broadside—neither of them heavy—the brigantine had sea room and *Perseus* didn't. Or wouldn't, unless Duckworth cut his anchor line and ran.

Grey feared Duckworth was waiting for him; Grey being *Perseus*'s essential cargo. For an instant Grey considered ordering backwater, but he feared this would only confuse the situation, and the jolly boat was almost within hailing distance now. At least his voice didn't have to fight against the tide.

"CUT, MAN," shouted Grey emphatically, waving to be seen and gesturing a cutting motion with one arm slicing down onto the other. "CUT AND RUN FOR IT."

It was their only hope. If *Perseus* could run clear, she had all the time in the world to come back for them—but if she were taken, England's fate might be sealed, to contend with France and a wealthy Spain combined against her.

He could see Duckworth standing at the leeward rail of the quarterdeck now. Grey repeated the cutting gesture, emphatically, like a wild man, all the while shouting "CUT YOUR LINES—CUT AND RUN."

And suddenly Duckworth understood. He ran out of sight, and a moment later he and the bosun could be seen running down the gangway, axes in hand. They began to hack at the bower line, quickly reinforced by a lieutenant. It seemed to take a lifetime, but with a gigantic snap the line was cut, disappearing underwater like a frightened sea serpent. Grey hoped the tension at the other end hadn't sent the rope snaking through the crew, killing the ones who weren't well enough clear.

Perseus was already filling her sails, and taking a sharp tack away from shore, with the brigantine on her larboard beam.

Still the brigantine flew no colors. It was sure now, she meant no good—but was she a pirate or a privateer? If a privateer, she would still be bound by the laws of arms. *Perseus*'s crew—or any crew she tried—could legitimately put up a fight to defend their ship, and expect to be treated as prisoners if they surrendered. The reason pirates flew a uniform flag—Jolly Roger with his smiling skull, and bones or swords crossed beneath—was to let a crew know that, just as pirates who surrendered would be hanged, so would any man who offered resistance. A fight with pirates meant no quarter given by either side. Pirates, of course, were prepared for this. Lawful crews frequently were not. All mariners knew the story of Black Bart raising Jolly Roger in Trepassey harbor at Newfoundland, early in the last century—prompting the entire crews of all twenty-two ships at anchor there to abandon stations and hide onshore. The lesson taken from the story varied from man to man. It was among the largest hauls in the history of piracy, but not a sailor was killed.

Grey, on the chance that *Perseus* would be forced to haul her wind and fight it out like a bear at the stake, was still ordering *stroke-stroke-stroke* towards her, but his eyes were on the brigantine. His eyes were on her when the black jack flew. So a pirate she was. And then came a flash from the brigantine's bows; bow chasers, probably long nines. Only one had fired. A warning shot that sailed through *Perseus*'s rigging. She ignored it; her Union Jack still flying defiance. Already she was putting distance between the pirate and herself.

The pirate fired a second warning shot; the other long nine. The ball hit *Perseus* near the waterline.

Afterwards, Grey couldn't be certain what exactly had happened, only that it was the realization of every navy man's greatest fear. Possibly *Perseus*'s powder monkeys hadn't closed the felt drapes that protected the magazine. Perhaps the shot had started a fire that spread with ferocious speed. Perhaps the shot had hit the magazine square and struck a spark, or the ball had simply been hot enough to touch off the powder directly.

All Grey knew for certain was that one instant *Perseus* seemed to be making good her escape—the next, she was engulfed in a monumental column of fire. More than a hundred yards away; Grey was blinded by it, and deafened. He was barely conscious of the wave it created, flipping the jolly boat and throwing him into the water. He dimly remembered rough hands pulling him roughly out of the water and throwing him into a pitch-black room, in the bowels of a ship. He dimly remembered the moaning of wounded men around him, occasionally breaking through the vicious ringing in his ears, which lasted until he passed out.

7

GREY HAD LITTLE EXPERIENCE WITH PIRATES, but he knew, or could guess, what would happen next. First would come the offer to join the pirate crew. Every ship at sea is always interested in restocking its supply of seamen. Simply sailing a machine of a blue-water ship's complexity meant two or three men a month were likely to be killed—falling from the rigging, being hit on the head by a block, washed overboard in a storm, blood poisoned by a cut gone bad. Add to that, attrition from fighting, and pirates were constantly pressing for fresh men—another good inducement for men not to put up a struggle once they saw a black jack flying.

Those who refused an initial offer might be asked to reconsider after one of their number was killed, generally in some deeply unpleasant way, for the holdouts' education and the pirate crew's amusement. Sharks were often involved. If the men still could not be persuaded to join, or were not able-bodied, they were bound for a dank prison and a long wait to be ransomed. If a man was lucky, there would be a wealthy countryman on some nearby plantation who would pay, or a close city with a home embassy, or an embassy of a friendly country, who would pay. If not, it was the slow process of letters home and the hope that relatives or parish churches could

raise ransom money. If that failed, it was the slave market. Sometimes the slave market was more immediate, when the prospect of a
good price seemed more attractive than the long wait for a confiscatory ransom that might or might not be paid.

In the meantime, the clock on England's future was ticking
down, and Montevideo seemed a terribly, terribly long way away.
Grey could easily have succumbed to despair.

For the moment, he was trapped in the bowels of the brigantine,
still in pitch black, with three of the oarsmen who'd rowed with
him to gather greens onshore; evidently the other three in his party
had been killed—either in the explosion or the wave that followed
it, or by the pirates who had fished Grey and the other survivors
out of the sea. There were manacles on his wrists, and the wrists of
the other men; the occasional jangle of the chains reminded Grey
that he was in company. As they had all come to their senses, there
was some discussion of the fate of the *Perseus*. Only Grey had seen
the explosion, as the oarsmen were necessarily faced the other way.
Over time, the four prisoners had drifted into silence, as each con-
templated his future, and the possibility that it might be very brief.

Grey was wondering if it was night or day when one of the oarsmen spoke up—the first time any of them had spoken, Grey thought,
in hours. Though maybe it just felt like hours.

"If they offer me to join up with them . . ." said a voice that Grey
recognized as belonging to an able seaman named Barrows. "If they
offer me to join up with them, I will."

"If you do," said Grey, "they'll tattoo Jolly Roger on your arm.
And if ever you make it back to the civilized world, you'll be hanged
as a pirate."

"Might better be hanged then as fed to the sharks now," said Barrows, after a moment. "And maybe I can explain that it weren't my
choice. I was obliged to join up with them."

"Maybe you can," said Grey.

"You don't think so?" said one of the other men, Dowdell.

Unable to see the oarsmen, the connection of the names and faces
and voices seemed to have become uncertain. He thought Dowdell

was fifteen or thereabouts. That's how his voice sounded anyway. Young, and with a fearful timbre to it.

"I don't know," said Grey. "I imagine that's what every pirate taken says, though. Much of the time it's probably true, but they tend to hang regardless."

"What would you do, sir?" said Dowdell.

"I'll join up with them too, if they offer," said the third man, Drumgoole. Another able seaman, a foremast jack.

"I don't know," said Grey. "Better to be called a pirate than a dead man; better to be a dead man than a murderer, I suppose."

"What will you do, sir, if they ask?" said Dowdell.

"Try to get a good price at the slave gallery," said Grey.

"You'd rather be a slave than a pirate? Than a free man?" said Barrows. He added, after a moment: "Coward."

Before Grey could answer, a hatch opened above them. The dim light that came through it was blinding.

"You," said a rough voice, in Spanish. "The captain will speak with you. *You.*"

The speaker pointed at Grey, then dropped a dowel ladder into the prisoners' hold. Grey looked at the ladder, and then at the three wretched seamen around him. Dowdell's eyes were red and swollen; all three looked like they were waiting to be summoned to the infernal regions.

"God speed you, lads," said Grey, taking hold of the ladder.

"God bless you, sir," said Dowdell.

THE PIRATE WHO'D DROPPED the ladder led Grey up from the hold and then back through the gundeck, where he passed under the eyes of a few dozen pirates. A few jeered, a few others whistled, one issued an ironic benediction. Grey asked his warder the name of the ship.

"*El Mosquito*," said the man, knocking on the door to the great cabin at the gundeck's rear, opening the door, and pointing Grey inside. The great cabin looked more or less like it did on all ship-rigged vessels: a large room with a wide sweep of windows at the back that stretched the width of the stern. There was no glass in any of them, just storm shutters that were, at this moment, fast to the ceiling. There was an air of dinginess to the place—totally absent were the obsessive cleaning and shining of the Royal Navy. The captain was recumbent on a sofa, a sort of ottoman mattress. He was twirling a finger in a long beard and reading from a duodecimo.

"Sir," said the captain, seeing Grey enter. "Sit."

He pointed to a rug on the floor in front of his couch. Grey had spent a number of years working and dealing with ottomans in Dalmatia and North Africa; still, concussed as he was, it took him a moment to remember how one goes about sitting on the floor in polite company, as opposed to plopping down on the ground as you might after a long march. Though perhaps calling this polite company was being too generous. In any case—the captain looked amused, watching Grey finally cross his legs, bent at the knee, and lower himself.

"Comfortable?" said the captain with a toothy grin.

"Exceptionally," said Grey, without expression.

"You are English?" said the captain; they were speaking Spanish.

"I am," said Grey. "Are you a Turk?"

"No," said the captain. "I am Spanish. I seized a Turkish barkentine once, and, well, I found its furnishing to be an improvement on my own."

"I see," said Grey. "May I ask where I am?"

"Aboard my ship, about a hundred sea miles west of Roque. On our way to Isla Cangrejo—do you know it?"

Grey shook his head. "A pirate island?"

"Yes. The southernmost of the markets of Comodoro Lafitte."

"Jean Lafitte?"

The captain laughed. "You know him?"

"Not intimately," said Grey.

"No, I thought not. But you know his work, then?"

"Rumors of it. I thought he worked further north."

"Indeed he does," said the captain, "but his franchise covers the entire Caribbean."

"His franchise?" said Grey.

"His markets," said the captain. "Which brings us to you. From your clothes—what is left of them—I gather that you are no seaman, but a supernumerary. From your clothes, and from this . . ." He picked up Grey's Girandoni repeater, which had been lying on the couch beside him. "What is it?"

"An air rifle," said Grey. "But I'm afraid it isn't for sale. Sentimental reasons, you understand."

"Your witticisms bring you rather close to the wind, sir," said the captain. "But an air rifle, you say. Most interesting. So this . . ." He held up the hand pump that was part of the rifle's ball-and-tool kit. "This fills it with air?"

"That's right."

"Well, perhaps someday you will have an opportunity to repurchase it. Which brings us again to you. You are not an officer."

"A passenger, sir, to Montevideo. And I would happily pay you to carry me the rest of the way."

"Pay me with what?" said the captain. "No, I think Cangrejo will be a better destination for you. You have people in Montevideo who will ransom you?"

"Yes," said Grey. "And at Recife too. If you take me there, they will pay you a very good price, and directly. No need to cut in the *comodoro*."

"And then, in Recife, to be hanged for my troubles?" said the captain. "I think not. What is your profession?"

"Priest," said Grey.

The captain laughed. "Bad luck to have a priest aboard. Perhaps I should maroon you. But no—you can read and write? Very good. You will fetch a good price. Your shipmates, I think I'll keep myself. But yes, you will fetch a good price."

"You deal much in slavery?"

"Oh yes, it's very profitable. I used to trade Black men, you know—and women," he smiled disgustingly, "but since the slave revolt in Haiti, white slaves command a heavy premium. Their owners find them less . . . uh, frightening. It was one of my main inducements to enter piracy. Ransoms are all well and good, you know, but a literate white man, and a priest to boot—nothing frightening about a priest, he won't rise against you, will he? Still, we'll try to ransom you first, might get even more than at an auction. So hard to predict auctions, you know. One day a man goes for a tutor, the next, his wife drives the bidders wild, and perhaps the day after, his son brings out the pederasts. But sometimes it's not worth the water it cost to bring them to market."

Grey nodded. "What's your name, sir?"

"Vargas," said the captain. "Will you remember me?" He laughed again. "I would ask you your name, but it doesn't matter—let's just hope the cost of putting you up in the ransomers' hostel doesn't cut too far into my profit of you. Very well."

He was thinking, twirling his beard again. "Yes, very well—now you will write your ransom letter. I will want . . . a hundred pounds for you. Sterling. Or else it's the market. So write well. There is the inkpot, and beside, a leaf." He pointed, and then resumed reading and twirling his beard.

8

WITH NO TIME TO ENCODE a more detailed message-within-a-message, Grey was able to insert, into his letter requesting a ransom from the British consul at Recife, only phrases that identified him as an intelligence man and a courier of dispatches or important news; this by making slight changes to the traditional closing of the letter: "I am, sir, *with all possible respect*, your *determinedly* obedient servant, Thomas Grey." He handed the letter to the captain, Vargas, who called for the warder pirate to return Grey to the prison hold. Depositing Grey, the warder ordered the three sailors to ascend. They did as they were told, and the hatch was sealed above Grey's head again, leaving him alone. The three sailors did not return.

When the brig docked at Isla Cangrejo—sometime later, hours or days, Grey wasn't certain—the hatch to the prison room was opened again, and Grey was brought on deck, past more jeering pirates. Among them—not jeering, but looking to various degrees deeply ashamed—were Barrows, Drumgoole, and Dowdell. All appeared to have cast their lots in with the filibusters.

It was twilight, but the sight of the harbor and the island that surrounded it frankly shocked Grey. Englishmen rarely concerned themselves with piracy; it was the privilege of their singular navy which escorted their merchant ships wherever the needs of commerce and empire took them. Grey knew, of course, that other nations trading in the Mediterranean, or the Caribbean, or in Canton, Batavia, Java, and so on, suffered considerable harm from pirates, but till this moment, he had never grasped the true magnitude of the industry. Hadn't the pirates' golden age died with Black Beard and Black Bart and Black Sam and Black Caesar and Black Bellamy? Grey reflected for a moment on the lack of imagination gone into pirates' noms de guerre, and looked around Crab Island.

It was only a mile or so off the Brazilian mainland, and it instantly put Grey in mind of Santorini or Deception—caldera islands, where the craters of dead volcanoes had given way to large natural harbors. Just the sort of geological phenomenon that Grey's late wife had reveled in . . . Was it five years now since they had sailed from Malta to the little monastic enclave of Santorini so Paulette could wander around, drawing the folds in the stone and collecting bits of ancient fish and insects?

Crab Island was smaller than Santorini, but not much; great sheer cliff faces dominated the harbor, which was brimmed with brigs and barks, sloops, snows, ships of every rigging; smugglers and pirates and, no doubt, rich *gentlemen* of the West Indies looking to buy what they ought not have. The shores all around were dotted with illuminated windows in shops and taverns and trading houses. Grey—still in his manacles—climbed awkwardly down the brig's accommodation ladder and into a cutter that ferried him and Vargas and a passel of eager pirates to a pier, where Vargas and his company marched Grey, with considerable fanfare, down a crowded market street. A sharp whistle turned Grey's head to a dirty, piratical-looking fellow at a spice cart—he met Grey's eyes for an instant before turning away again. And then Vargas was introducing Grey to a bizarre parody of a hotel: a prison where Vargas booked a cell for Grey, paying twelve shillings, in advance, for Grey's board.

The prison was a long, single-story building made of heavy oak, doubtless timbers that had once belonged to a ship. Grey's cell, near the end of a long hallway-full, was four wooden walls, one of them a heavy door, not locked but rather designed only to swing outward and barred from the outside. Opposite the door was a small window, about two-thirds of a foot square. No bars there; it was much too small to crawl through. Grey was just able to get his head out of it. Then, for an instant he worried he wouldn't be able to get his head back in again. There was a well-worn path along the prison's back side; no doubt a sort of banker came by to lend money to potential ransomees at absurd rates of interest. Probably vendors passed by to sell prisoners food at comparably confiscatory rates, or on confiscatory lines of credit. Grey wondered if that was how he'd have to obtain food and water, or would it be included in the price of the room? Aside from a drink from *El Mosquito*'s scuttlebutt as he was taken off, he had had neither food nor water for what felt like a very long time. He should have eaten some of those hog plums when he'd had the chance.

Here was a fellow now, rounding the corner of the prison and walking along the path, looking into cells as he went. It was the bearded piratical fellow who had whistled as Grey had been marched through the market, the one who'd been standing at the spice cart. Was there something about his appearance that was vaguely familiar? He had Grey's build; perhaps slightly taller; tanned skin and brown hair that was long, unkempt, and dirty. He saw Grey and approached, putting a finger to his lips. When he was close enough to be heard, speaking low but not so low as to give off the suspicious rasp of a whisper, he said:

"Well, well, well. Yes, I thought recognized you. Had some bad luck, have we, Mr. Caffery?"

He smiled at Grey. Grey stared at him. Grey had used the name Caffery during a recent assignment to Frankfurt, to help effect the defection of an important Frenchman. He recognized this dirty face, behind the beard and grime, and locks of long hair dangled over the eyes . . . but he was almost too astonished to believe it.

"Mr. Parker?" he said. "Philo Parker?" An American intelligence man; an opposite number of Grey's in service to the United States.

"No," said Parker. "Name's Bowen. Peter Bowen. And yours?"

"Grey," said Grey. "Thomas Grey."

"Mr. Grey," said Parker, "have you been detailed pirates too?"

Grey shook his head. "No, I hadn't planned on having anything to do with pirates; this was entirely their idea."

"Then what are you doing here?"

"Is that a joke? What are *you* doing here?"

"I've been detailed pirates," said Parker. "Don't they have newspapers in London? We've been fighting a little war."

"Were you at Tripoli?"

Parker nodded. "I was."

"Well, good work. Shame you haven't managed anything here yet."

"Patience, my lad, patience. We'll burn this hornets' nest too. Not everyone has a Helen-sized fleet, you know. Shame you noblest English haven't bothered yourselves about pirates."

"We don't bother them because they don't bother us."

Parker raised an eyebrow.

"Present company excluded. It was bad luck. A light ship and a lee shore."

"Well, lucky for you, the United States are here to save the day. Or will be, soon enough."

"How soon?" said Grey, his pulse quickening at the thought of disaster averted.

"Three days' time."

"Couldn't make it tomorrow, could you? I'm in a bit of a hurry."

Parker chuckled a short laugh and shook his head.

"I'm serious, though. I must get to Montevideo with all speed. What's the date?"

"July second."

"I'm damned, Parker—I've lost the best part of a week already. If I'm not in Montevideo by the middle of July . . . well, how will you feel about Napoleon running all of the French, Spanish, and British empires?"

"Not our first choice of outcome, certainly. But not our first concern either."

"Can you arrange something for me—something fast and

weatherly—for the moment following your nest-burning, three days from now? With fair winds and the good Lord's undivided attention, I might still make it."

Parker shook his head. "I'm afraid not."

"Then strike fast and weatherly; can you find me something that floats?"

"I'm sorry, Grey. If I possibly could."

"Parker, on my honor, this could not be a more urgent request."

Parker frowned at him. "In three days my navy attacks this island. And how long the freebooters may hold out, I've no idea. It could be over in a few hours—or it could take a month, fighting in the hills. That's the thing about pirates. Sometimes they fold up instantly and beg for mercy; sometimes, knowing they'll be hanged, they go to it pell-mell until every last one has been killed. All I can say for certain is that in the short term, there could be no question of sparing a ship or a crew."

Grey nodded and thought for a moment.

"Look, can you at least get me out of here? I'll hire a ship, or I'll pirate something myself. One of these gentlemen's yachts."

Now Parker thought for a moment. He scratched his beard.

"Yes," he said finally. "Yes, I can do that. But once I have you out, you don't know me and we won't speak again. I cannot risk my sub-rosity."

"I understand. I'm in your debt, Parker."

"Not yet, you aren't. Let's not count our chickens before they hatch."

"Prudent, but you forget: I'm already in your debt for those Frenchmen you tripped in Frankfurt."

Parker smiled. "Oh yes, I'd forgotten that . . . Yes, you are in my debt already, aren't you? Well, maybe someday I'll call it to account. For the meantime: Hold fast. I'll be back."

Grey nodded, and Parker walked away, continuing along the path in the direction he'd been going.

9

GREY WAS ASLEEP ON THE FLOOR of the cell, leaned up against one of the walls, when a pebble hit his forehead. He snapped awake and was instantly *shush*ed by the American Parker, whose face was at Grey's small window.

"Lord but you're a heavy sleeper," said Parker, in a loud whisper.

"Take these," he said, reaching a fistful of robust, foot-long ships' nails in through the window. "And this . . ." He handed in a wooden mallet hammer after them.

"The top beam here, running along the bottom of the window," said Parker. "Make bits of those nails, below the window here, something stout that you can seize a line to."

Grey saw what Parker was getting at, and began to hammer in the nails, in a roughly horizontal line, choosing spots in the wood that weren't too run through with dry rot. Occasionally he glanced out the window at Parker, who was making a hemp line into a harness for a pair of mules.

"Hammer faster," said Parker. "A little banging is unlikely to draw much attention from the main street, but there aren't many draft animals on the island, and the fellow I stole these from may come looking for them."

Grey hammered faster. It took something under five minutes to get half a dozen nails deep into the wall, with enough of their shafts showing for Grey to seize Parker's line to them as fast as fast can be.

"Pass me the bitter end," said Grey, and Parker fed the end of the line through the window. Grey couldn't help but notice that Parker was wearing, slung over his shoulder, Grey's Girandoni repeating rifle.

"And where in the hell did you get *that*?" Grey said, indicating the rifle with his chin while his hands began some old practiced knots.

"The air rifle?" said Parker, smiling. "I bought it off that Captain Vargas who led you in. He's the big number around here; he was holding court at a public house and I made him an offer. We settled on ten pound sterling and five Spanish dollar-eights."

"*Fifteen quid* for a *Girandoni*? He must have been drunk out of his skull, that——" Grey continued to loop his knots, unleashing a string of profanity at his captor.

"Indeed," said Parker, with a hint of a surprised chuckle; he was checking the lines around the mules' shoulders, satisfying himself that everything was shipshape. "Have you ever seen one of these in life? A fellow of mine—name of Lewis—owns one, and it's the most damned ingenious thing."

"Yes, Parker, I know it."

"Where do you suppose Vargas found one?"

"Oh, I'd dare venture a guess."

Parker looked up at him. "No. Yours?"

"It was."

Parker laughed. "Sorry, old man. Well, we can set matters aright after we have you out of here."

"If you have me out of here and on my way, I'll not only forgo the rifle, I'll have the transaction blessed by the Archbishop of Canterbury. Are you ready?"

Parker was giving a final tug on the mules' harness. "I am. Are you?"

Grey tugged the large coil knot on his nail bits. Immovable as the cornerstone of Canterbury Cathedral. "I am."

"Stand back, then."

Grey backed away from the window, and Parker began to lead the mules at a right angle from the prison's back wall. They were walking slightly uphill, through tall, reedy grass towards the edge of the tropical forest that covered most of the island.

The line's slack ran out, and the mules began to pull on the prison wall. They started to strain. The nails started to strain. The line was pulled arrow straight. Parker was urging the mules on with words of quiet encouragement—"There you are, boys—hearty fellows—heave and go, boys, heave and go." They pulled, harder, digging their hooves into the earth. "Come on, boys, you can do it, pull—pull—pull for your lives!" He smacked the one nearer to him on the rump, hard.

The wall of the prison began to bow out slightly. Then suddenly, like a rockslide—and with a loud snapping sound—it gave way—the bitted line took off half of the prison's back side. A gigantic hole gaped; Grey stepped through it, and as several other confused prisoners did the same, he headed for Parker. At the same time, Parker had his sword out and was slicing through the mules' hemp harnesses.

"Well, that was louder than expected," he said mildly, as chaos could be heard erupting on the prison's far side. "Time for that best form of valor, Grey; let's get the hell out of here. Into the jungle; out again on the other side of the harbor. I hope you can ride bareback."

The sliced coils of rope fell to the ground around the mules. Parker climbed aboard one and Grey pulled himself onto the other. Digging their heels in, they disappeared into the forest along a game trail just as a drunk piratical mob rounded the prison's corner.

With Parker leading, they made the best speed they could, pushing through branches and tangle, cutting vines, ducking boughs. After about a quarter hour, at a small clearing around a spring, they paused to listen for pursuers. After a minute's silence, they agreed they were home free, and Grey slipped quickly off his mule. There had been no water in the prison, and he hadn't had a decent drink of water in what felt like a lifetime. Adrenaline had powered him since Parker had woken him with a pebble to the forehead, but now—

seeing the fresh, clear water in front of him—the thirst burst back to the front of his mind. He was damned dizzy. He walked a few steps and dropped to his knees at the edge of the spring pool. He cupped his hands and brought a few gulps of cool water to his mouth. It was heaven.

Behind him, Parker hissed, "*DAMNIT MAN, MOVE. TO THE RIGHT TO THE RIGHT.*"

With the snap response of a marine following a battle order, Grey rolled to his right. Parker was off his mule, sword in hand, diving forward, down on one knee, slicing a large snake in two. A golden lancehead; Grey recognized it, though he'd never seen one. Half coiled to strike, now half a snake, it doubled back on what was left of its body, thrashing madly, now towards Parker, and sank its teeth into Parker's right leg, a few inches above his thick leather boots. Parker growled in pain, dropped his sword, used both hands to clamp down on the snake's head, peel it off, and throw it—writhing in a death rattle—away, into the jungle.

And Grey was jumping back to his feet, grabbing Parker's dropped sword and kicking away the writhing lower half of the snake. He used Parker's sword to make a shallow cut over the two fang holes below Parker's knee, and began to suck out blood and venom, spitting them away, returning for another mouthful, spitting it away, continually, for almost a minute, until Parker interrupted him.

"Grey, stop, listen to me. That may be helping—may have helped—but that was some kind of fer-de-lance, so I may not have much time, much coherent time." He was already ashen. "So listen to me, very carefully. There was a French ship *Tyrannicide*—you know of it? They also called her *Desaix*."

"Yes. She was at Algeciras. A seventy-four."

"Yes. Your fleet almost sank her there, ran her aground, but after Saumarez pulled back to Gibraltar, the French refloated her."

"She ended up foundering in the Caribbean, didn't she? In the year two."

"Yes, exactly. She was battered to pieces on the rocks at Cape Francis, and that was where the French left her—and her seventy-four guns. Jean Lafitte wasn't so easily cowed as your average frog, though. He brought an engineer from New Orleans and hired local divers and they and some of his seamen were able to recover some of those cannon. Four of them—eighteen-pounders. And he sent them here. That's why we—our navy, the American navy—hasn't been able to come in and clear this place out. At the cliff overlooking the mouth of the harbor . . . you saw it?"

"The cliff? Yes," said Grey, who had begun to clean Parker's wound with Parker's pocket kerchief and the spring water.

Parker winced, gritted his teeth a moment, and continued.

"Atop that cliff is a battery. Four eighteen-pound cannon. They make the harbor impregnable. And they themselves are impregnable. Most of the booters here are former man-o'-war's men. French, Spanish, British, Dutch, even American. Soldiers of fortune, and they're all still alive because they're good at their jobs. Your Captain Vargas more or less governs the island in Lafitte's stead, and the road to the battery is heavily guarded. And the battery itself is guarded—I barely escaped detection looking at it. There are two dozen men up there—not just to work the cannon, but to protect them. They get a few share-pieces each from every ship that makes harbor here, remitted to them by Vargas, so you can imagine they take their duties quite seriously."

Grey put his hands under Parker's shoulders and pulled him a few feet to the base of a tree, leaned Parker back against the trunk. Parker continued:

"I'm here to destroy those guns. Two of our frigates—*Congress* and *Constellation*—will rendezvous outside this harbor in, now, two days' time. They'll be waiting for my signal that the cannon have been destroyed, so they can enter the harbor and burn the establishment down. If they don't receive my signal, they'll begin a close blockade instead—a long, long process of starving the pirates out. But here's the rub, Grey: We knew that those cannon came from the wreck of *Tyrannicide*, but all we knew for certain was that they were eighteen-pounders in good condition—that, from a source of implicit trust. But they're not, Grey. I've seen them. They're not eighteens, they're thirty-sixes. Four monsters from the lower deck, the great guns. Double the weight of metal and five times the range.

"*Congress* and *Constellation* are expecting eighteens. They're going to sail into range—well into range—of those cannon. When they do, they'll be ducks on a pond. And then they'll be on the seabed, in minutes. One-third of our navy's flagships, gone in a flash, along with the best part of a thousand men. And there's no way to stop it, Grey, no way for me to get to them, no way to warn them. One-third of our navy's main force will be sunk unless that battery is destroyed. It has to be done, Grey. You have to do it."

Grey nodded. Could he spare two days for a man to whom he owed his life? But what about the lives of the men, and the women and children, who would be killed under a French reign of terror, if England fell? Montagnards in the House of Commons. Guillotines in the Court of St. James's. Too horrible to contemplate.

But two days was much less a delay than eternity, and if not for Parker, Grey would be dead. More than that, Parker was very possibly on the way to his own grave, a wound incurred saving Grey's life, on a misadventure to rescue Grey from prison, in an effort to make Grey's fulfilling his own duties possible.

No, there was no question at all. Grey would do his duty by God, and by God, there were few greater sins than perfidy and ingratitude. How sharper than a serpent's tooth . . .

"I will, Parker. I will. Tell me what you have planned."

"The harbor's very well guarded, but they don't bother about the outside of the horseshoe—you see what I mean? The island's shaped like a crab, with its claws out, but like a horseshoe, you understand?"

Parker was mumbling; Grey was pulling off his right boot. His foot and leg below the knee were a bright, fiery red and swollen like a balloon.

"I understand you, Parker; go on."

"The harbor's very well guarded, but the outside of the horseshoe is a sheer cliff, like some of the inside; all sheer, all vertical, above a rocky pebble beach. Like Chesil, but worse. Very difficult to land. But four of our marines are going to—they're going to skull on in a boat. For weeks I've been gathering line, taking it to the rendezvous, knotting and splicing. When the time came, I would lower it down the cliff face so they can climb up. You're not an alpinist, are you, Grey?"

"On occasion."

"You understand, that climb won't be possible without the rope. You need to get them off the beach, Grey. Get the rope down to them. They're bringing arms and slow match, to take the battery and to blow it up. See it gets done, Grey, will you?"

"I will, Parker."

"Pull the silverpoint out of my waist pocket, and the paper there. I need to draw you a map."

Parker closed his eyes and took a deep breath, willing his hands to steady, which they did. He drew a careful outline of the horseshoe-shaped island, marked the rendezvous with the marines and the location of the battery, noting elevations of both, drawing out what he'd seen of the battery's fortification, drawing in the road to the battery, and the rough paths of the game trails he'd used to avoid it.

Parker handed Grey the map. It was drawn, Grey saw, on the back of a letter. It was faint, written in silverpoint, but legible. Grey folded it, but had no pocket to put it in. Parker noticed this and laughed, wanly.

"Take my clothes, Grey, and take your rifle back, and take my pack. It has a striker in it, and some food. A signal lantern's hidden with the rope at the *X*; the signal from the marines offshore will be long-long-short-long; countersign short-long-long-short. It's there . . . I wrote it out . . ."

Parker cleared his throat, and mustered his remaining energy.

"There's a small chance I'll live through this, Grey, so leave me a bit of food and my sword, and then get moving. And God speed you."

Now Grey chuckled, mirthlessly.

"Don't be an ass, Parker—I'm not going to leave you here."

"Yes you damned well are, Grey. This is much too important for you to drag me along, you won't make it in time. Go. *Now, goddamn you*," said Parker, with venom in his voice.

"Mr. Parker, in a moment you'll be unconscious, and then I'm going to tie you to that mule like a sack of meal. I'll try to keep your head cool, and though I may have to take your leg off, I warrant you'll live through this."

Philo Parker was unconscious before Grey had finished speaking.

They had a long climb ahead of them, on switchback game trails to the caldera's top. Its lip? Rim, perhaps. In any case, Grey's first order of business was appropriating Parker's boots. Less against the climb than against the snakes.

10

THE CLIMB FROM THE INNER EDGE of the island horseshoe up towards the crater's rim took hours; not only—not even principally—because of the rim's height, but because of the increasing steepness of the paths. Made originally by whatever small animals ran wild on the island—some sort of feral pig, Grey supposed—they switched back occasionally, but apparently the feral pigs, or goats or jaguars or whatever they were, were very sure-footed, and in places, the incline exceeded forty-five degrees from level. Fortunately, mules laugh in the face of Newton and gravity, so, though slow, the going was steady. With the mules more or less content to be left to their own devices, Grey's principal concern was for the unconscious Mr. Philo Parker. Grey had fastened Parker's arms around his mule's neck, and his legs beneath its belly, making him look something like a jockey with an aggressive forward cant. Grey worried that the paths' steepest portions would see him slip loose and tumble down the thickly forested hillside, or else shift suddenly and pull the mule with him. In the event, neither happened, but it was far from the easiest ride of Grey's life.

It was eight or nine hours before they reached the crater's wide-rim plateau; Grey figured it was sometime in the late afternoon.

It was impossible for Grey to consider the time without worrying about Montevideo and the treasure fleet and the precious seconds pouring away through the hourglass. But for now, all he could do was muddle forward and pray that in helping Parker he would be helping himself along as well. The spring-soaked sleeve Grey had wrapped around Parker's forehead had lost any trace of coolness, and Grey spent some water from Parker's canteen on a new head covering; it wasn't near as cool as the spring water, but at least it was cooler than the sweat soaking Parker's face and hair.

The top of the crater's rim was much less thickly forested than the crater's interior, presumably because of the sharp wind that blew across it—incessantly, it seemed—and from which the interior of the island was sheltered. After the true Brazilian jungle through which they had ascended, the rim's foresting seemed like a return to some sort of civilization; like a forest in Asturias rather than in the Amazon.

Looking back into the crater's bowl, the harbor and market seemed extremely remote. On the crater's far side, Grey could make out no detail other than a gray smudge which he supposed to be the great guns' Martello tower; the battery to be destroyed. A thin wisp of smoke rose from it. If Grey could see the smoke from—what—eleven or twelve miles away?—then the fire it rose from must be considerable; the number of men it served, comparably considerable. Parker appeared not to be mistaken in the strength of the battery's defense. Grey disposed of the modest hope that he could simply sneak through in the dark of the night, throw a torch nearby the magazine, and be done with the enterprise himself. Then, instead of helping the American marines up, he could have helped himself and Parker down, ridden with them back to their mother ship—*Congress* or *Conglomeration* or whomever she was—and begged, in recompense, swift conveyance to Montevideo. Clearly that was not to be.

The point on the rim that Parker had marked on his map as the sight of his rope and signal light; adjacent to the spot where the marines would make their ascent, was something near half the distance between the point Grey judged they had emerged from the crater, and the spot where the battery stood. If the crater were in the vicinity of twelve miles across, its circumference—had it been a full crater rim rather than a fractional one, and if Grey remembered his tables—would be more or less forty miles. Grey figured he was just over halfway around the rim from the spot where the battery stood, so—in rough and round numbers—about ten miles to the rope, ten more to the guns. Distances neither inconsiderable nor insurmountable. But either way, as the marines wouldn't signal from offshore till an hour before sunrise—which Grey guessed was about eight hours away—he had time now to check Parker's bite and change its dressing.

Grey slid off his horse and slid off the bandage he'd wrapped around the upper portion of Parker's lower leg. It was a darker, blacker red now, but Grey smelled nothing that suggested dead or dying flesh, which was a very good sign. Of course, Grey's experience in wounds were with those inflicted by falls, balls, bullets, and splinters; he had, frankly, no idea whatsoever about the nature of snake venom; no guess as to the mechanism by which it worked. Paulette would have known . . . she had remarked a few times on snakes, though the only thing Grey remembered now from those remarks, which were in connection with a certain Maltese hedgehog said to be immune to snakebites, was that a snake's bite either turned the blood dangerously thin or dangerously thick, or caused the quick death of flesh in the bite's vicinity. Parker's pulse seemed strong enough, so his blood presumably had not congealed to a jelly. And his wound was not bleeding, so it had likewise not turned into . . . Grey tried to think of a liquid that flowed more quickly than water, but couldn't. Surely there wasn't one, was there? In any case, the bite had apparently not turned Parker into a hemophiliac. So if the flesh were not yet dying, perhaps Parker was winning against the poison. Or perhaps in an hour he would be dead. Grey could not honestly tell himself he had a clear notion of Parker's condition. He did, though, remember his late wife saying that, like spiders, snakes' bites tended to be less severe than generally thought—whereas centipedes, innocuous and worm-like though they might appear, should be given as wide a birth as possible.

After checking that none of the rope loops holding Parker fast to his mule had caused burns that themselves might become infected, Grey resumed his own mule and their ride towards the rendezvous, allowing himself cautious optimism.

II

WENDING QUIETLY THROUGH the rim's woods, it took
Grey and his company two or so hours to reach Parker's
point indicated. Per Parker's map, a tree ten or so yards
back from the outer edge would have a gigantic coil of rope around
its trunk, and the signal lantern tied beside it. Grey hoped no one
had chanced upon them and become curious, though happily there
seemed to be no indication that anyone other than Parker, and now
himself, had been up here.

Grey turned his small convoy towards the outer edge of the caldera's rim, towards the outer cliff face. The wind increased as they
approached the precipice; at about ten yards back from it, Grey tied
the lead mule to a tree; untied from it Parker's mule and tied that
mule to a tree as well, and left the animals to pick relaxedly at the
thick tropical grass, as Grey continued on foot. There was no point,
he believed, in searching for a single tree in a forest while mounted,
and in any case, he wanted to get some blood back into his legs.

He walked up to the verge, steadying himself with a tree,
against the wind. It wasn't yet threatening to knock him down, but
with fewer and fewer trees to diffuse it, it had become considerable indeed, and was vigorously tossing around his short hair. Grey
looked over the edge. Probably at some point in the distant past the

island had sloped down to the water, as did the outer edge of Santorini; some eternity of Atlantic waves beating against Isla Cangrejo, however, had worn it sheer. Far below—five hundred feet? or thereabouts?—Grey could see pillars of rock that had sheared off the cliff face and now lay broken on the rocky beach like the ruins of some gigantic, ancient temple. It was no wonder that Vargas—or Lafitte, or whatever cohort decided these things—saw no need of keeping watch over it; it was the very definition of inhospitable. Grey half expected to see it festooned with ships, like Scylla. In fact, as he considered it, there must certainly be wrecks beneath him, and in daylight he would probably see their skeletons, picked clean by scavenging pirates and crabs.

But no sense dwelling on it, Grey told himself; there was much still to be done and but dwindling time in which to do it. A few yards back from the edge, Grey walked parallel to the cliff's face, looking inward, looking for Mr. Parker's tree. It would have been useful had Parker been able to describe some feature of the tree, or its close— something that might help bring him directly to the spot indicated. But of course, Parker hadn't intended, or foreseen a need for, anyone other than himself finding it.

But in due time—after five or ten minutes' walk—Grey found the tree, wearing its immense coil of rope. About five hundred feet, presumably, of one-inch line. Grey hoped Parker was a good hand at splicing. Had Parker been to sea as Grey had? In the course of their acquaintance, they had exchanged only a few hundred words; it had never come up. And as a rule, Grey didn't like to pry into any private affair other than those of an enemy government.

Grey took his bearings and then returned to the mules, who were contentedly clearing the grass beneath their respective trees. Parker was still laid atop his mule like a sack of grain, still unconscious. His leg still lacked the smell of dying flesh. Retying the second mule to the first, and taking the first by a handful of mane to get him going in the right direction, Grey took the convoy to the rope tree, and there began to make ready for the American marines.

After unloading the useful contents of Parker's pack, he made a pillow of it and laid Parker on the ground, the pack beneath his head. And then he began to uncoil the rope. Normally this sort of repetitive work would get Grey humming a work chantey in his head; now all he could do was figure over and over the delay he was adding to his voyage to Montevideo.

Aloud, he admonished himself to focus.

12

GREY GATHERED THAT THE MARINES were off either *Constellation* or *Congress*, which must be somewhere out there, in the Atlantic, with its sidelights doused. Their boat would be lowered, and then their home frigate would disappear back over the horizon, to wait for the next night's rendezvous. Then, as a feeling of total isolation—with which Grey was intimately familiar— set in, they would begin rowing towards the seaward coast of Crab Island, which would, in the darkness, be invisible. They would aim for the sound of large swells crashing on rocks. When it had grown appropriately loud, they would pull up their oars and wait for Grey's signal, and hope that the earliest colors of morning light would be enough to get them safely through the rocks and onto the beach. They couldn't dare to wait longer; though the Cangrejo harbor's mouth was on the landward side of the island, and though this rough and rocky exterior was of little use to anyone, ships approaching the island or leaving it would have watches set, and one glimpse of the four men rowing towards the cliffs or climbing them would throw the whole operation into a cocked hat. With this in mind, it would have been better to approach before the first hints of dawn. But the approach, let alone the climb, would be dangerous enough in a little light. In none at all, it would be mortal. So timing was everything.

Grey checked, one last time, that the end of the giant coil was immovably fast to the stoutest tree in the vicinity, and then, using Parker's jacket as a windshield, Grey lit the signal lantern and walked towards the cliff's edge, standing as close to the verge as he reasonably could. He sat down, cross-legged—as if on an Ottoman's carpet—and waited, staring out into the darkness. Waiting to see the magnified twinkle of the Americans' signal light.

Back from the cliff's edge, where there were trees enough to break the wind, it was warm, verging on hot, and extremely humid. Here at the edge, with the wind howling in from the Atlantic, and a nontrivial updraft from its collision with the cliff face, it was cold and blustery. Grey put on Parker's jacket, and wished he had a cigarillo or a pipe or anything in the tobacco line. Tobacco was, in essence, Grey's only vice, and being deprived of it chafed his already irritated humor. All he could hope was that soon the intoxication of action would take his mind off it. As it was, the only thing seriously contending with tobacco for his thoughts was the ever-present tick in his head of a clock winding down to the moment his mission to Montevideo would fail.

The wind started to blow harder, and the stars—as bright here as at sea (id est, a great o'erhanging firmament; a majestical roof fretted with golden fire)—started to dim. Clouds were moving towards the land. Soon the stars were invisible. The first drops of rain hit Grey's face just as he saw light flash offshore:

Long-long-short-long.

Grey opened the dark cover on his own signal light and answered:

Short-long-long-short.

The game was afoot. (Follow your spirit, and upon this charge cry "God for Harry, England, and Saint George!") As Grey returned to the rope coil, he wondered if Americans regretted dissociating themselves from the home of Shakespeare. Grey's father, who had spent some years in the American colonies—had in fact met Grey's mother there—was himself a great lover of Shakespeare, and had often remarked on the curiosity of no American town, no matter how small, lacking a fair-weather Shakespeare company.

No longer coiled around a tree; coiled rather, Bristol fashion, on itself, the task of feeding the line over the cliff edge was not too great. The only difficulty would be in ensuring it reached all the way to the ground. For that—and unable, in the darkness, to see any detail on the cliff's face—Grey had only the hope that the place at which he'd chosen, in the waning light of the previous evening, to lower the rope, contained no hidden snags that might imperil the rope's descent. He hoped too, as he lowered the line hand over hand, that the Americans now rowing ashore would have strength enough left in their arms, backs, and legs to make the climb. It would be a hard one. The rain was growing heavier.

At his height of about five hundred feet above the sea, Grey's horizon was something over twenty-five miles away. The first light wouldn't reach the men in the boat for several minutes more, but Grey could now see faint reds breaking through black clouds. Red sky at morn, sailors forlorn. It was going to be a filthy day; a storm was rolling in. Grey squinted down at the sea beneath him. He could just make out the white lines of breaking waves. He searched for the marines' boat. No sign of it yet.

The climbing rope was weighted with an iron plumb; even so, Grey could see it being blown back and forth. Well, there was nothing to be done about that. Not from the top, anyhow. The men at the bottom might try seizing it to something, though it was possible their weight on the rope would be enough.

There they were!

For a moment Grey thought his eyes were giving him the lie, but no, there they were—fighting with a heavy surf on the beach. Landing a boat over surf is an art, and one that requires a good deal of practice, which doubtless these Americans had. But there was no amount of practice that could prepare you for landing a boat through a storm surge. Most souls lost in shipwrecks were lost within a few yards of dry land. Grey found himself instinctively reciting the Lord's Prayer as he kept his eyes locked on the tiny boat, far below, trying to time its landing, trying to coast in on a wave that would deposit it on the beach, and the right way up.

There they went—they'd picked their moment and now the four men were pulling hard as they could, trying to stay on the crest of a wave. Grey could feel every move each man was making. He was tightening his arms, unlocking his knees, swaying in the rhythm of the oarsmen far below, though he couldn't make them out.

The boat's stern swung out to larboard; the men on starboard would be pulling double quick—short, choppy strokes, trying to straighten it out again. The wave broke beneath it, and the boat was on the shore—at an angle, but upright. Grey could see the dots of men leaping out, grabbing their oarlocks, heaving the boat higher onto the beach before another wave could break over it.

The next wave did break over it—but the four men kept the boat steady, even as it filled with water; fought against the undertow pulling it back towards the sea. Grey saw one man fall; instantly the retreating wave pulled him back off the beach, into the surf. But the other three kept the boat steady, and now they had it above the break point, out of danger. Now one of the men was grabbing an oar and running down the beach with it, holding it out, pulling his foundered mate out of the water. Now all four dots of men were on the beach, with their boat, doubtless catching their breaths. They couldn't wait long, though, to find Grey's rope—that is to say, Parker's rope—and begin to climb it. Not because day was breaking. Because the storm was getting worse.

13

ON THE ROCKY BEACH BELOW—to call it a pebble beach would have been too generous—three marine privates were looking to their sergeant, Patrick Neville, who'd just fished one of them out of the sea. All four were catching their breaths, but Neville gave them just half a moment before setting back to work.

"Eaton, Presley: Get the bows from the duck bag and string them. O'Bannon: Make sure the wax on the dry match is intact. I'm going to find our accommodation ladder."

No one chuckled at the mild witticism; they were tired already, and knew they had very much still to do. Neville raised the signal lantern and used it to sweep slowly along the face of the cliff, where it met the beach. Finding the rope wasn't hard; it twisted in the wind, rolling back and forth over the cliff face, dragging its lead plum with it; occasionally whipping the weight into the air.

Neville went up to it, caught it as it swung past him, steadying it, and looked up. The top wasn't quite visible, but it looked as if Mr. Parker had chosen his spot well, with the rope lying against roughly smooth rock (he very slightly smiled to himself: "roughly smooth") and no obvious jagged outcropping on which his men might be impaled. He looked back to his men, now each carrying a small pack, with short arrows protruding from its top, and a short composite bow beside. Presley held out a strung bow for Neville; O'Bannon held out Neville's pack, which carried the long, slow-burning fuse with which they would be able to set fire to the battery magazine without, in the process, committing suicide. Neville slung the bow diagonally across his back—shoulder to hip—and tightened the belt sling so there'd be no slack, no sudden weight shift to shake him off the rope. The pack followed it; as he fastened it over the bow, he said:

"Presley, Eaton, check the other's pack. O'Bannon, check mine. The wax was sealed?"

"All dry and sound, sir." He gave a tug on Neville's pack. "And this is tight and fast."

"Good," said Neville. "Turn around and let me check yours."

O'Bannon's things were tight and fast too; as were Presley's and Eaton's. So far everything had gone precisely to plan; now Neville had to make a considerable change.

"Boys"—he was twenty-two; they, between eighteen and twenty—"the plan of course was for me to go first—first into the breach—but this rain's getting harder, which means the climb's getting harder. So O'Bannon's going to go first, then Presley, then Eaton, and I'll bring up the rear."

"I'm glad we've agreed that I'm a stouter fellow than Presley," said Eaton, with a grin.

Presley slapped the back of his head—"Like *fun* you are," and for a moment the tension broke and the four men chuckled.

"If I'm going first, sir, I ought to carry the match," said O'Bannon.

"No," said Neville. "You'll have enough to worry about, forging the path up."

"But sir—"

"That's enough, O'Bannon; there isn't time. Up you go."

A moment's hesitation, looking at Neville, and then O'Bannon was grabbing the line, looking up to where it disappeared in hazy gray darkness. He pulled once, hard, to see it was sure, and then he began to climb, carefully, pacing himself, hand over hand. Neville took hold of the rope beneath him, to anchor it as O'Bannon climbed. For O'Bannon, the climb looked effortless. He was a Vermonter from a line of lumberjacks, with arms like Samson. They were all very strong climbers; that's why they were here. But Neville didn't feel any compunction at sending O'Bannon in his place, first up the rope. He could easily handle it.

But now they had to wait. Its having been known that Mr. Parker would have to splice the line himself, the decision had been made for only one man to climb at a time. And with the storm, Neville couldn't even watch O'Bannon's progress. All he could do was wait for three emphatic upward tugs on the rope—the sign that the man climbing had reached the top and the next could begin.

As Neville, Eaton, and Presley watched, O'Bannon receded from view and disappeared. The sun was rising, but it was rising behind the storm clouds and did them very little good. It was just the sort of day a man wants to spend in front of a fire with a good book, a glass of lager, and a girl's lap to lay his head on. No such luck today, thought Neville, wiping rain from his eyes. The rain was coming in hard and fast, at a steep angle, towards the cliff face, where strange eddies of wind whipped it into a heavy spray, like the spray of the surf through which they'd just come.

Of course, all four men were thoroughly accustomed to being soaked to the skin. Still, it was funny, thought Neville . . . when you're warm and dry, you never take a moment to appreciate it.

14

As the storm worsened, Grey lost sight of the Americans, but a few moments later he could see the rope tauten, and he knew the first of them must have begun his climb. He—the first American marine—appeared out of the dark haze of rain about a hundred feet below the clifftop. Grey watched him climb. His progress was impressively steady, even with the freshening wind pushing against him and his pack, twisting them first one way, then the other. As he reached the verge where Grey was kneeling, Grey had to resist the impulse to offer a hand to pull him the last few feet; as rain-soaked and slippery as his hand was, it would have been a damned foolish substitute for the rough, easy-to-grip rope. The American pulled himself up and over, and then pushed himself up onto his haunches, then to his feet. Without a word to Grey—only a nod, as he caught his breath—he reached down to the rope and tugged it hard, three times. A moment later the rope went taut again.

The American knelt down and began to catch his breath. He was powerfully built, over six feet standing, Grey guessed, with a deep flush on pale skin and hair that was probably a sandy blond when it was dry. After a few puffs, he looked up at Grey.

"Are you Mr. Parker, sir?"

"No, I'm Mr. Parker's deputy. The name's Grey."

"O'Bannon," said the American, extending his hand. "You're English?"

"I am," said Grey. "Are you . . . Irish?"

O'Bannon shook his head. "American."

Grey nodded. It wasn't the man's name that had made Grey wonder, but his species of Yankee accent, which seemed to have a sort of County Mayo roll to it. Though there seemed to be some East Anglia in it as well.

"Are you the senior man?" said Grey.

"No," said O'Bannon. "That would be Sergeant Neville. He'll be along. What happened to Mr. Parker?"

"Snakebite," said Grey.

O'Bannon nodded and then moved closer to the edge, looking for his next compatriot to emerge from the storm.

15

THREE STOUT TUGS ON THE ROPE told Neville that Presley had made it; now it was Eaton's turn, and as Eaton began, Neville couldn't help but say a silent prayer for them all. When it occurred to him that he was alone on the beach (even if he hadn't been, the howling wind would have made it impossible to hear words spoken six inches away), he repeated the prayer aloud, and quite forcefully.

It was an agonizing wait, but when the next three tugs came on the rope—when he knew his men had all made it safely to the top— he felt a swell of relief build up inside him. He took a last look at the rope's iron plumb, wishing it were a little heavier—he had no one to anchor for him, of course—but he wasn't really worried. He'd grown up beside a Philadelphia shipyard, and had been laying rigging and climbing ropes since he'd learned to walk. He dried his hands one last time—sticking them up under his jacket, feeling for a dry bit of shirt—and then grabbed the rope and began. It was old hat. Even in a damned serious storm.

16

EATON, WHO CARRIED WITH HIM a few small essentials of a surgeon's chest—bandages, needle and thread, a phial of laudanum—was crouched over Parker, removing the bandage on his leg and the compress on his forehead, evidently with the notion that the fresh rainwater would be better for him than the sweaty cloth. Presley, O'Bannon, and Grey, meanwhile, were at the cliff's edge, waiting for the sergeant Neville to appear out of the storm. With every passing moment, the wind seemed to strengthen, and the swings the rope took, whipped around by it, seemed to increase in their frequency and violence. But the rope remained taut, which told them Neville hadn't fallen. So they waited, unable to do anything else, until Eaton called Presley to help him move Parker to slightly higher ground, out of standing water. Grey and O'Bannon continued the vigil.

And then, suddenly, there he was, inching his way upward: first a shape in the rain, and then a distinct figure only fifty or sixty feet beneath them. His brow was badly gashed; pouring out blood which was just as quickly washed away by the rain; a swing of the rope away from the cliff must have dashed him against it. Grey could see his eyes, blinking incessantly; every few feet upward, Neville violently shook his head, doubtless trying to clear his vision.

A sharp updraft again pulled the rope away from the cliff face; as it blew back inward, Neville, twisting in the wind, was able to get a foot pointed towards the rock and absorb the blow with a leg. He climbed on, now just thirty or forty feet beneath them.

"We could pull him the rest of the way," said O'Bannon.

"It would take twenty men to pull this rope up with a capstan," said Grey.

O'Bannon nodded; he'd known that, of course, but he was nervous, and grasping. Grey could hear the tension in his voice. He remembered being a marine of O'Bannon's age, still too young truly to accept that sometimes you had to wait and let the game play out.

Another updraft blew Neville away from the cliff face. Again he swung back like the weight on a pendulum, legs braced for impact. But a cross-draft caught him and spun him and he crashed into the cliff face shoulder-first; his right shoulder dashed into the rock, and instantly Grey and O'Bannon could see something was wrong. Neville's right arm was dangling uselessly at his side. He tried to bring it up over his head to keep climbing but couldn't. He slid a yard backward down the rope before wrapping his feet tightly around it to hold it in place, then began to try again to climb, with only one hand on the rope. He made no progress at all; clearly he could barely hold on; Grey and O'Bannon could see him unable to brace himself against blows into the rock. Neville was entirely at the mercy of the wind.

O'Bannon was throwing off his pack, ready to go down after him. Grey put a hand on his shoulder and pulled him back from the edge.

"Do you have a knife?" said Grey, shouting into O'Bannon's ear to be heard over the howling wind.

O'Bannon nodded, now drying his hands to begin his climb down to his sergeant.

"No," said Grey, again into O'Bannon's ear. "Stay here. Give me the knife. When I signal, all of you heave."

O'Bannon was frozen, unsure what to do, instinctively unwilling to defer to a stranger from a strange land.

"Damnit, man, I know what I'm doing!" shouted Grey, with the wind screaming around his and O'Bannon's heads. "There's no time! Give me the knife!"

O'Bannon's hands went to his belt and slid out a large hunting knife; he handed it to Grey, who was throwing off his (Parker's) jacket.

"Remember!" shouted Grey. "On my signal, pull us up; all three of you!"

O'Bannon nodded. Grey clamped the knife in his teeth, sat down, and pulled off his (Parker's) boots. He took hold of the rope and slipped over the edge.

Fearing Neville, with one hand, wouldn't be able to hold on much longer, Grey—as he had a thousand times in his life, sliding down backstays at sea—circled his shins around the rope and slid down, tightening them to bring himself to a stop a good ten feet above Neville, not wanting to risk sliding too far and knocking the man to his death. He climbed down a few yards more so the soles of his feet were just above Neville's left hand, white-knuckled as it hung on to the rope. Grey wrapped his right arm around the rope, made sure he had a solid grip, and then used his left hand to take the knife out of his mouth and bellowed:

"SERGEANT NEVILLE, CAN YOU HEAR ME?"

"YES," bellowed Neville.

"I NEED TO GET BENEATH YOU. IS YOUR GRIP ON THE ROPE STRONG ENOUGH?"

"YES."

"HOLD FAST THEN," said Grey, before returning the knife to his mouth. He gripped the rope with all his might, with his hands, and then released his feet. Lowering himself hand under hand, he descended till he was eye level with Neville; his hands just above Neville's single grip. Their eyes met for a moment; Grey's were blanks; Neville's betrayed well-in-hand concern and confusion. Now also holding on with only his left hand, Grey snaked his right under Neville's damaged shoulder, around his back, and grabbed the rope again, with his right arm encircling Neville's rib cage beneath his armpits.

"I'M GOING TO HOLD YOU UP FOR A MOMENT," shouted Grey as best he could, the knife clenched in his teeth muddling his speech, "SO YOU CAN WRAP YOUR WRIST AND ELBOW AROUND THE ROPE—GET A BETTER GRIP—YOU WON'T BE ABLE TO USE YOUR LEGS."

It took Neville just a second or two to understand what Grey was getting at.

"ALL RIGHT," he said. "ON YOUR WORD."

Grey made sure of his grip, and his hold on Neville, and was about to tell him to let go when an updraft swung them away from the cliff face and then crashed them back into it. Grey was able to absorb most of it with his legs. He made sure of his grip again, on the rope and on Neville, and—through the knife in his teeth—shouted "GO."

In lightning-fast but jerking motion, Neville let go of the rope and laced his arm around it, letting the rope pass behind his wrist and twine around his arm down to his elbow. An instant later Grey felt him take his own weight again.

"ALL RIGHT?" said Grey.

"ALL RIGHT," said Neville.

"I'M GOING TO CUT NOW," said Grey.

Neville nodded. With every ounce of muscle at his disposal, Grey gripped the rope with his right hand, under Neville's shoulders. With his left, he took the knife out of his teeth, reached down as far as he could—to about the level of his and Neville's knees, and began to slash at the rope. It took four good hacks to cut it through.

The instant the rope was cut, Grey dropped the knife and grabbed the rope with his left hand. The wind began to toss them around like a kite in a storm. Grey looked up, through the rain in his eyes, and shouted to O'Bannon. He knew O'Bannon couldn't hear him, but hoped that O'Bannon could see his lips moving.

And so he did. Slowly but steadily, Grey felt the rope drawn upward. It took a few very long and agonizing minutes for them to reach the top, where the rough hands of three American marines grabbed them and pulled them over the top, and dragged them away from the edge.

All five men were panting. O'Bannon was the first to speak.

"Thank you," he said to Grey.

"Sorry about the knife."

O'Bannon chuckled. The thanks were echoed by Presley and Eaton, and then Neville had his breath caught enough to speak.

"I'm deeply in your debt, sir."

"Think nothing of it," said Grey. "I needed the exercise."

He lay back, flat on the ground, and let the warm rain cool his hot and flushed face.

17

NEVILLE'S ARM WAS BROKEN. Eaton intended to set it, but Grey took over, having considerably more experience in broken bones than the young marine. Before the arm was set, the first thing Neville said—after thanking Grey—was to ask where Mr. Parker was.

"There he lies," said Grey, pointing with his chin, snapping the bone back into place and tightening a splint around Neville's arm.

Neville sucked air through his teeth. Grey slipped the arm into a sling and helped him to his feet. Neville thanked Grey again and walked towards Parker. Parker was still unconscious, but perhaps slightly less pale? It was possible he was through the worst of it. Grey knelt and again sniffed around Parker's bite wound. Still no smell of flesh-death.

"What happened to him?" said Neville, looking down at Parker's face.

The rain was beginning to let up; the storm was blowing further inland—might be over the mainland by now—but the rain was still heavy enough for there to be no sense wiping Parker's brow. But Neville did anyway, as he knelt beside Grey, doubtless out of habit in dealing with feverish colleagues, and not knowing what else to do.

"Snakebite," said Grey.

"Where are his boots?"

"I'm wearing them," said Grey, who'd put Parker's boots on again after the climb and the breath-catching. "He was very keen on making certain one of us two was still on his feet when it came time to bring you up here, and bring low the pirate battery. He's asked me to assume command in his stead."

"I'm afraid I don't understand," said Neville, standing.

Grey stood as well.

"He asked you to assume command? Why?"

"Because he worried that his lack of consciousness might impair his ability to make command decisions."

"Yes, very amusing, sir. You are an Englishman. I am the next-ranking American. Mr. . . . . ?"

"Grey. Thomas Grey, late a captain of His Majesty's Royal Marines."

"Well, that's all very well, Captain Grey—and I don't want to appear ungrateful for what you've done—but you could be Lord High Admiral of All His Majesty's Ships at Sea and it still would give you no authority to lead a detachment of the American military."

"I don't claim authority from my former rank; I merely use it to reassure you. I derive my authority from Mr. Parker's fervent request, and my having given my word to do as he asked."

"I would have to hear that from his own lips," said Neville.

"Well, that's fine," said Grey, "as you're going to stay here and keep watch over him. And then you can hear it from his own lips the very moment he regains his senses.

"As for you three," he said turning to the other Americans, "Make ready. We've a long walk ahead of us. I'll carry the slow match."

"*No*, sir," said Neville. "I appreciate your intentions, but I don't know you from Adam. You may have given your word, but so have I, when I took my oath. I have my duty to do, and intend doing it."

"Then let me put it to you this way, Sergeant Neville. I told Mr. Parker that I would ensure the destruction of that battery, and that's exactly what I'm going to do. You can lead your men there, or they can come with me. But I warrant you: I've been doing this sort of thing for much longer than you, and I've a third again as many functioning limbs."

"We'll go together," said Neville.

"No we won't," said Grey. "You'll slow us down and already we're behind your navy's schedule. Add to that, I don't wish to see Parker left alone while he's unable to defend himself."

Neville had no instant answer to this, so Grey went on:

"The only question you have to ask yourself is, what is the more important duty: maintaining your authority, or achieving your object. I should add—the cannon aren't eighteen-pounders. They're thirty-sixes. So your frigates will already be in range come morning time; tomorrow morning. At first light, I gather."

Again Neville was silent; the other men murmured among themselves. Thirty-sixes? The largest cannon any had ever seen was a thirty-two; it was the largest cannon the British made. There were rumors that the French used thirty-sixes on a few first-rates, but they'd been abandoned for shaking the ships' knees to pieces.

Then Neville spoke.

"What assurances can you give me that you'll do as you say?"

"None," said Grey. "Other than my word of honor."

Neville resumed his silence. Then he extended his left hand; the other being bound in a sling. "Very well, Captain Grey. I pray you won't let me down."

Grey took Neville's left hand with his right. "I won't, Sergeant. And I thank you. If you need to move, there are two mules tied up there; we won't be able to use them."

Now Grey turned to the other three, Eaton, Presley, and O'Bannon.

"Give me the sergeant's pack and bow, but leave him the hunting knife." As Grey said this, he was examining Parker's map. "We've a long walk ahead of us, so I hope you've caught your breaths. Follow me."

He looked up at the sun a moment to get his bearings. Now unobscured by clouds, it forced the thought into Grey's head: one more day behind his own schedule; one day closer to Spain declaring war on Britain.

18

THE FOUR MEN—Grey leading, then Presley, Eaton, and O'Bannon—walked in single file along the caldera rim, believing they had about ten miles before them. Erosion had forced them back from the rim's verge into the trees, where the rain had left rivulets to be crossed and molasses-esque mud to be trundled through. Grey concluded that even two miles in an hour would be an optimistic speed. Much slower than that, however, and they would arrive at the battery after dark, and—notwithstanding Parker's sketch of the fortifications—Grey wanted to get a look at it while there was still daylight. After that, they could retreat somewhat and rest till nightfall; but before, it would be a forced march. Grey had Parker's sword and led the way with it, slashing through the boughs and bushes that blocked their path.

The three Americans said very little. Doubtless they were relieved at Grey and Neville having amicably settled their disagreement over command. But they were young men. Very young men; roughly half Grey's age (was he getting old? or, in his middle thirties, was he in his prime?). Even if they'd been at sea since they were six—which, given that they were American rather than English, was unlikely—they would still be enough in their salad days to find the sudden change in plans discomfiting. Add to that, the likelihood that none had ever been in a jungle before, and that none of them—Grey included—knew just what lay ahead of them. So their reticence was unsurprising. Under different circumstances Grey would have tried to get them talking—it's never prudent to go into the breach shoulder to shoulder with a stranger—but he was frankly exhausted. He'd been exhausted before the climb up the crater; he'd been exhausted before hanging Parker's rope, and he was damned exhausted after going down to get Neville. He would keep going—if he was blessed with no other quality, he could push himself very hard and very far—but he simply didn't have the spare breath to make conversation. So he continued to slice away obstructionist plants (probably supporters of the Foxite Whigs in Her Majesty's loyal opposition), and try to keep his huffing and puffing to a tolerable level. If the Americans found this evident want of breath distressing, they kept it to themselves.

After two or three hours of this—and perhaps little more than two or three miles passed—Grey proposed a five-minute repose. They were in a moderate clearing, and, while mindful of Grey's warning to, for God's sake, beware of snakes, each lay down on his pack. The Americans ate some dried beef and suggested Grey would find some for himself in Neville's pack, but he demurred. He did, however, give in to curiosity, and by gently depressing the tip of a giant leaf, tipped the rainwater gathered thereupon into his mouth. There was a hint of waxiness to it; otherwise, it was the freshest, clearest water he'd drunk since Tenerife. He said this to the Americans and they followed suit, each in turn agreeing that a drink of fresh leaf water was a consummation devoutly to be wished.

They resumed their walk, gradually turning south along the crater rim. The harbor's mouth was more or less the south side of the island, the bottom of the horseshoe. The further south they went, the less intense the wind, and the thicker the jungle. Progress slowed further, with Grey now rotating with the Americans, each of them taking a turn in the lead, slashing vegetation so that none would end up with a dead arm. The sun reached its zenith and began to slide down towards the west. The hours ran by, with no breaks called.

They were headed, by dead reckoning, towards the place on Parker's map where a game trail could be rejoined (how Grey longed for the easy walking of a game trail).

They didn't find it till early evening, which would have worried Grey more if the trail didn't so dramatically ease their passage. Soon the trail was running along near the inner edge of the crater rim, and—just as Parker's map said it would—running above a wheel-rutted dirt road, curling up from the harbor, which the men could now see far below them. It was tempting to decamp to the road, which, though hardly the Appian Way, was four or five times wider than the game trail, looked reasonably well packed, and was—well, a road. But from what Parker had said before he lost consciousness— in re avoiding roads and the profitability for pirates of working at the battery—Grey suspected there might be an evening watch of men traipsing upward, or even riding up in a munitions cart or something. Did they have gunners in practice, using the 36-pounders? Given how relatively recently the great guns had been warped onto the cliff, it was a reasonable question. On the other hand, powder would not be in short supply here, what with every merchant ship carrying *some*, and virtually none that were taken offering any resistance, Vargas must have accumulated a considerable stockpile. And of course, they could cast as many 36-pound balls as they had iron to melt. And no doubt every ship that couldn't be repaired had been stripped for nails. So in all probability, the gunners here were well in practice. Had they ever fired at a ship in anger? Who could say.

Grey's guess—or was it Parker's intelligence, rather?—had been right, and as the evening darkened and the four men continued along the game trail, the voices of a crowd of pirates began to reach them. Singing something that sounded a little like "Blow the Man Down," but in Sabir, the bizarre Mediterranean lingua franca: a mix of Portuguese, Spanish, Catalan, and Occitan, a dozen Italian dialects, Greek, Turkish, Hebrew, and Arabic. Grey had never heard it sung before. It was not a euphonious language.

They were coming up towards the battery, along a switchback road, which meant the pirates likely sounded closer than they were.

Parker had said that there were more than a score of men working the cannon—would they all be relieved by the evening watch, or just a portion of them? In the worst case, two dozen men would be coming up the road. Could an ambush be laid in time? The Sabir singers couldn't be more than ten minutes away. It would be chock-ablock, but it would be easier to kill them now than once they were within the battery's defenses.

They would be armed—with dirks, daggers, short swords, saps—maybe pistols, possibly rifles. It was only the powder weapons that worried Grey; the sound of a single shot, even in this close air, would carry at least a mile, and would lose them any chance of taking the fort by stealth. If there was going to be an ambush, it would have to be a silent one.

Each of the Americans had a bow on his back, as did Grey. He wondered how lethal they'd prove. For his own part, Grey knew how to use one, but he was no Robin Hood. As a rule, the only Englishmen who were handy with a bow and arrow were poachers and aristocrats' children. No one else had much use for them. In Britain, that is. No doubt they were still used by the more backward Europeans. They were a medieval relic, but of course, so was most of the continent.

But in the United States? Grey had never given it much thought. From anecdotes of America's western frontier that occasionally reached the London papers, Grey gathered that, where bows and arrows were concerned, Americans were more perforated than perforating.

No, it would be better to use knives and Parker's sword. Even if the Americans could handle their arrows, Grey couldn't be sure of himself, and this was not a job he would let out of his charge. As Grey had left Neville his knife and thrown O'Bannon's away, they had among them just two knives and the sword—which was fine, because Grey wanted one man with the Girandoni air rifle, just in case things got out of hand. It was a good deal louder than a knife, but still a damned sight quieter than a powder gun.

Quickly, Grey put his plan to the Americans. Of course, Ameri-

cans were the world's preeminent practitioners of ambush warfare—
it was how a rabble of armed civilians won their independence from
the empire. Grey and the marines were on their haunches, in a rough
circle; when he asked which of them was the best shot, each raised a
hand or pointed to himself. Grey snorted amusement.

"Which of you is worst with a knife, then?"

The hands all went down again, and after a moment O'Bannon
spoke up to say, "Not to be rude, sir, but I'm afraid it's probably you."

Grey cocked half a smile. "I think not, O'Bannon."

"If I may, sir, who's the most cunning enemy you've fought
against?"

Grey shrugged. O'Bannon continued.

"Sir, if you've never fought an Indian, or never fought with an
Indian beside you, then you don't know how to go to war with a
knife."

"I've fought with Indians, O'Bannon."

"I don't mean them of the East Indies, sir, but the West Indies.
That is, West Indians. American Indians."

"Yes, I know, O'Bannon, but I'd reckon our Gurkhas over your
Mohawks against any lay worth naming."

"I'd take that bet, sir. But either way—did you grow up fighting
with your Gurkhas? Or even against them?"

"I can't say that I did."

"See, sir, every American—even those that go to sea later—
grows up in the woods, and every American's got a little Indian in
him. It's one of the things that makes us Americans, and not Englishmen. And makes us better in a fight than you English sorts. I don't
mean to be rude."

"I'm not offended, O'Bannon, but I'm not persuaded either."

"But placing that to one side, sir—why would we use knives
rather than the bows? It's what we brought them for."

"I'm not much of a hand with a bow. And there may be a score
of pirates coming up the road. Up close, with knives and a sword,
we can make quick work of them. But how fast can you shoot those
bows?"

The Americans looked at each other and smiled.

"Pretty fast, sir," said O'Bannon.

"Fast enough to kill a score of men? If just one lives and escapes, we're sunk."

"We'll get 'em, sir. And if I might suggest, you can stand a little on up the road, and if we miss any of them, you can finish 'em off with the sword. Though I don't expect you'll need to."

Grey sucked his teeth. O'Bannon's logic was hard to deny. On the other hand, Grey didn't like the idea of sitting back and letting other men do the fighting. But his pride was, perhaps, not the chief concern in the matter. In any case, if he nocked early, he felt fairly certain he could stick one pirate at least.

"Very well, colonials. We've only moments to get into position, so place yourselves."

IT WAS AN ANXIOUS ten minutes later when the pirates rounded a bend in the road and came into sight. By that time, O'Bannon, Presley, and Eaton were all concealed in the forest undergrowth beside the road: two on one side and one on the other, and strangely unconcerned about crossfire. Grey was about thirty yards beyond them, with an arrow nocked, trying to pick out any one of the Americans. There was still some daylight left, but he couldn't, for the life of him, make a one of them out. They weren't wearing the regular uniforms of American marines; instead each man had a common brown felt jacket of the sort you might see on any common man in any town in Europe or America. Now they seemed to blend entirely with the greenery around them. Or perhaps it was just that the greenery enveloped them; the jungle, back inside the cradle of the crater, had returned to its former density.

He wondered if they could see him, and resolved to brush up, when all this was over, on his woodsmanship. Before taking their places, the Americans had remarked on turkey shoots, and then explained to Grey what they were. Grey knew that a turkey was an oversized chicken, but had never seen one, and hadn't been familiar with the Hoyle's Rules for hunting them. Per O'Bannon, turkeys walk in a line, and when you hunt them, you start at the line's back and work your way forward—that way, the turkeys nearer the front of the line will try to escape by continuing forward, instead of scattering. Though turkeys were, according to O'Bannon, not overburdened with intellect, this technique was said to work on men as well. If this were true, it would be very well worth knowing, and Grey was eager to see the theory in action. With turkeys in mind, therefore, the Americans would let the pirates pass them before opening fire on those in the rear. Grey, meanwhile, would forbear firing unless the turkeys began to run in some other direction than onward as the road led them.

Grey adjusted his grip on the arrow, which was quite short— suited in length to the small composite bow, of the sort the Hungarians favored; which they'd evidently adopted from the Mongols during a past epoch. Grey had used them before, but being a patriotic Englishman, he would have preferred a longbow. He drew the arrow back to half-cock and waited.

And then it began. The pirates were not walking in organized files, of course; they were a jumble, and a quick count put them at sixteen in toto (a relief, Grey assumed, for two-thirds of the men then on duty). The three furthest back suddenly stumbled and fell. Grey had heard nothing, but could see the arrows in their backs. The other nine pirates spun around to see what had happened, and three more of them were shot, and after some shouts and stumbling, fell. Grey could see arrows protruding from their chests.

There were ten left now, and they were running up the road towards Grey's position. Another three got arrows in the back and fell. Then the three beyond them. Now the four survivors were only a few yards ahead of Grey.

His instinct was to drop the bow and draw his sword, but it would be a damned foolish thing to do, stepping into the line of fire. In any case, before he'd have had time to step out of his cover, three more arrows were let loose, and three more pirates fell. The last man standing got an arrow in the chest from Grey, and before he'd fallen, three more in his back.

Grey stepped out of cover. Sixteen pirates lay on the ground. A few were trying to crawl away; a few others were groaning. None of them would live—their insides were too badly cut up; an arrow was a nasty weapon. Grey drew his sword and put the yet-living pirate closest to him out of his misery. He nodded to the three Americans, who took his cue and walked among the dead to deliver coups de grâce to the dying, firing arrows point-blank into their skulls.

Grey and the others proceeded to recover the arrows from the dead men, then dragged their bodies to the leeward edge of the road and heaved them downhill, into the jungle, where they would shortly rot or be eaten. They kicked dirt over any obvious signs of the massacre—blood and handprints—and then climbed back off the road and onto the adjacent game trail.

None said a word until they were all back on the trail, on their haunches, recovering their breaths.

"Gentlemen: Consider me impressed."

"Thank you, sir," each said in turn.

"All right," said Grey, "we've killed one watch. That should leave forty or so still to kill. Do any of you need any rest?"

"No, sir," said O'Bannon.

"O'Bannon," said Grey, "you're in the habit of speaking for your colleagues."

"Yes, sir. Only as I've been at this a bit longer'n they have."

"Well, that's fine. You all seem like stubborn sorts, so just in case I get killed before you, there ought to be a bit of order here."

He nodded to O'Bannon. "Who's next-senior to you?"

"Eaton, sir."

"Very well. Presley, if all three of us are dead, you're in charge. Eaton, same goes for you if O'Bannon and I are killed. And O'Bannon, for the time being, you're the ranking officer. Now, let's move. In a few minutes it'll be night, and the dear only knows what happens if our work isn't finished by morning."

Of course Grey knew too. The American frigates would be sunk. A thousand men would be killed. And scenes of the treasure fleet weighing anchor played over and over and over in his head.

19

PARKER'S MAP LED GREY and the Americans back up towards the lip of the crater, to a spot where they could see the battery encampment laid out before them; a bare patch of volcanic rock sticking out towards the harbor; a peninsula in miniature, no more than half again an acre. There was breastwork where the road from the harbor ended; inward from that were four poorly constructed wooden longhouses, where, Grey presumed, two dozen men were able to escape downpours, and keep some stores besides. Then a giant rainwater cistern, which Grey presumed was their giant scuttlebutt; water for drinking and bathing, and—most important for any battery—to fight fires with. And beyond that, a single well-constructed building—well constructed in the sense that, unlike the others, it looked as if it wouldn't have to be rebuilt twice a year when the tropical storms had their druthers. It was masonry, and must have been a gigantic trial to build; there was no question what it was. Inside would be barrels of powder, hundreds of 36-pound iron balls, and four monstrous cannon.

"What was Neville's plan?" said Grey to O'Bannon.

"For us to enter the camp by stealth, silently kill anyone guarding the cannon, set the slow match burning, and retreat to the jungle."

Grey nodded. "That isn't going to work."

"No, sir," said O'Bannon. "We were expecting cannon of half the size and a guard of fewer than ten."

Below them the camp was alive with men standing or sitting around fires, eating and drinking.

For a moment neither said anything.

Grey nodded. "What's the range on these bows?"

"Random shot would be near a hundred yards, in an arc. No more than twenty straight on."

"Could you hit those barrack buildings?"

"Yes, sir."

"Have you got a striker?"

"Yes, sir; we all have."

"Have you got any liquor?"

There was a moment's pause.

"Eaton has a small bottle, sir, for physic emergencies."

"What sort?" said Grey to Eaton.

"Gin, sir. Navy strength."

"Good," said Grey, nodding his head, thinking, then nodding again. "Good. Now. Those wooden barracks were pretty well soaked last night. They've had most of a day to dry out beneath a hearty tropical sun, but they may still need some help catching fire. You're going to soak rags in gin, tie them to a few arrows' heads, and loose them into the roof of the barrack furthest from the battery. Can you? We need them blazing."

One by one, the Americans nodded.

"Good, lads. It should turn the place to chaos; when it does— when every man's attention is on putting out the fire—I'm going to walk through them, into the battery, start the match burning, and walk back."

Again the Americans nodded, one by one. No one needed to say it would be a damned dangerous undertaking; at that moment there didn't seem any other course to suggest. Grey hoped that whoever the son of a bitch was responsible for the 18–36 pound error, he was expiring slowly from a particularly unpleasant venereal disease.

"Now: Fire only the barrack furthest from the battery; closest to us here. If one catches, they'll see an accident. If we touch off two of them, they'll know something's afoot.

"Likewise, they'll know something's afoot if they see the arrows as points of light in the black jungle. So once they're lit, fire away, quick as you can. Am I clear?"

"Yes, sir," said Eaton and Presley.

"What if they do realize something's afoot, sir?" said O'Bannon.

"Then God help us, O'Bannon. We'll have to make certain no signal is sent to the harbor. We'll have to kill them all. Posthaste."

"Yes, sir."

"It would be a damned ugly business, but if it comes to that, remember they're not men, they're pirates. They're savages who give no quarter and expect none in return. God will have mercy on them; we will not."

GREY GAVE THE PIRATES a few hours to drink and retire. There seemed to be some ill will in the camp, which Grey suspected had something to do with the lateness of the relief watch. So far it didn't seem to have amounted to much. No doubt timekeeping and punctuality had gone by the board before.

When he felt he'd put the arson off as long as was useful, Grey roused the Americans, whom he'd told to try to get a few hours' rest. It took a few minutes to get the fire arrows ready. Grey wouldn't shoot; their target was near fifty yards away, and he couldn't be sure of his aim. When each of the Americans had his arrow nocked, drawn, and aimed, Grey used Parker's flint striker to get each of them going. O'Bannon first—he let loose while Grey lit Eaton's arrow; Eaton, while Grey lit Presley's. O'Bannon's arrow hit its mark; so did Eaton's. In his rush to loose, Presley aimed wide. His arrow landed in the tufty volcanic ground and extinguished itself. Grey hoped no one had seen it land.

It took only seconds for the barrack to be burning like Dante's inferno. Grey had underestimated the tropical sun's powers of desiccation. And almost as quickly, a line of bucket men sprang up between the cistern and the burning building. Parker had said these were at-least-somewhat-disciplined man-o'-war's men. Clearly he was right—to an extent. Even as the water began to move, men were running, terrified, out of the burning building. A few others, probably those most indignant at the delay of the relief watch, seemed well into their cups, and ran around haphazardly or watched and laughed.

But Grey wasn't looking at any of them. He was looking at one pirate standing by himself, looking down at Presley's stray arrow. Grey watched him pick it up and look it over—and watched as he began to understand what it was and what it meant.

The man began shouting to men around him; no one would listen; all were intent on putting out the fire. But he wouldn't be deterred. He managed to peel a few men from the bucket lines to listen to him. What he said, Grey could only guess, but an instant later this knot of men—seven of them—were filling buckets and running towards the battery.

And Grey was grabbing the Girandoni off his back and firing at them. At a hundred and fifty yards, the Girandoni was still accurate, and more than likely deadly. That was just about the range to these six bucket men. Grey fired at the first in the line—no turkey matter here—and he fell. Grey tilted the barrel back, clicked the thumb loader, and another ball was in place. He killed the second bucket man in line. Another tilt and reload, and he fired at the last man— the third, fourth, fifth, and sixth in line had already disappeared into the battery. The seventh in line fell, with one of the Girandoni's .46-caliber balls lodged in his back. But four men had made it inside. And Grey knew what they were doing.

"We're blown, lads; fire at will. Start at the head of the road and work inward. No man escapes. Kill them all."

20

GREY FELT SICK.

He'd killed the lion's share of the pirates himself; his repeating rifle was a staggeringly effective instrument of death. He could fire twenty shots in the time it took a Baker or a musket to fire two. The Americans had put down the rest with arrows. The fire had spread from the first barrack to the next, then to the third and the fourth, leaving nowhere for the pirates to hide. Some had run for the road, bringing them almost head-on to the barrage of arrows. A few had used the cistern for cover and tried to return fire with their Baker rifles—but had been unable to figure out where to return fire to: with no powder flash from the air rifle, and obviously none from the arrows, the pirates looked helplessly into the night, trying to find something at which to shoot. Grey had picked them off with the Girandoni, along with a few others who tried to make it to the stone magazine. It had been like shooting fish in a barrel. And Grey's contention that pirates were not men and deserved no mercy had proved much easier to make than to believe. In a few moments more, the only survivors would be the four bucket men who'd first run to the battery. Before dealing with them, Grey and the Americans had to walk among another near score of bodies, delivering coups de grâce, checking for heartbeats, making sure the dead were really dead. A few men had burned to death, and the stink of their charred flesh filled the air. Grey had rarely been part of something which so profoundly revolted him. Just a few days earlier he'd seen a clipper full of men he knew and liked blown to shivers; here was the carrion of the earth's scum, but the death affected him much more deeply. First the sixteen men on the road—now twenty more here. He didn't wonder if he'd done the right thing; he was certain he had. But it was such a godforsaken thing. A massacre. So methodical a massacre. He felt as if his soul had been soaked in blood, and that there was no way to get at it, to clean it off. He had a sudden inclination, though not a Romanist, to make confession and receive some sort of immediate, divine cleansing. Release the charge in his soul. But he couldn't. He stabbed Parker's sword through the heart of a dying man, to end his suffering. The man died with a final cough of foam blood.

That was all. Now, the cannon.

21

GREY AND THE AMERICAN MARINES stood just outside
the small stone door that led into the long, low masonry
building where the battery and magazine were kept. Four
pirates, they believed, were inside; no doubt in defensive positions.
No doubt the first non-pirate who stuck his head in to see would
have it blown off.

Though, needless to say, neither the bows nor the air rifle were
fired using sparks and powder (that is to say, they weren't, in the
strictest terms, "fired" at all), Grey was hesitant to blindly fire either
a bow or the Girandoni into a magazine. Between the Girandoni's
lead ball and the steel heads on the arrows, the chance of a spark
between metal and stone was not trivial. The pirates on the inside
had the benefit of knowing where the magazine's powder was kept.
Grey and the Americans had not, and Grey wouldn't take the chance
unless it were unavoidable.

No, he had a better idea. The Girandoni fired balls using gouts of
compressed air, each of which pushed with the force of a rifle's powder charge. A rifle loaded only with powder can still knock a man
down, at point-blank range. Grey had never tried this with a Girandoni, but here seemed a fortuitous time for the experiment.

The Girandoni was already loaded with a lead ball. Gesturing for the Americans to cover the door, he pinched the Girandoni under his arm, with the barrel tipped forward, and let the shot roll out. He returned the ball to the twenty-two-shot magazine tube that lay alongside the barrel, and gestured for the Americans to stand back.

Grey approached the door and then, with his right hand on the Girandoni's trigger guard and his left on its butt plate, stuck it through the stone doorway—aiming right, which from the outside one could see was the only direction the opening's passage led—and pulled the trigger.

There was a whoop of air, sort of like the sound of a punch to a man's gut, and the startled shout and crash of a man falling backward.

Now Grey stepped through the door, prepared to fire again; what he saw preempted him. A single pirate lying on his back, looking dazed.

Grey waved the Americans to follow, and to restrain the dazed man, then proceeded up the stone hallway, coming after a moment to another doorway on his left. Actually, to two doorways, with their joint opening split down the middle by a stone wall. On the right he saw the magazine—dozens of barrels of gunpowder. On the left, he got his first look at the monstrous cannon, the 36-pound great guns; brass and gleaming in the early morning sun.

This was the first moment Grey realized they'd been at this now all through the night, and dawn was breaking. But for this moment he had no time to consider that.

Assuming there would be men waiting just inside each of the two new doorways, he reached the Girandoni into the battery room and fired another blank blast of air. No response. He peeked his head in. The room seemed empty—aside from the cannon. He repeated the process in the battery room. Again, nothing. Again the room seemed empty, aside from a baker's dozen barrels of gunpowder. He began to search among the barrels, expecting to find pirates hidden among them. He repeated this search in the cannon room. There was no one. He returned to the entry hall.

"Where are the other three men you came in with?" he said to the pirate he'd knocked over—then in the process of having his hands bound by Presley.

"Gone," said the pirate, in Spanish.

"Gone where?" said Grey.

"Jumped."

"Jumped?" Grey could hardly believe it. "When?"

"Just minutes ago. They tried to wait for daybreak. To try to avoid the rocks. I was going to jump too, but . . ."

He was shaken from the Girandoni's blast, and apparently, afraid of heights. Grey would have been too, if the prospect was jumping from the battery's mouth down to the harbor. A plunge of hundreds of feet. Even if a man landed in water, Grey doubted he would survive. It wasn't until that moment that Grey truly understood the terror the midnight massacre had caused.

. . . Unless the man was lying and the men were hidden somewhere, waiting to spring out. Grey put this to the man, who said, with a glassy look to his eyes, that Grey could see for himself. Grey walked back to the battery room. Its front, obviously, was open, so the cannon could fire out. Grey walked between the two cannon nearest the door and looked down from the edge. So close to the water that the waves were now lapping at their corpses, lay three broken bodies.

No wonder the fourth man hadn't jumped.

Next Grey went to the magazine. As he'd suspected, he found four empty buckets there, and the powder barrels with their lids off. Dipping his hand into each barrel, he found it carefully moistened— not drenched, but poured through with enough water to make it unfirable until thoroughly dried. It was an eminently sensible precaution in case of attack. A fire lit in here, by an attacker, would now do as much damage as a fire lit in a room filled with barrels of sand. Grey returned again to the bound pirate.

"Where are your other powder stores?"

"We have none."

"For your rifles?"

"Those I presume you burned away, along with everything else."

Grey nodded. "Very well," he said.

He stood and addressed the Americans. "Gentlemen, we shall be doing this the slow, old-fashioned way."

After throwing the powder kegs into the sea, just to be certain they would be set to no mischief once they'd dried, the four men, using the pull ropes for running the guns out, ran them out to the battery's verge. It was a slow job, and an exhausting one, given their small number. But foot by foot, they pulled the draw ropes back: the ropes that ran through pulleys and pulled the guns forward to their firing position after each shot's recoil. Inch by inch, the first gun rolled forward until its carriage was touching the low wall meant to keep its crew from accidentally running it over the cliff's edge. Then, using four handspikes used normally to train the guns left or right, and a pair of loose bricks for fulcrums, they levered the carriage up, pulling, pushing, giving everything they had, until the cannon's muzzle was tipped down enough to carry all away. The four men ran forward to watch as the great brass gun fell, and saw it tear and splinter into glittering hunks of metal on the rocks below.

There were only three to go, and on the horizon they could see the marines' ship—the USS *Constellation*.

22

B Y THE TIME the last cannon fell and shattered, *Constellation* had a position commanding the mouth of the harbor; behind her, USS *Congress* was taking in sheet, preparing to slip into the harbor itself and open fire on anything that put up any resistance. Would there be surrenders? No doubt some of the men on the island would claim simply to be merchants selling legally obtained merchandise at a free port. Some might get away with it, and those with even slight hopes were more likely to try an American court than an American warship. Many of the pirates, however, knowing they could fight and die or surrender and be hanged, would choose the former. They might at least, that way, end up in a good chantey tale.

Able to see the American marines' utter exhaustion, and utterly exhausted himself, Grey suggested they take a few moments off their feet, have some water and eat some of their provisions. After drinking their fill at the cistern, the four men climbed to the now-empty battery's roof and watched *Congress*, barely making steerageway, pass *Constellation* and glide into the center of the crater-harbor of Isla Cangrejo. There was a crackle of small-arms fire from an oak building on the shore. *Congress* fired on it with her bow chasers, reducing it instantly to tinder. A suicidal sloop at anchor fired a single carronade filled with grape, which tore through *Congress*'s rigging but seemed not to do much damage, at least from where Grey sat. *Congress* returned fire with half a broadside, and the sloop was instantly stove in and sinking. That was the last shot fired in defiance of the American frigates, for the moment. Tiny specks of white—sheets or shirts or whatever was on hand—began to appear in windows and doorways of the harbor-side town. Grey could see American marines lining up on the decks of the two frigates (he assumed they were marines, anyway—they looked damned peculiar wearing blue instead of red). He saw the frigates begin to lower boats to put them ashore. Like watching a flock of sheep on a distant hillside, Grey could see pirates begin to stream out of the town and into the jungle. At this, *Congress* began a true bombardment—firing grape and chain over the town and into the escaping miscreants. He watched the fusillade tear through the forest. Grey could feel the concussion of the frigate's broadsides shake his lungs.

Though utterly exhausted—as he was—there was no time for dawdling. The cannon were destroyed—which meant that Grey could again devote his full energy to getting back on his way; back to his own desperate job, involving many more than four cannon, two frigates, and a thousand men. After just a few minutes' respite, he ordered the Americans back to their feet and began a forced march to where they'd left Parker and Neville. It would take hours for the pirates fleeing the village to reach the crater's rim—if that's where they decided to go—but to get Parker et al. to the harbor and safety, the fled pirates would either have to be gone around or gone through, and Grey wanted to press the advantage the Congressional bombardment was giving them. As none was wearing a uniform, it shouldn't be hard to pass down to the harbor undetected. When you're running away from a fire, do you stop to look at someone running in the other direction?

As they left the volcanic outcrop where the cannon had been housed, Grey had a pang of regret that he'd proved unable to destroy the building that had housed them. While it no longer posed any threat to the frigates, no doubt some of those pirates now retreating into the jungle would end up finding refuge inside the masonry, and the Americans now putting ashore might be in for a devil of a time getting them out. But he'd done what he could, and he had grander-scale things now to concern him.

Using the vacant road as far as they could, before turning off it into the jungle, Grey and the Americans made their best time back to the place they'd left Parker and Neville. The last third of the journey was through jungle into which Grey, O'Bannon, Eaton, and Presley had personally hacked a path only a day earlier. Grey was astonished to see in places the path was already recovered by new growth. When a plant moves faster than carriage traffic in London, one has to wonder if it's really fair to deny it a place among the animals. Perhaps it was time to include vines among the cattle and creeping things. There was no doubt they crept. As neither Grey nor any of the Americans had spare breath with which to make conversation, the men walked in silence, and Grey ended up musing for several hours on the metaphysical nature of plants. He felt rather light-headed and kept circling back to the same thoughts, which repeated in layers like a fugue. Did plants move or just increase in size? After all, a pile of books couldn't be said to move just because you kept placing new books on top. Grey resolved to write a letter to his particular botanist, Kefauver, posing the question.

Grey hoped he would soon have a chance to sleep.

When they found Neville he was pacing nervously at the edge of the cliff, looking out to sea, absently running his hand over the back of his neck, where the sling for his broken arm bit into his skin. Parker was sitting nearby, back against a tree, with his eyes closed, a flush in his cheeks, and a wide smile on his face.

"Are you awake, Parker?" said Grey, nodding to Neville as he went to check on his snake-bitten friend.

"I am, Grey. And I can hear our guns firing."

The sound of *Congress*'s broadsides had felt surprisingly close until Grey and the marines had passed out of the crater. Now on the rim, they seemed surprisingly distant, but could still be distinctly heard.

O'Bannon, Eaton, and Presley had followed Grey out of the forest, looking pleased. Neville still looked nervous as he approached them, looking them up and down for signs of wounds.

"Are any of you injured?"

"No, sir," said O'Bannon. "Shipshape and Boston fashion."

"Very good. It came off then? We heard no explosion of the battery."

"Yes," said Parker. "Until we heard the sound of our own cannon, I can tell you, I was quite worried. What happened?"

"They soaked the powder, so we had to tip the cannon onto the rocks."

"But they're destroyed?"

"Utterly."

"And the powder?"

"Thrown into the sea."

Neville exhaled loudly; Parker's smile grew a little wider.

"Splendid. Thank you, Grey. That's at least eight hundred American sailors and marines saved. Not to mention the pirates dealt with. Quite a good few days' work, eh? By all of you."

"Your countrymen did most of the heavy lifting, but I was glad to do what I could, Parker," said Grey, "if for no other reason than to help settle the score between us."

"Yes," said Parker, his head leaned back against the tree and his eyes closed again. "I've saved your life, what, two, maybe three times? You've saved mine once, and Neville's, and the eight hundred men on those two frigates. So I think the score is three to eight hundred and two."

"I'm glad you figure it that way, because I do need to ask you for a favor. More than one, actually."

"A ship to Montevideo? Choose any of the prize ships in the harbor and I'll get you men to sail her; I believe I can guarantee that, at least, when I explain our debt to you."

"And there are three men among the pirates, they were taken prisoner with me. Barrows, Dowdell, and Drumgoole. They signed up with Vargas, but only under threat of death. If I can find them, I'd like to take them with me. If I can't, I'd like your word that they'll be given free pardons. A week of piracy isn't worth hanging for."

Parker nodded. "Barrows, Dowdell, Drumgoole. If you don't take them along, I'll see they're sent to your West Indian fleet."

"I am much obliged to you, Parker. Now we should cut along— not a moment to lose. Can you ride, if I hold the lead?"

"I think so," said Parker. Grey reached a hand down and pulled Parker to his feet. Soon he would have a naval surgeon look at his leg, but for the moment, thought Grey, he seemed to be out of danger. The swelling was going down, and nothing suggested anything more complicated than a residue of bruises. The mules were where they'd been left; Grey helped Parker onto the first and then turned to Neville, who was engaged in lively discussion with his three young privates, who were relating their raid blow by blow.

"Sergeant Neville," said Grey, gesturing to the second mule, "may I give you a leg up?"

Neville shook his head emphatically. "No, thank you, Captain Grey—I'm well rested, and of all of us, I'm quite certain, you're most in need of some time off your feet. To be blunt, sir, you look like hell."

Grey smiled. "Well, you know . . . you're right. I won't argue with you then. Will one of you lead Mr. Parker's mule?"

"Yes, sir," said O'Bannon.

"Parker, how long is it back to the harbor?"

"If we aren't held up, three hours. I was about to say we ought to wait for the bombardment to stop, but I believe it has. Our marines must have landed."

Grey nodded. "Shall we?"

"Let's," said Parker, who gestured weakly forward.

On his motion, the six men and two mules began their slow walk back towards the battery road.

23

THE RIDE WENT SMOOTHLY ENOUGH THAT, at some point, Grey fell asleep. It wasn't until a switchback in the road, only a few hundred yards above the harbor, that he woke, at his name being called by Parker.

Grey took a moment to remember where and who he was; why he was sleeping on muleback. Parker was pointing at something. Grey looked to see what it was. There was a shrine—at first Grey thought it was some sort of pagan setup, filled with gods, but after blinking a few times and getting a better look at it, he saw it was a shrine to every patron saint of sailors. The pirates, apparently, were taking no unnecessary risks. Saint Brendan, Saint Phocas, Saint Nicholas, Saint Christopher, Saint Clement, Saint Francis of . . . somewhere. Saint Elmo. The harbor was well covered. And sitting cross-legged on top of the shrine's wooden housing was a man, tipping the bottle. Grey recognized him, but it took another long moment to remember who he was. Vargas, captain of the *Mosquito*, potentate of Crab Island. And now he was looking at Grey.

"Why, Friar Grey," said Vargas, slurring his words slightly, "we meet again. It's funny, I had a feeling, when you escaped our hotel, that you would bring me to no good." He looked back at the harbor, where both American frigates were now at anchor. "I don't see how, but somehow I feel certain this has all to do with you. Am I right?"

"Not precisely, Captain. I was mostly along as a supernumerary."

Vargas snorted. He was still looking at the harbor, and the end of his little fiefdom.

"Yes," he said, "we had a good run."

"Apparently so," said Grey.

"Yes," said Vargas. "Yes we did. Soon I'll be hanged from one of those mainmast yardarms."

"That seems likely," said Grey.

"First, though," said Vargas, throwing his bottle into the shrine; it shattered, and knocked one or two of the patrons' wood statues over. "First, I'm going to kill you."

With his left hand he unfastened his sword belt, and with his right he drew his sword. The belt fell to the ground, and he stood at the ready.

"You're drunk, Vargas. It would hardly be a fair fight."

"On the contrary," said Vargas. "Because I'm drunk, perhaps it *will* be a fair fight."

"I gather you realize I'm not actually a priest."

"You astonish me, Friar," said Vargas, dryly. "Come. Lay on." Those last few words he spoke in English.

Grey looked at Parker, who shrugged. "He's going to die one way or another, might as well give him a decent exit. Not to mention that he's holding us up."

Grey nodded and climbed down off his mule, drew Parker's sword and took a few steps towards Vargas.

"*En garde,*" he said.

Vargas lunged forward, thrusting at Grey's chest. Grey stepped to his side, sliced down at Vargas's arm, cut it clean off just above the elbow, then—on a rising backhand—cut off his head. Vargas's body crumpled to the ground. Grey wiped his sword on Vargas's coat.

"A good riddance of bad rubbish," he said. "Frankly, the yardarm would have been more appropriate."

"Yes," said Parker, "but you haven't the time for luxuries at the moment. Let's get on."

"Hold on a moment," said Grey, kneeling by Vargas's severed arm. "The impudent bastard was using *my* sword. I wonder if he has my watch . . ." Grey checked the dead man's waistcoat pockets.

Parker chuckled and shook his head. Grey gave up on his watch and extracted the hilt of his sword from the dead hand's grasp.

"It reminds me, though," Grey continued, "that I have these to return to you."

He slipped his now-recovered sword through his belt and carried Parker's back to its owner, along with the Girandoni air rifle, held out at arm's length.

"Thank you," said Parker, taking the sword and slipping it back into his own belt. "You keep the rifle."

Grey hesitated. "I can't accept it."

Parker laughed. "Because it's too valuable? Grey, I paid for it perhaps half a hundredth part of its true worth. In any case, I would take your refusal as a most grievous insult."

Throughout this argument, the four marines were rolling their eyes or smiling or winking at one another. After another moment's hesitation, Grey swung the Girandoni back onto his shoulder and smiled.

"Thank you, Parker. I'm most grateful."

"The pleasure's mine, Grey. Now again—let's get on."

Upon its capture, the entire contents of the Isla Cangrejo harbor had passed into the possession of the American navy. With the harbor town now having capitulated in its entirety, the company of American marines were forming ranks in the town's muddy streets, preparing to march into the jungle and smoke out the pirates therein. The junior captain of the small frigate squadron—Captain Hugh Campbell—was standing on the quay, directing and administering things, as his boat crew tried to fend off a crowd of merchants attempting to plead their innocence.

"I'm glad it's Campbell," said Parker.

He and Grey had dismounted; O'Bannon had commandeered a boat hook for him to use as a walking stick, and then Parker had directed Neville and his boys to get some food, drink, and rest. Neville and coterie were still detached from their ship's company and under his command; before sending them off, he told Neville that, until they heard different, they remained under his command, and not to let anyone try to tell them otherwise. With that done, he and Grey had begun navigating their way through the press of men around the harbor's edge, for Parker to report and for Grey to secure transportation.

"Campbell commands *Constellation*; the commodore is Captain John Rogers of *Congress*. Rogers may not be the most belligerent man in the world, but he's certainly among the top two."

At that moment Campbell spotted Parker in the crowd, and ordered a path cleared for him.

"Mr. Parker," said Campbell, extending his hand and warmly shaking Parker's, "what a fellow you are. I saw the last of the cannon fall with my own eyes, and I gather they were a sight larger than eighteens. I daresay you saved our ships, sir, and our bacon with it. If I'm not preempted by the commodore, will you take dinner with me on the barky? I want to drink your health, and Sergeant Neville's health, and health to his men, and then hear the entire story in excruciating detail. Where is Neville? What's happened to your foot?"

Parker smiled; Campbell was in action a serious, quiet man, but at all other times, remarkably garrulous.

"The foot's fine, thank you, sir. I sent Neville and his boys off for a meal and a rest; I trusted you wouldn't mind—they've been on a pretty rugged trail for near three days with hardly a stop to catch their breaths. And it would be my great pleasure to dine with you."

"Yes of course, though do please have Neville et al. come and see me when they've something recuperated—I want a shake of their hands."

"Certainly, sir."

"You know, I suppose, that Neville's to be made sergeant major, and the boys promoted to corporal."

"I do, sir, but I'm reasonably certain they do not—it will be a pleasant surprise."

"Yes. Yes, I'd wanted to raise O'Bannon straight to sergeant, since he was due a promotion to corporal in any case, but with the Barbary stuff, everyone and his younger brother seems concerned about the rapid inflation in rank. They seem to be worried we'll run out of privates and ordinary seamen. Will you introduce me to your accompaniment, there, sir?" said Campbell, smiling at Grey and extending his hand.

"This is Mr. . . ." Parker looked at Grey; Grey nodded. "Thomas Grey, formerly of George the Third's Royal Marines, more recently a pirate captive and hostage on this island, and the man who commanded the destruction of those cannon—they were thirty-sixes, by the way, sir—commanded their destruction after I lost a fight with a snake." Parker gestured mildly to the bandage protruding from his torn-up pants leg.

Campbell turned to his coxswain and said, "Pass the word for the surgeon," and then turned back to Parker. "Mr. Parker, please to sit down," he said in a tone of voice that made it clear this was an order. He indicated a quay-side crate for Parker to sit on, and then turned to Grey.

"Mr. Grey, a pleasure. I am entirely confused as to how this came about; I hope you'll enlighten me."

Grey shook Campbell's hand. "The pleasure is mine, sir."

Parker interjected, "I think, sir, it would be best if I were to explain the situation. In the meantime, there's a considerable degree of urgency in one matter, if you could possibly accommodate me."

"You must be joking, Parker. Name it."

"I need a fast sloop from among the prize ships, a crew to work it—including, if they can be found, three English sailors taken prisoner along with Mr. Grey—and ships' stores to provide for a voyage south to Montevideo."

"Ah," said Campbell, "this I will have to discuss with the commodore. What is in Montevideo?"

"I've no idea, sir," said Parker, "but I've given Grey my word we would get him there."

Campbell looked at Grey, then Parker, then nodded.

"Then we mustn't let him down."

24

BEFORE THE SUN HAD SET, a sloop which had begun the day with the name *El Zorro*, which was now rechristened USS *Hornet*, sailed out of Cangrejo harbor under the command of an American lieutenant named Isaac Chauncey. Grey was sound asleep in a tiny cabin, to starboard and slightly abaft the mainmast. Somewhere before the mast, he expected Barrows and Drumgoole were asleep as well. Dowdell was absent. He'd slit his wrists on his second night ashore as a pirate. Grey had arranged to have a stone marker placed over his body in the potter's field where it had been buried, and for the minister off USS *Constellation* to say a few words. He'd been forced to borrow money from Parker for the purpose. Parker had assured him it was no problem, as Grey would be entitled to a share of the prize money from the pirate flotilla's capture. They had parted on the quay with a handshake and the agreement that, should either find himself in the other's country, they would toss off a bumper together.

Now Grey was on his way again, to save England and democracy and so forth, having lost something like twenty days; maybe a little more, depending on how long it took to re-round Cape St. Roque. The last thought he had before falling asleep was, wouldn't it be a miserable joke if *Hornet* ended up prey to a different pirate, and Grey had to do this all over again.

HE AWOKE THE NEXT MORNING feeling like a new man. With the inevitability of rain during the voyage, fresh water was of little concern. Lieutenant Chauncey—or rather, now wearing the traditional pro forma title, Captain Chauncey—had invited Grey to breakfast and expressed his enthusiasm at being "Captain Chauncey" again—said he'd had temporary command of a light frigate, but when it had ended, he'd despaired of getting another command before all the pirates had been swept from the ocean, God forbid. He said this with tongue in cheek, though Grey knew that, to a certain extent, he was in earnest; the traditional Thursday toast of the Royal Navy—which Grey had drunk perhaps a thousand times in his life—was "to a bloody war and a sickly season." Meaning, "to the clearing of the ranks above us, so we can move up the list to better and better postings."

This of course was also said with tongue in cheek. A large proportion of toasts in His Majesty's navy were somewhat flip. Sunday, Monday, and Tuesday were entirely in earnest: to "absent friends," "our ships at sea," and "our men." And of course, no matter the day of the week, there was at least one entirely earnest toast: "to the king." However, from there, the expected good humor of a ship's gunroom came on. On Wednesday, the toast was to "ourselves," with whoever was least sober traditionally adding, "as no one else is likely to concern himself with our welfare." On Thursday, to "a bloody war," on Friday, "a willing foe (and sea room!)," and to cap the week off, "to wives and sweethearts (may they never meet)." The last was somewhat in keeping with Nelson's famously indiscreet remark that, beyond Gibraltar, every sailor was a bachelor. The two that preceded it, for all their evident flippancy, were reflections of most navy men's sincere desire to fight. A man can prove himself in battle, but for that, you need a battle. Many brave men went their entire careers without once firing on an enemy, never making names for themselves, retiring as so-called yellow admirals, or worse, as aged lieutenants who were never posted captain; as objects of pity. So Chauncey was understandably in a good humor. Which is why, with the inevitability of rain and little concern over drinking water, he had invited Grey to take a postprandial freshwater bath, and even offered the use of his razor for Grey to shave.

And so Grey was feeling like a new man, standing on deck, watching the American bluejackets go about their business. He was pleased to see Barrows and Drumgoole learning the ropes—not that American rigging had diverged overmuch from English, but as Chauncey had it restrung from its curious pirate gaffing, Grey saw a few notable differences.

And he saw something more surprising than that. There was, evidently, a minuscule marine detachment on the boat—at least three men, one per watch, as there was a single American marine standing at the break of the quarterdeck, ready to beat the men to quarters. When the watch changed, the marine coming off duty turned to Grey, and Grey saw, to his considerable surprise, that it was O'Bannon, in his freshly sewn corporal stripes.

O'Bannon, of course—not being an officer—would not step onto the quarterdeck unless it were in the course of some duty. But Grey, of course, went straight forward and clapped him on the back, and shook his hand.

"O'Bannon, stout fellow; how did you find yourself here?"

O'Bannon smiled broadly. "Well, sir, last evening, when they were fitting out a complement for the new *Hornet* here, Mr. Parker came to tell us of our promotions. He told me there was a general sense that I should have gone up two steps, but there was nothing, for the moment, that he could do to effect it. So instead he offered me my choice of duties, and I told him I was rather curious to see what it was you were so keen to do in Montevideo. The others volunteered too, I might add, to come along, but apparently Campbell or Rogers or someone wouldn't hear of it; can't have a sloop's complement be a sergeant major and three corporals. And what with the continuing action on Crab, sir, a single corporal was all they were prepared to spare, and a couple privates with him."

"O'Bannon—you're the ranking marine on the sloop?"

O'Bannon smiled even more broadly, his backwoods lumber twang becoming very pronounced: "I am, sir."

"Well, permit me to give you joy of your first command, Corporal. I haven't a doubt you'll carry it well."

"Thank you, sir," said O'Bannon, and then, not knowing what to add, saluted.

Grey, whose sense of courtesy prevented him pretending any American rank, replied with a nod. And then added a small wink.

O'Bannon broke his stoic saluting expression for a final smile, and Grey suggested he get some rest.

"Just as you say, sir," said O'Bannon, dropping the salute and turning to disappear down the fore hatch.

"Old friends?" said Chauncey, as Grey resumed the quarterdeck.

"Yes," said Grey. "Comrades-in-arms."

Chauncey nodded. "Nothing like a war with the French to heal the wounds of a revolution, aye?"

Grey smiled. "No, I suppose there isn't."

THE RUN SOUTH along the Brazilian coast was uneventful; *Hornet* ran well with the wind on her beam, and the easterlies blowing from Africa kept her around six knots most days. No *Perseus*, to be certain, but a respectable speed, and Grey was allowing himself to be optimistic. He would certainly miss the treasure fleet's earliest possible sailing day of July 15th; he would, however, arrive a month or so ahead of its last possible sailing day of September 1st. All he could do was hope, pace, and wonder to what extent the Spanish habit of midday sleeping had expanded with their empire.

In four weeks, they had passed the mouth of the river January, with its large, thriving Portuguese city—which, under different circumstances, Grey would have been eager to wander in a few days. In five weeks from Crab Island, the headlands of Punta del Este hove into view, and by noon the following day, Montevideo was in sight.

Strictly speaking, Spain and Britain were still at peace. Grey might know Spain's San Ildefonso treaty commitments, but it was entirely possible that he was the only man in the Western Hemisphere who did. Even the men making the decisions regarding the treasure fleet were likely unaware of its larger importance; the requirement of keeping the transportation of vast amounts of wealth secret hardly needing explanation. Yet there was considerable coolness between the Spanish empire and the British, for any number of Ildefonso-independent reasons. Spain had supported France in supporting the American revolution. Spain and Britain had very nearly fought a war when, in 1789, Spain began to seize British commercial ships trading furs at Nootka Sound on the far-north American Pacific coast. Spain claimed exclusive right to trade in the Pacific, citing a papal bull from three hundred years earlier. Protestant Britain threatened to destroy Spain's vastly weaker navy unless its merchantmen were released, which they were—ending Spain's multicentury monopoly on the world's largest ocean. A few years later, when the French revolution began to spiral out of control, Spain allied with Britain to stop it, and remained Britain's ally until 1795, when the infamous Godoy negotiated a separate peace. So, even without a shortly-to-be-declared war, Anglo-Spanish relations were not collegial.

Relations between the Americans and Madrid were not splendid either. Spain had supported the American revolution in hopes of weakening British claims in North America, but that didn't stop her hating the idea of Republicanism. The Spanish government feared revolution—not so much in Spain as in their myriad new-world colonies. However, on the western side of the Atlantic, Spanish America and the United States got along quite well, as trading partners who, post 1776, were no longer shackled by London's transatlantic protectionism. In consequence, they were getting rich together—which meant that Grey's arrival in Montevideo under the Stars & Stripes received a much warmer reception than it would have under the Union Jack.

Salutes were fired on both sides, and after *Hornet* had dropped her anchor, an invitation arrived for Chauncey to present himself at the governor's residence. The jolly boat which arrived with the invitation carried Chauncey ashore. Grey came along, promising to meet Chauncey later in the evening to discuss their respective plans. Chauncey had been ordered to ferry Grey to his destination, no more, but he wanted to know that Grey had made it into the hands of the British consul before weighing. In any case, he wished to resupply. O'Bannon rode ashore as well, having assigned himself (with Chauncey's permission, of course) as Grey's escort. Confidentially he told Grey he was simply eager to see Montevideo firsthand. Grey believed this, but only in part. In any case—

Chauncey and Grey parted at the dockside, with Chauncey off to the governor's residence. Chauncey's Spanish escort pointed Grey in the general direction of the house of the British consul, and Grey set off with O'Bannon beside him.

In their more than a month at sea, Grey and O'Bannon had become good friends. Notwithstanding their difference in age—Grey was nearly old enough to have been O'Bannon's father—they had two things principally in common: service as marines, and a perpetual state of curiosity. O'Bannon had already been four years at sea in the Caribbean, but prior to the Cangrejo battery detachment, had never been further south or further east than Tobago at the bottom of the Windward Isles. He had asked Grey to begin by naming and describing to him every capital city in Europe. Conversely, Grey, whose mother had been born in New England; whose family still included Yankee lumbermen, had never been further inland in the American Northeast than Boston, and wanted to know, in detail, the country and business of his patrimony (matrimony, somehow, did not seem to be the right word). O'Bannon described, to Grey's immense fascination, his first river voyage—not on a boat, but on what O'Bannon called a "raft" of logs; loose logs, shepherded through decreasingly tiny tributaries into the Connecticut River and then to Hartford, with American woodsmen jumping from log to log, ever mindful of the near certainty that any man who fell in would be crushed or—more likely—drowned, unable to resurface from under the acres of lumber. Logjams were frequent, as the raft moved over rapids or waterfalls. Even though the log drives were timed to coincide with the spring thaw and the river's annual flood, sometimes the only way to break the jam was with powder kegs. O'Bannon's fascination with the immense power stored within the seemingly innocuous black dust led him to stay in Hartford, at one of the city's nascent arms factories. From making rifles to using them in defense of his countrymen seemed an obvious jump, after the six frigates began to recruit ships' companies to contend with the piratical French.

So back and forth they went, Grey illustrating the old world, O'Bannon the new world. O'Bannon probed, with intense interest, for every detail of the Parthenon Marbles Grey had alluded to, and Grey had done his best to capture the intense beauty of the drawings which Elgin had had published, while imagining to O'Bannon the way they had looked in situ, before the Turks had decided to use the Parthenon as a gunpowder magazine, and had accidentally blown it up. Grey, meanwhile, was eager to have O'Bannon teach him some Iroquois, to which he agreed, if Grey would reciprocate by teaching him true French (as opposed to habitant trapper French). O'Bannon's duties, between standing a watch and supervising the others, kept him occupied for about twelve hours each day. He reserved six, more or less, for sleep, and one for eating with and becoming better acquainted with his two-man company. The remaining five hours were almost invariably spent in conversation with Grey. Now, as they walked towards the house of the British consul, the monthlong conversation simply continued where it had left off, with a discussion of the southern skies: a new world to O'Bannon, with new constellations and no polar star. O'Bannon wanted in particular to know what the Magellanic Clouds were made of. Grey wasn't certain, but was willing to speculate.

The home of the British consul was not far from the docks; not especially grand but not shabby either, with a garden separating it from the street, filled with peculiar blooming bushes of sorts Grey had never seen before. Having lost, in the explosion of the *Perseus*, the various documents given him by Sir Edwards, giving him broad plenipotentiary authority over the British Plate colony consul, he had to fall back on a series of innocuous passphrases to identify himself as one of Sir Edward's men and an agent of His Majesty's secret intelligence service. The phrases were tucked into a letter of introduction which he'd written for himself aboard the *Hornet*, and which he now presented to the British consul's butler. And now he and O'Bannon were seated in the garden waiting for a response.

"So," said Grey, after a moment's repose on a stone bench by a fountain, "what do you imagine will be next for you? I gather from Mr. Parker that after Cangrejo the squadron of *Congress* and *Constellation* are set for the Mediterranean, to relieve the part of your fleet that's been on station there dealing with the remaining Berber pirates."

"I believe so, sir," said O'Bannon. "In fact I'm looking very much forward to it; I understand the fleet's rendezvous is at Syracuse, and I am anxious to get a look at it, perhaps see some of the Naples while my ship's provisioned."

"Syracuse? Not Valletta?"

"No, sir. They decamped from Valletta after one of your captains refused to return some of our deserted sailors, who'd received thirty-odd pieces of silver to help make up a watch."

Grey shook his head. "This business of men moving fleet to fleet will come to no good, O'Bannon."

O'Bannon nodded. "The impressment in particular, I believe. Though this running business certainly does us no favors."

Grey nodded.

O'Bannon continued. "Though this does raise a certain vexed question regarding Barrows and Drumgoole. I understand, rather than working their way back to a British ship as Mr. Parker had allowed for, they would like to have their names entered in our books. Otherwise they can't be paid—but then they'll have to serve out at least a year. Which they say they're happy to do; evidently they were pressed into your navy from the merchant fleet, and have come to see that as the basis for their problems. At least that's what my boys say is the word before the mast."

Grey nodded. "Well, I can't say I blame them, though they play a dangerous game with being hanged as deserters. Though, on the other hand, I don't suppose one can be accused of having deserted a ship that's exploded."

"You wouldn't think so," said O'Bannon.

Grey tapped his fingers on his knee. With time being of the essence, the long sea voyage from Cangrejo had been trying. That, of course, was an unavoidable fact of life. But now that he was finally here—had finally made it to Montevideo near a month after his intended date—to have to sit in the garden tapping his knee was verging on too much to take. He had been tempted to send Barrows or Drumgoole—or even O'Bannon, whom he'd come to trust more or less implicitly—to begin nosing around the docks, seeing if there were any news of the treasure fleet, but of course that would have been an impossible risk to run. No, there was nothing to do but wait.

Grey noticed O'Bannon noticing the anxious tapping of his fingers, and stopped.

"Do you play tennis in the United States?" Grey asked, just as the consul's butler reappeared and asked him to step inside.

"I'll wait where I am, sir," said O'Bannon to the butler, "if you've no objection."

"None, Corporal. I'll have some water sent out to you."

"Thank you, sir, very kind."

Grey stepped into the consulate; the floor was dark red wood and the walls whitewashed. The butler led Grey to a sitting room at the back of the house; the windows looked into a glass hothouse, filled with orchids. The man Grey assumed to be the British consul was removing a pair of heavy cotton gloves; he had Grey's letter of introduction pinched in the crook of his elbow. Grey wondered why you would need a hothouse so close to the jungle, but perhaps these were especially sensitive orchids.

"Mr. Grey," said the consul, tossing the gloves onto a low end table, "welcome. Before we discuss serious matters, if I might intrude a more trivial subject: Do you know who won the Clermont Cup this year? I'm somewhat behind on the sporting news."

This was a countersign to the passphrases in Grey's letter. Grey completed the exchange:

"I'm afraid I don't remember his name—only that his sire was Eclipse."

The consular nodded. "Very well. I'm Matheson. What can I do for you? Have a seat, won't you?"

"Thank you, sir. Allow me to come directly to the point," said Grey, sitting on a couch opposite the hothouse windows; opposite a couch where Matheson now sat. "There's a fleet of ships that will deliver an enormous sum of treasure assembling here at the Plate, to Spain, before the end of the year. I must, with all possible speed, learn the details of its cargo, the ships involved, and most importantly, the date of sailing. Is there anything you can tell me?"

Matheson thought for a moment. "Spanish convoys—merchant convoys, navy convoys—sail very regularly from Montevideo; it's their principal port here. I've not had any reason to be concerned with their contents, and I'm afraid there are too many of them for me practically to concern myself with their comings and goings—particularly as we are at peace with Spain. My business with the harbor, so to speak, is more or less exclusively concerned with the maintenance of rights of British merchantmen and sailors. And occasionally arranging help for one who has been arrested, or for any in the area who have been taken for ransom—not a common, but certainly not an unheard-of, problem in these waters."

Grey nodded, declining to add his own experience in that line to the discussion. There wasn't time.

"Have you any reliable contacts in the colony's government?"

"I have, but none to whom I could put this sort of question. They are social contacts, rather than hire and salary. There's a great deal of wealth accumulated here, so there is more for a Spaniard to lose from bribes than to gain by them."

Grey nodded. "Who is their senior naval officer?"

"Detailed to the station, you mean?"

"Yes."

"That would be Vice Admiral Juan de Pareja y Mariscal; he is their port admiral."

Grey leaned forward, stared for a moment at the floor, and then looked up again. "Do you know where he lives?"

25

GREY ASKED O'BANNON to make his apologies to Chauncey, and to say that, if the *Hornet* were still in the offing one day hence, Grey would be pleased to wait on Chauncey at the captain's convenience. He also asked O'Bannon if, before carrying this message back to the *Hornet*, he wouldn't mind cleaning one of the two small pistols Grey had just borrowed from Matheson. O'Bannon was, of course, happy to do as Grey asked, but reluctant to leave Grey when the cleaning was through. He figured that if Grey was intending to go about the city carrying a brace of pocket guns, he must have a reasonable expectation of finding himself in a scrape. Grey assured O'Bannon he would be fine; that this was part of the Montevidean excursion he could not discuss, and sent the young American on his way.

Aside from its unusual foliage, Montevideo had very much the feel of a European city—the streets were well made, and in some places, paved with stone. Aside from a messy knot around the harbor battery, they were laid out square. Aside from a small hill—on which sat the harbor battery—and a large hill looming up in the distance, the city was essentially flat. This, perhaps, was the reason for an evident paucity of pack animals; or perhaps it was just Grey's imagination—but either way, the city smelled much less manured than a normal metropolis. Perhaps in recompense, the smell of fish was abnormally strong. But as they say, a change is as good as a rest.

The port admiral's decently large home was towards the edge of town, where the buildings were less cramped. It was surrounded by a head-high stone wall; walking past the iron entry gate, Grey was able to see an elaborately manicured garden of flowers and hedges, and in the middle, a two-story-tall stone house.

Grey continued past it, on a long, slow circle around nothing in particular, arriving back at the admiral's garden wall just as the night became dark enough to hide him from prying eyes.

He took a moment to make sure no one was coming; then to tie a kerchief over his nose and mouth. He grabbed the top of the garden wall and pulled himself up and over, and dropped down on the far side, on a soft but close-cropped lawn. Somewhere not too far away, a voice hummed a Spanish tune. The hummer was obscured by a hedge, but Grey presumed him to be a night watchman of some sort, and waited silently, in a crouch, while the voice passed. It was going left; after a short interval, Grey began to creep to his right, looking for a gap in the shrubbery. After about twenty feet, he found one, and looked inward towards the house. There were a pair of Spanish soldiers standing at the front door, which was a few dozen yards to Grey's left. Straight ahead was the house's front left corner. And now, to Grey's right, came the soft pad of footsteps on grass. Grey froze against a hedge and tried to look verdant.

A Spanish guard in a shako loomed into view. He was smoking a cigarillo, and the glowing tip bobbed through the darkness as he passed—coming within three feet of Grey, but not seeing him. Again Grey waited a few moments for the soldier to get a discreet distance away, and then turned onto a path through the hedges that led inward towards the house. After three more rows of hedges—or were they flowering bushes of some kind?—either way, after three more rows of them, they gave way to flower beds. Looking carefully around and holding his breath to hear as clearly as he could, Grey made certain there were no more night-watch soldiers about, and then crept another ten yards or so to the corner of the house.

Looking up, there were several small terraces outside second-story windows. The house's exterior wall, however, was too smooth to climb. About halfway between the front left corner, where Grey stood, and the rear left corner, was a rain pipe that emptied into a shallow channel—a gutter to carry the doubtless heavy and frequent rainfall away from the house and the flower beds. The pipe looked . . . somewhat sturdy. Not all Grey could have hoped for, but it was worth a tug, in any case.

Ducking under a pair of first-floor windows, Grey moved along the side of the house. He put a hand on the rain pipe and pulled. It didn't move. He put a second hand on it and pulled harder. It didn't move. He put his hands higher and pulled himself up. It took his weight. He began to climb it. At the level of the second floor, he reached out for one of the second-floor terraces—first with his hand, then his foot. Neither could reach it, so he continued upward to the shingled roof, pulling himself onto the red clay tiles and climbing gently inward to the central peak.

He had no fear of slipping—the soles of his boots were scored, and the clay shingles were rough. Being slightly too confident, therefore, in his balance as he reached the roof's pinnacle, a gust of wind nearly knocked him over. It might have sent him tumbling down the roof and back into the garden if he hadn't been able to grab a chimney to steady himself.

The chimney was warm and slightly smoking. Grey assumed these were remnants of a fire for a brisk winter's night in the southern half of the world. That the fire was dying, Grey hoped, indicated that the master of the house had retired for the evening. Descending slightly from the roof's peak into its lee, Grey made his way to the back of the house. In the center of the rear wall was a terrace twice as wide as the others. Grey hoped this would belong to the master's bedroom. He saw no light coming from the room; perhaps Admiral Pareja y Mariscal was an early-to-bed, early-to-rise sort. Setting a foot on the iron rain gutter that ran along the roof's sloped edge—checking it could hold him—he turned inward, dropped down to a crouch, grabbed the gutter, and lowered himself over the side.

He let go of the gutter with one hand and looked below him, then dropped about five feet to the terrace. He landed with a thud, but that couldn't be helped. He waited for a moment in a crouch, listening to hear if anyone would stir inside the room to which the terrace was attached. When no one did, he stepped inside.

The room was black as pitch, but there was a single line of light at the bottom of a door into an evidently illuminated hallway. Grey was using it to guess the dimensions of the room when, somewhere to his left, a match was struck. It was held to an oil lamp, and a moment later the room was lit with a gentle yellow glow.

A girl of twenty or so was lying in a large bed, staring curiously at Grey. For a moment Grey stared back, waiting to see if she'd scream for help. Instead, she just looked at him, with the smallest hint of a wry smile. He held a single finger up to his lips, to ask for quiet. The girl smiled more widely.

"Do you speak French?" said Grey, in French.

After he was through, he wished no one to know their intruder had been English.

"I do," said the girl, with a Spanish accent. "Might I ask who you are?"

"I am a bandit," said Grey, in his most charming tone of voice.

"You are dressed rather nicely for a bandit," said the girl.

Grey was wearing a black jacket, brown trousers, and black boots: a reasonably fine suit of clothes lent to him by Chauncey.

"You're very kind, madam—I am a bandit of the upper class. My banditry is sport, making game of my own people, you see—it lends excitement to my dull and privileged life."

The girl's smile turned skeptical. "Should you not then confine yourself to burglarizing the French?"

"I would normally, madam, but as they say, when in Rome, you must burglarize Romans."

The girl laughed quietly, then said, "You have twice called me 'madam.' It is mademoiselle."

"Oh, indeed?" said Grey. "You are not the admiral's wife?"

"I am not," said the girl. "His wife is in Spain——and as old and gouty as he is."

"Ah," said Grey. "I take it you are not his daughter, either."

"I am not," said the girl.

"You are a kept woman?" said Grey.

"I'm a prostitute," said the girl.

Grey stifled a laugh.

"You are forward, mademoiselle."

"You are the one who has crept into my bedroom in the dark of night, monsieur," she said.

"Touché," said Grey. "I wonder if you might direct me to the admiral's bedroom."

"This is his bedroom," said the girl, "but I'm afraid you are simply not to his taste."

Grey chuckled. "Can you tell me when he'll be along?"

"If he's not here by now, the old bastard has fallen asleep at his desk."

"And where is his desk?"

"In his study. Across the hall."

"Thank you, mademoiselle," said Grey. "I am only sorry not to offer you custom before moving on."

"I'll be here all night," said the girl. "If you wish to pass through again on your way out."

"Could I afford you?"

"After robbing the admiral? Perhaps."

Grey smiled and stepped towards the door.

"*À tout à l'heure,*" he said, and made his exit.

As he stepped into the dimly lit corridor, he checked that it was empty with a hand resting on one of his pistols. Happily, there was no one about. He crossed the corridor to the facing door, opened it silently, and stepped through into a lamplit room. At the opposite wall——positioned so, in the daytime, he would look out on his entry gate——was Vice Admiral Pareja. He was slumped back in his chair, snoring softly. Grey walked over to him, removing a pistol from his pocket. He pulled the admiral's chair back from his desk—which, to Grey's surprise, did not wake him. Grey aimed the pistol at the admiral's face, just far enough back to be in focus, and then lightly kicked the admiral in the shins.

The admiral stirred, slowly. He opened his eyes slowly and saw first the pistol, then Grey holding it. His eyes went wide with confusion and fear.

"What is going on? Who are you? What is the meaning of this?"

He spoke in Spanish; Grey answered in French.

"Do you speak French?" he said.

"Yes," said the admiral.

"Good," said Grey. "Let me explain carefully and completely. There will soon sail from your port a convoy of ships carrying treasure, bound for Spain. You can give me the convoy's particulars, in toto, and live. Or you can deny that you have them, in which case I will kill you. Then I will rifle your files, find the information I'm looking for, and spread the rumor that you not only told me what I needed to know, but afterwards fell to your knees and wept like a woman, begging for your life. I apologize for this ungentlemanly coercion, but you must understand, I am in great haste and will not trifle."

The admiral looked at him, looked at the pistol, then back at Grey. Grey was deeply irritated to see the admiral steel his resolve.

"Do what you will," said the admiral. "If you thought I would value my life or even my reputation above my country, you were mistaken."

The man had called Grey's brag. As it was out of the question that Grey would actually kill the man to make a point, he instead grabbed the back of the admiral's chair, threw it to the ground, and rolled the admiral onto his face. He bound the admiral's hands behind his back and stuffed a kerchief into his mouth. Grey was prepared to search through every scrap of paper in the office, but the obvious first place to look was a small iron safe on the floor beside the admiral's desk.

Grey knelt beside the admiral and began to search his pockets, finally finding his keys on a chain around his neck. Grey opened the safe with the first key he tried; inside the safe were two small gold ingots, several more of silver, and under them, stacks of papers, in individual files bound together by string.

Perhaps unsurprisingly, the top file was the records of the treasure fleet. Grey took it to the desk, untied it, and began to leaf through . . . There were extensive notes on the treasure's assembly in Montevideo, and its contents . . . It was loaded aboard not galleons, but four Spanish frigates: *Medea*, forty, *Fama*, thirty-four, *Mercedes*, thirty-six, *Santa Clara*, thirty-four. He knew them all, by reputation. They were good sailors; not as fast as the frigates the French made, but fast. He continued through the file. The final leaf of paper was a fair-writ copy of a sailing order . . . for August the 8th.

Eight days ago.

Grey had missed it.

He was too late.

He had failed.

His breath caught in his chest. He felt as if he'd been punched in the face.

There was a knock on the door.

"Pardon me for intruding, sir," came a Spanish voice from the other side. "I was on duty at the front door and thought perhaps I had heard someone fall. Are you well, sir?"

Grey folded the complete file and slipped it into a pocket. Then he grabbed one of the gold ingots and walked to the door. Just as the soldier on the other side was starting to knock again, Grey pulled the door open, and with his right hand—with the small gold bar clutched therein—he delivered a murderous straight punch to the soldier's jaw. The soldier went out like a snuffed candle and crumpled to the ground. Grey stepped over him, looked up and down the hall, and reentered the room of the admiral's professional mistress.

She was awake, sitting up in bed, looking excited by whatever commotion she had heard in the corridor.

"Spend this for me, would you?" said Grey, tossing the gold bar onto her bed as he passed through the room.

She looked at it and then looked at him, just as he was stepping back out onto the terrace.

"*Au revoir, bandido,*" she said.

Grey ignored her, stepped up onto the terrace railing, and dropped down into the garden. A few moments later he was over the wall, stuffing his kerchief-mask into a pocket and walking quickly as he could back to Matheson's house. As he did, a thought played over and over in his head: *Medea*, forty, *Fama*, thirty-four, *Mercedes*, thirty-six, *Santa Clara*, thirty-four. Fast frigates with an eight days' sailing advantage. An enormous head start. Already they could be something like an eighth of the way to Spain. Could they be overtaken?

GLAD TO FIND the British consul still awake, Grey strode into Matheson's office without waiting to be announced, and came straight to the point.

"Mr. Matheson—forgive the intrusion—do we have any ships here? The Spanish treasure fleet has sailed. It is imperative—*imperative*—that I catch up to them."

Matheson nodded solemnly and gestured for Grey to take a seat. Grey was too agitated to sit.

"Well, we've no navy ships here," said Matheson. "Do you mean English ships?"

"Yes," said Grey.

"A few," said Matheson. "Hulking West Indiamen. You must have seen them in the harbor."

"Yes," said Grey. "Is that all?"

"I'm afraid so," said Matheson.

"What are the fastest ships of which you're aware? In the harbor or in the vicinity of the Plate. I need something that can get at least twelve knots. We must pay whatever is required."

"There's a clipper," said Matheson, after a moment's thought. "A Baltimore clipper, named *Cervantes*. She is said to make fourteen."

"Very good," said Grey.

"However, we won't be able to buy her. She's a private yacht belonging to an immensely wealthy Frenchman. He fled down here after the Haitian revolution; he owns an estate a few miles up the coast, towards the river mouth. I believe he uses the yacht mostly to travel back and forth from Buenos Aires; there is some belief that he is illegally dealing slaves from the interior. In any case—whatever his business—there seems little hope of his selling us the sloop. Even if he were not already too wealthy to make the proposition attractive, he is French. And even if he is not a patriot, selling her would be more than enough to put his head on the block if ever word of the sale made it back to Paris."

Grey was scratching the back of his neck. "She's not a sloop of war . . ."

"No," said Matheson.

"About a hundred feet long?"

"That's right."

"I could sail her with a crew of . . . eighteen. Does that sound right to you, sir?"

Again Matheson thought for a moment. "Yes, I believe so. Watch and watch."

Grey nodded again, thinking. "Eighteen men . . . How many sailors do you think we could get out off those West Indiamen?"

"I'm sure I could muster you enough to sail her, if you had her—but that's the question, isn't it? How do you propose inducing the Frenchman to give her up?"

Grey looked at him with an ironic, mirthless half-smile. "Piracy."

26

O F COURSE, it was not piracy in the strictest sense. As a
plenipotentiary representative of the Court of St. James's,
Matheson had the power to issue letters of marque—which
would legitimize an act of piracy as an act of war carried out by
licensed agents of His Majesty. That is to say, Grey and his assembled
men were not pirates, but privateers.

There was, though, the remaining question of Spain's neutrality.
Taking a French ship under a letter of marque wouldn't violate the
law of arms, but it would violate the terms of Britain's use of neutral
Spanish ports. Obviously, in a matter of weeks—one way or the
other—this would no longer be a concern. But for the moment, it
was. Especially with a number of English commercial vessels, not to
mention English subjects, available in Montevideo and Buenos Aires
for retaliatory arrest, the matter had to be approached delicately.

With no royal marines to enforce impressment, eighteen sailors had to be abstracted from the British West Indiamen by buying out their contracts and offering exorbitant enlistment incentives
(the Adam Smith approach to naval recruitment). And without permission from a flag officer, the American captain Isaac Chauncey
could not offer any direct assistance either in the cutting-out of a
French ship, or in the violation of Spanish neutrality. In fact, with

Grey unwilling to provide details as to why the enterprise was so essential, Chauncey was forced to take rather a dim view of the proposal, within or without the aegis of a letter of marque. Still, with a lingering feeling of indebtedness to Grey from the destruction of the Isla Cangrejo battery, Chauncey did make a single concession: that O'Bannon, at O'Bannon's insistent request, would be allowed to assist Grey, who would otherwise be without the help of any other trained soldier; West Indiaman sailors being feisty and fighty, no doubt, but with no practice or discipline. However, if O'Bannon were to go along, he could not be wearing an American uniform. And without a uniform or a letter of marque, he would be guilty of piracy. Grey dealt with this final conundrum by issuing O'Bannon—on Grey's own authority—with the temporary rank of acting sergeant of His Majesty's Royal Marines. As only an acting, warrantless officer, O'Bannon would have no oath to take—O'Bannon made it very clear he would take no oath to Britain, nor in any way indicate fealty to a country other than the United States. But since a temporary rank needn't be confirmed or even accepted, it was a moot point; only the labyrinthine legalism mattered, and on that count, he was protected.

To avoid the appearance of involvement, Captain Chauncey insisted on weighing before the cutting-out took place, taking with him Grey's promise to deliver O'Bannon to Gibraltar, where he could rejoin the American fleet. At the last minute, Drumgoole and then Barrows decided they too would come along; do their duty to God, king & their country. So now, two longboats purchased by Matheson rowed inland along the coast of the *Bahía de Montevideo*, the first coxswained by Grey, with Barrows and nine merchant sailors rowing, the second by O'Bannon, with Drumgoole and nine merchantmen rowing. Many of the merchantmen had, at times in their lives, belonged to the Royal Navy—all of them through impressment—but even so, most had seen scrapes before. But to avoid chaos, they would stand back and let the hitherto professional fighting men attend to the fighting. Grey's instructions to them were only, first, to join the fight if they saw they were needed,

The Montevideo Brief | 165

and second, not to kill anyone if they believed killing could in any way be avoided.

Two longboats, eleven men in each of them, rounded a headland just after sunset on the day following *Hornet*'s arrival in Montevideo. and began to pull into a small, sheltered harbor. Starting with the inside of the headland, a long J-shaped beach stretched up towards a wide, manicured lawn, studded with blooming trees, and behind them, a palatial wooden house. Where the lawn met the beach, a wooden pier met a gravel path, and stretched over the water for about twenty yards. Several small boats were tied there. Further out from the beach, in deeper water, the clipper *Cervantes* tugged gently at its anchor line. So far as Grey could see, she was defended only by a single small cannon on the lawn, which likely as not was used for signaling rather than fighting.

With a whispered reminder to row slowly and quietly, the two boats crept towards the clipper. O'Bannon's pulled to the clipper's taffrail; Grey's continued forward to the bower line. With O'Bannon signaling he was ready, Grey grabbed the bower line and pulled himself through the anchor port, sliding silently onto the deck. At the same time, O'Bannon grabbed the taffrail and pulled himself up and over it. The other twenty men remained in the boats, holding their collective breath.

Grey had assumed the clipper would be manned by a skeleton crew, and so it was. The rigging was empty. A man sat on a stool by the wheel, sleeping. Another was asleep leaned against the binnacle. Two more were asleep laid out on makeshift sailcloth mattresses. No doubt belowdecks it was too hot and close to sleep. Finally, just feet from Grey's right elbow, a man stood—awake—gazing back towards the lawn and house beyond it. There was the glow of torch-light in a dozen windows; perhaps the man in the bow was daydreaming of being asked to attend some gala party. It didn't matter. Grey got silently to his feet, walked silently up behind the man, threw his right arm around the man's neck, and choked him to unconscious-ness before laying him softly on the deck.

Grey looked aft. The man who'd been asleep at the wheel was

similarly laid out; O'Bannon had already moved to the man who'd laid himself against the binnacle—slowly circling an arm around his throat, which woke the man up and then put him back to sleep.

Now Grey and O'Bannon converged on the waist. Grey put a finger to his lips, then put up a palm telling O'Bannon to wait; pointed two fingers to his own eyes, then pointed at the sleeping men, telling O'Bannon to keep watch over them. Grey slipped down the main hatch onto the main deck. There wasn't much to be seen there. A mostly empty room for men to sling hammocks, behind which was a single, comfortable cabin—for the owner, Grey assumed. Its door was open for airing and Grey stuck a head in. Nothing especially remarkable. It was longer and narrower than a normal great cabin; contained a wide-slung cot, a writing table, and lar- and starboard galleries through which fresh air could pass. He turned back to the crew's quarters. There was a reefed sailcloth partition where the ship's mainmast passed through the deck; Grey assumed the ship's officers, such as they were, slept behind it and the men before. The front third of the main deck, separated by a waist-high wall, served as the sail locker—spare cloth, hemp, and cord. Just before the mast was a steep companion ladder down into the hold, which Grey followed. It was stocked with barrels, half or more empty, but the rest filled with salt beef, hardtack, peas, and slightly slimy fresh water. Enough provision for a short sea voyage; presumably the run to Buenos Aires and back—this was an unexpected boon, as Grey had assumed he would have to keep the men going on rainwater and the provisions they carried until they reached a Portuguese port further up the coast. This would easily be enough to get them to the Rio Janeiro, where they could take on enough to get them back across the Atlantic. But Grey shook his head. He wasn't here for housekeeping, he was checking for concealed men. When he was satisfied there were none, he returned to the weather deck. O'Bannon was standing just where Grey had left him, over two still-blissfully-unaware sleeping sailors.

"The barky's empty otherwise," said Grey. "Let's seize these two up, and we'll put them on those headlands, along with their less conscious compadres."

O'Bannon nodded, and at that moment a man dropped out of the rigging, landing just feet behind Grey, seized Grey around the neck, and attempted to bring a knife to bear on his throat. O'Bannon leapt forward, grabbed the man's knife hand, yanked it away from Grey, and punched inward into the man's elbow. It snapped, the man screamed, Grey twisted away, and O'Bannon twisted free the knife, took hold of it, and used its hilt to bludgeon the man unconscious. It all happened in less than five seconds.

Meanwhile, the sound of the struggle had woken the two sleepers—but seeing two armed men standing above them, they quickly surrendered, and were bound, hands behind their backs, one each by O'Bannon and Grey.

"Thank you, O'Bannon. There's one I owe you."

"On the contrary, Captain Grey, I checked the rigging and didn't see him up there," said O'Bannon, looking again up into the rigging, making a more careful examination this time.

Grey was looking up too. "Neither did I, the inconspicuous devil."

Satisfied the rigging was genuinely empty, O'Bannon decided the knife he'd just saved Grey's life with was not a keeper and stuck it into the gunwale for general use, and Grey leaned overboard to address the two longboats filled with sailors.

"The ship is ours, lads. Come aboard."

From somewhere in the blackness, a voice called out, "She ain't a ship, sir, she's a fore-and-aft."

There was the sound of a scuffle, and the sound of someone being tipped ignominiously into the water, and then Drumgoole's voice:

"Sorry about that, sir, we're coming aboard, and most of us dryfoot."

"Very good, Drumgoole. Get them to the capstan, won't you? We'll begin with the boats and then take up the anchor."

27

AMONG THE EIGHTEEN SAILORS seconded from the merchant fleet, there was a middle-aged sailing master named Mogg who'd long awaited his first captaincy. Only this eagerness, he claimed, induced him to depart his otherwise stable and satisfactory merchant employment, though Grey suspected there may have been some love of king & country that played into it—men of a certain sort, and Mogg seemed to be one of them, tended to be cynically embarrassed to remark on such things. In any case, he now had command of the ship, under Grey's supervision. Grey offered O'Bannon passage either as a guest or in any official position he was inclined to take—suggesting that in the absence of any marines to command, he might like to act as boatswain. O'Bannon said in fact, if he might, he would like to apprentice himself to the sailing master-cum-captain, explaining that he had never been satisfied with his incomplete knowledge of the mechanics of sailing. To both Grey and the new captain Mogg, this arrangement seemed ideal. Drumgoole instead became boatswain and captain of the first watch, and Barrows boatswain's mate and captain of the second.

Once they were at sea, with the trades on their starboard quarter and the men adjusted to the unusual rig of the clipper, they made extraordinary time: a regular fourteen knots. Grey believed they must be doubling—at least—the speed of the Spanish treasure fleet. Or was this just confusing hope with logic? Though of course, either way, it didn't make a jot of difference. The cards had all been dealt now, bets had been made—fortunes staked—and all that remained was to show hands. The game would play out, but Grey no longer had the ability to improve his odds. All he could do was await the turn.

And that was what he did—leaving the sailing to the captain and crew, and pacing, pacing endlessly, back and forth along the taffrail, or sometimes climbing the foremast and clinging to the crosstrees, both to take some cool air and from the idle hope he might catch a glimpse of the Spanish fleet. Grey now knew exactly the route they were taking, and for what port they were headed—Cadiz—and felt that the clipper *had* to be gaining ground. And fast. And, though again wary of confusing hope and certainty, he felt certain of overtaking the Spaniards' frigate foursome before they could make harbor. The question was only: *How far* before they made harbor? Would there be enough time to find and assemble a British fleet to bring the Spanish to action? Of that, there was no telling.

And then, on the morning of September 24th, just south of the Canaries, Grey was sleeping comfortably in the cot of the owner's cabin, near dawn, when a knock came on his door. It was the captain, and O'Bannon with him; they ushered Grey up on deck, where everyone was speaking in hushed, excited tones. Every man was on the leeward, larboard rail. The captain handed Grey a glass and pointed. Hull down on the horizon, stretching in a loose formation, front to back, over several miles of sea, were four sail.

Grey took hold of the spyglass with his teeth and ran up the mainmast, stopping momentarily for a long look from the maintop, then continuing up to the crosstrees, to confirm what was already an utter certainty boiling in his chest:

The four sail were his four Spanish frigates. Though they flew no colors, there was no question at all . . . but just to be certain, Grey counted their guns. And they were just as described. *Medea*, forty; *Fama*, thirty-four; *Mercedes*, thirty-six; *Santa Clara*, thirty-four. Grey climbed back down to the maintop, slid the rest of the way on a backstay, and, back on deck, returned Captain Mogg his glass.

"How much longer would you say it will take them to reach Cadiz?"

Mogg, afraid of straying out of his depth, hesitated and said, "At least eight days."

"And how far are we from Gibraltar?"

"Three, likely. No more than four."

Grey nodded. These had been roughly his guesses too, though he hadn't wanted to prejudice the captain by saying so.

"Very good, Captain. Please get us there, flying with wings as eagles."

"Very good, sir," said Captain Mogg.

28

I N THE EVENT, Mogg was perfectly correct. On the evening of the
fourth day, the Rock loomed into view—and Grey had a course
laid straight for a ship of the line flying the broad pennant of the
commanding officer: Admiral of the White William Cornwallis.
Not willing to wait on lowering a longboat, Grey had Mogg put the
clipper beneath the entry port of the giant HMS *Robust*, seventy-four,
and beg permission to seize to her. Himself, Grey did not wait for a
reply but ran up the accommodation ladder, stepping into the entry
port on the main deck, saluting the marine there, and requesting
permission to come aboard.

This forward approach to accession onto a flagship caused a certain degree of confusion. After several minutes, with a young marine
private peeking at him from the corner of his eye, Grey was greeted
by the *Robust*'s third lieutenant:

"Good evening, sir; I'm Lieutenant Franks—may I ask what your
business with *Robust* is?"

His face was the cold stoic of Royal Navy officers preparing to
deal with battles or rudeness.

"Good evening, Lieutenant Franks; I'm Captain Grey of the
marines, here on urgent business from the Admiralty."

Grey had written out the standard letter of introduction, complete with the secret passphrases that would let Cornwallis know he was one of Sir Edward's intelligence men, but Grey, feeling the oppressive crush of time, added, in hopes of speeding matters along: "The admiral may remember me from an occasion at Haddon Hall in the late nineties, when we spent a considerable length of time discussing the prospect of integrated bullet cartridges. And please emphasize that this is a matter of the utmost urgency."

Lieutenant Franks was somewhat confused by all this, but Grey gestured a dismissal with a tilt of his head and Franks walked off at a good speed, leaving Grey to wait impatiently. The remark about Haddon Hall was not one of naval intelligence's passphrases; it did in fact happen that Grey and Admiral Cornwallis were, in a small way, social acquaintances. With his occasional spells of haunting the Admiralty, for many years now Grey was acquainted socially with many post captains and flag officers, though generally by no more than name and sight. Cornwallis was a somewhat different case, owing to his famous good nature. He was well known for his close companionship to his men, who admired him so greatly that they'd awarded him the distinction of a sea chantey in his own lifetime, widely sung throughout the fleet. "Billy Blue" was both the title of the work and Cornwallis's nickname before the mast; the piece was a ballad work song commemorating one of his great victories, known somewhat ironically as "Cornwallis's Retreat."

In '95, Cornwallis had been commanding a small squadron of seven ships and had had the misfortune of happening on a large French squadron of twenty-nine. In normal circumstances, such a dramatic mismatch of force would have led to a quick surrender—but instead of giving in, Cornwallis had retreated a short distance, far enough to "see" imaginary British reinforcements beyond the Frenchmen's horizon, to whom he'd sent the semaphore signal "enemy in sight." Then he'd heeled his ships around and begun a no-holds-barred attack on an enemy of more than four times his strength. Confused by his aggression and concluding that the signal to reinforcements could be no ruse, it was the giant French fleet who retreated, in ignominy. Tapping his hand anxiously on his thigh, Grey began to hum the song, and sing it inwardly:

It was just at break of day,
We were cruising in the Bay,
With Billy Blue in Sovereign *in the van,*
When a French fleet bound for Brest,
From Belleisle came heading West,
'Twas so, my lads, the saucy game began.
Billy Blue, oh Billy Blue, here's to you and here's to you.
Washing decks was hardly done
When we heard the warning gun,
And we saw them black and clear against the sky,
Thirteen big ships of the line,
And with frigates, twenty-nine,
On the easterly horizon drawing nigh.
Billy Blue, oh Billy Blue, here's to you and here's to you.
We'd the Triumph *and the* Mars,
And the Sovereign, *pride of tars,*
Bellerophon *and the* Brunswick *known to fame;*
With the Pallas *and the* Phaeton,
Frigates that the flag did wait on,
Seven ships alone to uphold England's name.
Billy Blue, oh Billy Blue—

Lieutenant Franks tapped Grey on the shoulder and asked him to follow. Franks led them up the main companion to the weather deck, then aft and up onto the quarterdeck, at the rear of which was the admiral's great cabin. On the poop atop the admiral's great cabin—which was atop the flag captain's great cabin, at the rear of the weather deck—was the flag captain himself, the man in charge of the flagship while the admiral ran the fleet. He had his hands clasped behind his back and was looking down at the clipper *Cervantes* making fast to his ship. Being out of uniform, Grey dispensed with the formalities of saluting the quarterdeck. Just before Grey and Franks passed out of sight beneath him, the flag captain turned and gave Grey a curious, searching look before adding a polite nod. Grey returned the nod, and Franks knocked on the door of the admiral's cabin.

"Come," came a deep voice from inside.

Franks opened the door; Grey nodded to him as well—and to the door's marine guard—and stepped inside. Franks closed the door behind Grey, remaining on the outside.

"Captain Grey?" said Admiral William Cornwallis, rising, answering Grey's instinctual salute; so much for not being in uniform. "In fact I do remember our conversation at Haddon Hall, but let us dispense, for the moment, with reminiscences. I am told your business is urgent, so please to state it. And to have a seat."

He pointed to a chair opposite his desk, and opposite the windows of the great cabin, which showed the sun dipping below Spanish hills.

"Yes, sir; thank you. Did you have a chance to look at my letter?"

"Not yet, Captain Grey."

"Then let me add to it that I don't believe I've been aboard a flag since the year *Royal George* was laid up in ordinary."

"So you work for Sir Edward," said Cornwallis, resuming his own seat; recognizing the passphrase. "That elucidates the situation somewhat. What can I do for you?"

Knowing Cornwallis was a serious man, Grey excluded the drama he might have used to persuade a more trivial officer of the gravity of the situation:

"We have recently discovered the details of a secret treaty compacted by Godoy and Napoleon; under whose terms Spain will join the war on France's side as soon as a final shipment of gold, silver, and sundries is safe in its coffers. Specifically"—now Grey read from the notes he'd taken from Pareja y Mariscal's safe—"seventy-five sacks of wool, one thousand six hundred and sixty-six bars of tin, five hundred and seventy-one bars of copper, eight hundred sealskins, sixty barrels of seal oil, one hundred and fifty thousand gold ingots, and gold and silver coins of various denomination, equaling four million two hundred and eighty-six thousand five hundred and eight dollars."

Cornwallis cocked his head and gave out with an impressed whistle.

"Quite so," said Grey. "Without that treasure, Spain will be neutered. As she means to go to war with us, the Admiralty had decided to deprive her of it."

"Very sensible," said Cornwallis.

"The treasure will arrive at Cadiz sometime in the next few days. It is carried aboard four men-o'-war—the frigates *Medea*, *Fama*, *Mercedes*, and *Santa Clara*. Do you know them?"

"Yes," said Cornwallis. "And I think we can match their strength. Unfortunately our old *Robust* here gives her name the lie: her knees are shot and even a rolling broadside will break them, until she's firmed up with new bracing. But I'll give you Captain Moore in HMS *Indefatigable*, forty-four; he should be ready to sail at the break of dawn. I've also got Captain Hammond in *Lively*, thirty-eight, Captain Sutton in *Amphion*, thirty-two, and Captain Gore in *Medusa*, thirty-two. They can be ready to sail in no more than two days' time."

Cornwallis had dipped a pen and begun to write.

"I suggest, though, you ship with Moore at once; the others will join you posthaste; that is to say, they will join *Indefatigable* in patrolling the roads to Cadiz."

Cornwallis blotted the paper upon which he was writing, slipped it aside, and began to write on another.

"Those are orders for you," said Cornwallis, "and these are for Moore. Please to deliver them to his hand."

Cornwallis blotted the second leaf and handed both to Grey. "If there's nothing else, Captain Grey, I'll let you go."

He rose from his seat; so did Grey.

"Very briefly, sir, two other small matters. I have accounts of the circumstances leading to the discovery of this fleet, and the destruction of His Majesty's sloop *Perseus*."

Grey pulled them out of his jacket. "If you could have them conveyed to the Admiralty."

"Certainly, Captain," said Cornwallis.

"And the sloop I came in on—we cut her out a few weeks ago,

at the River Plate—incidentally, from a French slaver; I've no idea if she's a legitimate prize, but she's a fine sailor and would make a good tender. In any case—aboard the clipper I came in on is an American marine; one of several Americans who proved indispensable to reaching this point; it's all in my account there. In any case, sir, he's aboard the clipper and I've promised to return him to his fleet. I believe they'll be touching here on their way to make hay with the Berbers. I wonder if you could accommodate him till then—and see no hungry captain tries to press him."

Cornwallis nodded solemnly. "Certainly, Captain Grey. Send him aboard and I'll attend to him."

"Thank you, sir."

"Tell Franks to have my cutter lowered while you attend to any final affairs on your clipper, and we'll ferry you over to *Indefatigable*. And when this is all over, perhaps we can take a moment to celebrate with a discussion of the newest advances in riflery."

Grey smiled. "Thank you, sir."

He saluted. Cornwallis answered it, then waved for Grey to get going.

29

B ACK ABOARD THE CUTTER *CERVANTES*, Grey quickly gathered
his few surviving possessions, and O'Bannon, and thanked
the clipper's small crew, adding an expression of hope that
they'd get some money out of her, as it was possible she'd be condemned as a lawful prize. This drew a huzzah.

O'Bannon, for his part, was reluctant to miss the grand finale of
the voyage, particularly as Grey had never been able to fully explain
things to him; O'Bannon knew that Grey was intent on intercepting
a Spanish convoy, but no more than that. O'Bannon asked to join
Grey on *Indefatigable*. As much as Grey would have liked to accommodate him, this would be a bridge too far—bringing a foreign
soldier onto a warship engaged in a secret military enterprise. As
sorry as he was to put O'Bannon off, there were certain consider-
ations of loyalty. And though he was certain beyond any shadow of a
doubt that O'Bannon was a loyal friend, he was equally certain that
O'Bannon was a loyal American, and inasmuch as the interdiction of
officially still-neutral ships would be a legally uncertain area, Grey
felt it would be imprudent to involve a third sovereign party. Grey
couched the rejection in these terms:

"O'Bannon, dear heart, you can come along as an acting sergeant of His Majesty's Royal Marine Forces, in uniform. Anything else would be impossible to effect, but I leave the choice up to you."

O'Bannon sighed and extended his hand to Grey for a final shake. "I know you understand why I couldn't possibly do that."

"Of course," said Grey. "I wish it were otherwise. I hope you won't think ill of me for it."

"Perish the thought, Grey. None is here so vile that will not love his country."

The rest of the quotation went: "If any, speak, for him have I offended." Grey smiled and shook O'Bannon's hand.

"It wasn't long ago that I agreed with another friend of mine—French chap, you would have liked him—to meet at Philippi. I hope to see you again before that."

"Likewise," said O'Bannon. "Mr. Parker told me it's possible you'll favor us with a visit to Boston someday. As he described it, your 'old hometown.'"

Grey laughed. "Good luck with the Barbary pirates."

"Good luck with the English," said O'Bannon.

Grey chuckled again. Legalities aside, he felt no personal compunction about the Spaniards' ships. Declaring war and declaring one's intention to declare war were the same, as far as he was concerned. It did raise some question, somewhere in the back of his mind, regarding the line that separated seizing Spanish treasure as a soldier and seizing it as a pirate, but it was a question for another time. Perhaps he would put it, someday, to his minister. His attendance at church had been rather lax since his wife died; she had always been the motive. It would certainly do him no harm to solicit a pastoral opinion.

In any case, O'Bannon was on his way up the *Robust*'s accommodation ladder, and Grey was moving to *Cervantes*'s leeward rail to step down onto *Robust*'s blue cutter, which would ferry him to *Indefatigable*.

It was a short ride across the harbor. Grey watched *Indefatigable* as they approached her, and wondered at how utterly different she looked since he'd seen her last. She was a different ship. She'd been built, in the eighties, as a sixty-four-gun ship of the line, a third-rate. But with the French building their third-rates at seventy-four guns, and the Americans changing frigate warfare with their six heavies, a decision had been made a few years earlier—sometime in the mid-nineties—to razee *Indefatigable*; cut off her top deck and relaunch her as a forty-four-gun heavy frigate. Grey tried to picture the spot in the air where he might have stood on a weather deck that no longer existed. Somewhat bizarrely, given how dramatically her current shape differed from her original plans, she was a damned fine-looking ship: a sleek single-decked beauty that looked to the manner born. And, as a single-decker, she'd been spectacularly successful, taking near two dozen prizes and sinking a dozen others. Her razee was probably the most valuable decapitation since Robespierre's.

The blue cutter ran alongside and Grey climbed the accommodation to *Indefatigable*'s weather deck. He hoisted himself through the entry port at the break of the quarterdeck, saluting it (in for a penny, in for a pound) and requesting from the officer of the watch permission to come aboard, adding that he carried orders from the flag. A moment later he was being escorted to Captain Moore's cabin.

The officer of the watch knocked twice on Moore's door.

"Yes," came a not overloud but resounding Glaswegian voice from inside.

The midshipman leading Grey opened the door and stepped back for him to enter, closing it behind him. Standing behind a wide oak table, under a brass kandili that lit the room and swung gently back and forth with the rocking of the ship, was Captain Graham Moore, with a sour look on his face and his hands clasped behind his back.

"Captain Grey," said Moore, in his thick Scotch brogue.

"Captain Moore," answered Grey, matching Moore's sour expression with one of his own. "So we meet again."

"So we do," said Moore.

He made an exaggerated sneer, and Grey burst out laughing, followed shortly by explosive laughter from Moore, who now rounded the table, grabbing Grey's right hand for a vigorous shake and then slapping him on the shoulder for good measure.

"Tom, you old cockscomb, how in dear's name are you?"

"Oh, fair, Graham, pretty fair. And you?"

"Oh, pretty fair myself. What do you think of my new bark here?"

"A damned prettier sight than her captain."

Moore laughed.

"Take a seat, lad, and tell me what you'll have to drink? I've got ardent spirits from the homeland, and some exceptionally good rain-water Madeira that floated in a few days ago."

"Madeira would suit me splendidly, Graham, always assuming you'll join me," said Grey, dropping down into a cushioned cane chair opposite Moore's desk.

"Well, Tom, you've twisted my arm."

Grey laughed as Moore extracted a bottle from the stern lockers and poured a pair of drinks. He handed a glass to Grey and clinked it with his own. "Your health, lad."

"Yours," said Grey, and they both drank.

It was splendidly dry and crisp. Grey sucked his teeth. "Oh— very good."

"Isn't it, though?"

Moore sat down opposite him, and for a moment they sipped in silence, until Grey reached into his jacket and pulled out Cornwallis's orders.

"Billy Blue sends orders to Captain Moore," said Grey, tossing the folded page onto Moore's desk. Moore opened it and read.

"I'm to be commodore of a force of four frigates, to rendezvous beyond Cadiz."

"Give you joy of a broad pennant," said Grey, raising his glass. "Your first?"

"Aye," said Moore, smiling. "The orders say you'll instruct me as to what to do with it."

"I will," said Grey. "The immediate matter is this: You will meet and take four Spanish frigates."

"So I see," said Moore, rereading his orders—lingering on the temporary promotion therein. "I'm instructed to use all possible means to avoid a fight, while under no circumstances permitting the

Spanish ships to land at Cadiz, or anywhere else on the continent, but to direct them to Gibraltar."

"Just so, Commodore Moore."

Moore smiled at hearing the title for the first time, while continuing to study his orders.

"I see here the commodore of the Spanish fleet is Bustamante."

"Yes," said Grey. "José de Bustamante y Guerra. Are you acquainted?"

"With his work," said Moore. "Smart fellow in the scientific line, you know."

"I didn't."

"Yes—he led an expedition around the Spanish Americas, the Spanish Pacific, Canton, down to New Holland."

"The Malaspina expedition?"

"Just so," said Moore. "Bustamante and Malaspina planned it together, as an homage to Cook's voyage. Did some fine work mapping the Americas' Pacific coast."

"Sounds an interesting chap," said Grey.

"Yes. Perhaps in a few days we'll have a chance to have him to dinner."

Grey nodded. "God willing. Coachee believed you'd be able to sail with the first tide. Was he right?"

"He was," said Moore. "We're provisioned for a cruise to Port Royal, so I daresay it won't be any problem lingering at Cadiz."

"Damned fine," said Grey. "Perhaps I can finally get some sleep tonight that's worthy of the name."

"Well, you're requested and required to tell me about this Spanish frigate fleet first, but start by finishing your drink."

Grey nodded, leaned a little further back in his chair, and took another sip of Madeira.

"So," said Moore, "how long has it been?"

"Oh, years, I should think," said Grey. "I don't believe we've met this century."

"Have we not?" said Moore, shaking his head. "Well, I suppose it hasn't exactly been a time of leisure for either of us."

Moore had long been a sort of adjunct officer of naval intelligence; one of a number of relatively senior officers whom Sir Edward called on for assignments of particular delicacy. Though Moore was a few years Grey's senior, they had been introduced to the Banksian world of daggers and dark lanterns at the same time, and had consequently developed a friendship not only of comrades-in-arms, but of classmates. Last Grey had heard of him, there were murmurs of Moore being seconded to Sir Edward from the West India station on an emergency basis sometime in the year one. Grey had been in Malta at the time, and of course he would not ask Moore any details of his work that Moore didn't volunteer. Moore's mind seemed to be running along the same course—no doubt he was wondering what Grey had been up to this century, but wouldn't inquire. Instead, his only reference to Grey's work in Malta was to raise his glass and say, "Paulette."

"Paulette," said Grey, and the two men drank to Grey's dead wife. Grey drained his glass.

"So," said Moore after a moment, "the treasure fleet."

30

THERE WAS STILL A HEAVY MORNING MIST on the water when, less than half a day's sailing from Gibraltar, *Indefatigable* reached her patrolling ground a few horizons west of Cadiz. It was September 29th. Grey spent the day pacing up and down the quarterdeck, occasionally stopping to exchange a few words with Moore, who was consumed, all the day long, with readying his ship for a fight. All day long the high-pitched *ting-ting-ting* of a blacksmith's shop came from the gundeck, where the thirteen crews that worked the deck's twenty-six 24-pounders were at work with hammers, files, and chisels, working away any impurities in the five or so hundred tons of iron shot the ship carried. Having a smaller job, the crews of the quarterdeck and forecastle's combined twelve 12-pounders had, by the late afternoon, finished with polishing their balls and moved on to scouring the guns' barrels, cleaning their touch holes, checking their arresting lines, and greasing their axles, running them in and out and ensuring everything was taut and smooth. By the time the gundeck crews were doing the same, the upper-deck crews had moved on to scouring the insides of the six gigantic 42-pounder carronades, which, for all their enormous destructive power, had a woefully short accurate range. Consequently—with the strong tendency of His Majesty's gun crews to pride themselves on their aim——the carronades were treated with, if not contempt, a distinct absence of affection.

The sun set without any sign of the Spanish, or any sign of English reinforcements. Moore had had a cot for Grey slung in his own cabin: the great cabin, where there was more than enough room. The two men played chess late into the night. Grey hoped Moore's confidence in battle wouldn't be shaken by Grey's relentless victories; he explained his training at the hands of the great mathematician Atwood, about which Moore was very interested to hear. Later, when Grey made a careless, fatal move, Moore let go with a torrent of incomprehensible Scottish oaths intended to make it clear that he would not tolerate Grey losing intentionally.

The next day, fight preparation continued. Blocks and tackle, rigging, sheets, and spars and so on were all inspected, repaired, and where at all suspect, replaced. No sign of the Spaniards, or of the English; nor on the next day.

On October 2nd, HMS *Lively* appeared on the horizon, and was soon part of a two-ship patrol working north and south over the approaches to Cadiz. The day after that, *Indefatigable* and *Lively* were joined by HMS *Medusa* and HMS *Amphion*. On the evening of the third, Commodore Moore entertained Grey and the three subordinate frigates' captains at a lengthy, heavy dinner of several courses and a great deal of wine (enough that Grey hoped the Spaniards wouldn't arrive for the few hours following). On October 4th, the four-frigate fleet sailed up and down, keeping stations at the extremity of sight. With each ship having, from its mainmast lookout, a view of about seventeen miles in any direction, the four frigates were able, at rest, to keep watch over a sea lane near ninety miles wide. Their pacing patrol expanded that by more than a third again.

And as they patrolled, every man on each of the ships—as word of their mission (or approximate word, anyway) had now spread to every man jack among them—was an expectant father waiting for news of his wife's delivery, looking up at the watch at the mastheads, waiting to hear a shout of sails sighted to the southwest. No shouts were forthcoming.

On October 5th, 1804, at dawn, with the coast of Portugal in sight to the east, a sail appeared on the horizon to the west. By six bells in the morning watch, the four Spanish frigates were hull up and forming a line of battle. The four English frigates did the same, and keeping the weather gauge—that is, keeping themselves between the wind and the Spanish—the English approached. Before the start of the middle watch, the two small fleets were within pistol shot of one another, in a state of cold martial tension. Eight warships of two nations not at war.

It was a few minutes before ten in the morning when Moore lowered his spyglass and turned away from the Spanish flagship *Medea*, addressing his quarterdeck.

"Ascott," he said to his first lieutenant, a man in his early thirties, "have a boat lowered, and bring Mr. Grey over to *Medea* under a flag of truce."

"Sir," said Ascott, with a salute and a quick turn to the waist.

Moore turned now to Grey; waved him closer. In his thick Scotch voice, he said, "Mr. Grey, please carry my compliments to Spanish commodore Bustamante and inform him of my orders. We do not wish to fire on him, and we do not wish to rob him, but he must surrender command of his ships and allow us to bring them into Gibraltar."

Grey nodded. "Very good, Commodore."

Moore extended his hand; Grey shook it.

"Good luck, Tom," said Moore.

Then he turned back to the *Medea*, where he could see his opposite number staring at him, waiting for Moore and the British to make the first move.

It was at precisely eight bells in the first watch that Grey joined Ascott in the captain's cutter, and the captain's coxswain got its crew rowing for the Spanish flag. The sea was low and the crossing took only ten minutes. In Spanish, Grey shouted a request for a line to seize to and permission for himself and Ascott to come aboard. Both requests were granted, and a moment later Grey and Ascott were standing on the Spanish quarterdeck.

Bustamante approached them with his hands clasped behind his back. Ascott saluted him and was ignored.

"Gentlemen, what is the meaning of this? We are at peace, and your interdiction of my ships is an act of war."

Grey answered him. "My apologies, Brigadier Don Bustamante"— the slightest hint of surprise crossed Bustamante's face at being so addressed; having not given his name—"It is the belief of my government that your ships are engaged in an act preparatory to the declaration of war by your government. Until the matter is resolved, Commodore Moore of His Majesty's ship *Indefatigable*, in company with His Majesty's ships *Lively*, *Amphion*, and *Medusa*, has orders to bring your fleet into Gibraltar, where the matter can be dealt with at the level of our diplomats."

"If your diplomats would like to discuss the business of my ships, I would be most happy to entertain you this afternoon at Cadiz."

"I'm afraid, sir, that that won't be possible. While emphasizing his desire to avoid bloodshed on either side, Commodore Moore must formally ask for your surrender. You will be treated with all dignity suitable both to your rank and to a guest of His Majesty's Royal Navy; you will not be asked to relinquish your sword. But you and your officers must quit your ships until we've brought them into Gibraltar."

"I assure you, Mr. . . . ."

"Grey. Thomas Grey."

"I assure you, Mr. Grey: That will not happen. May I take it from your lack of uniform that you speak not for your navy but for your government?"

"I speak for the commodore, Don Bustamante."

"Well, it is of no consequence. Return to *Indefatigable* with this message: These are ships of the Spanish Armada, answering only to His Majesty Charles the Fourth, *Rex Hispaniarum et Indiarum*. The British navy has no authority to detain or delay me. Any other action will be considered by my command an act of piracy, and will be dealt with as such. When your boat has safely cleared our ship, we will continue to Cadiz. Tell your commodore."

"I will, Don Bustamante," said Grey. "If I may add a final word: It is the view of our fleet that a de facto state of war exists between our two countries. No compunction will be felt on the part of our fleet in using force to stop you."

Bustamante had turned away, to face *Indefatigable*, and said nothing more. Grey and Ascott climbed back down to their boat, and at the first bell of the middle watch, were back on *Indefatigable*'s quarterdeck.

"What word from Bustamante?" It was a pro forma question from Moore; already the topmen were taking reefs out of *Medea*'s sails and her gun crews stayed ready at the cannon.

"He says he's going to Cadiz, and we've no right to stop him."

Indefatigable's topmen were prepared to loose sheets as well; so were those of the other six frigates. And every gun crew remained at its gun.

"Pass word to the forecastle," said Moore to Lieutenant Ascott, "to fire a warning shot across *Medea*'s bow. And signal down the line to expect that fire will be returned."

A moment later, just as the *Medea* began to make headway, the warning shot was fired. While the shot's booming echo was still bouncing back and forth between the two battle lines, *Medea* answered with a broadside, aimed at *Indefatigable*'s mainmast. *Indefatigable*'s rigging was torn up, and the mast splintered in places, but it was not seriously damaged—and now, all eight frigates began to lay into each other, in belligerent pairs—firing broadside after broadside; the Spanish, to leeward, aiming mostly at masts and rigging, hoping to damage the English ships enough to slip away—being to leeward, they had open room to run with the wind at their backs. The English, meanwhile, poured broadside after broadside into the Spanish gundecks, dismounting dozens of cannon and killing scores of men. Moments after the barrage began, the space between the battle lines was so utterly filled with powder smoke that the ships could no longer be seen from one another's decks, and the only reference points by which to aim were the orange stabs of flame the cannon made as they fired.

And then suddenly the smoke changed from a dull gray to a bright orange-red, as if the ships were inside a cloud at sunset. *Indefatigable* began to shake violently; Grey was thrown off his feet and slid backward across the width of the quarterdeck, as the ship heeled sharply away from the Spanish line; he came to a stop with his back against the windward rail. A cannon—a gigantic, 24-pounder cannon, surely weighing at least what a bull elephant does—flew over Grey's head. For an instant he believed he was dreaming. This notion was reinforced by a light rain of gold and silver coins, landing on the quarterdeck like hailstones.

And for an instant the firing stopped, and wind began to clear some of the smoke. The voice of a marine in *Indefatigable*'s mizzen top broke into the sudden quiet:

"On deck there! The *Mercedes* has gone up!"

Grey—and everyone else on the *Indefatigable*—and everyone on the other six frigates—jumped to his feet and locked his eyes on the place where, a hundred seconds earlier, there had been a thirty-six-gun ship. Now there was nothing there but bits of timber and cloth, and some spars fastened together by scraps of tarred rigging, some of it on fire. A moment later, most of the wreckage was pulled under by the corpse of the ship, to which it was still attached. Again Grey pictured a scene of sparkling coins, lit by the high, late morning sun, drifting down into the darkness, to be lost forever in the depths of the bottomless Bay of Portugal. He saw chests break open and pour out bricks of silver and gold as the wrecked ship that had carried them sank past in the background. Shaken as he was, Grey was pulled out of this daytime dream by the resumption of firing— now, it seemed, only from the British ships; the surviving Spaniards had been much closer to *Mercedes* and were much the worse for it. It took just one more rolling, scattered fusillade from the British battle line for a cheer to break out—from *Indefatigable* at the van to *Medusa* at the rear. The Spanish colors were coming down. *Medea*'s lowered first. *Fama*'s and *Santa Clara*'s followed a moment later.

Over the sound of his ringing ears, Grey heard Moore—doubtless through ringing ears of his own—shouting orders to his quarterdeck to fly the signal to put down boats to search for survivors from *Mer-*

cedes; then to prepare prize crews to take possession of the three surrendered frigates.

FORTY SPANIARDS WERE PULLED from among the floating splinters of *Mercedes*; they were taken aboard *Amphion*. *Lively*, *Medusa*, and *Indefatigable*, meanwhile, were beginning to fill the boats emptied of survivors with English sailors: prize crews to take the captured ships into Gibraltar. *Fama*, seeing the English ships at ease, dropped her sails and put before the wind, hoisting her colors again as she did. A terrible sight. *Medusa* instantly took off in pursuit of her, but was quickly overtaken by *Lively*, easily the fastest ship in the small fleet. And compared to *Medusa*, *Lively* was relatively unharmed by the explosion of *Mercedes*. Her only serious injury being two men of a forecastle gun crew sliced in half by a wooden angel that had been *Mercedes*'s figurehead.

From the quarterdeck of *Indefatigable*, Grey and Moore stood side by side, handing Moore's glass back and forth, watching *Lively* run *Fama* down. *Fama* had started her water and a moment later began tipping her cannon into the sea. It was no use. Perhaps if she had thrown overboard the treasure she carried, she might have escaped. It didn't matter. *Lively* was in range of her bow chasers now, and a single shot punching through *Fama*'s fore- and mainsails brought her colors down again, this time for good.

"Excuse me, sir," said a midshipman who had come up behind Moore and Grey. "You had asked for the butcher's bills."

Moore turned towards him. "Yes?"

"No word yet from *Lively*'s surgeon, sir, but *Amphion*, *Medusa*, and ourself combine for seven dead and eighteen wounded. Also quite a few cases of deafness, but Mr. Pennworthy thinks they're most likely temporary."

"Very good, Mr. Ellermann. Carry on."

"Sir," said Ellermann, saluting and departing the quarterdeck.

"Well," said Moore, turning back to Grey as he slipped his spyglass into a pocket. "Ghastly shame about the *Mercedes*, but I'd say that, one thing taken with another, this went rather well."

31

OORE TOOK THE CAPTURED FRIGATES into Gibraltar, where they were repaired and recrewed. To begin a joyous, verging on excessive, landborne fête, Admiral Cornwallis announced that Moore would continue as commodore, detailed to sail the captured ships to Portsmouth, and personally to deliver Cornwallis's dispatches relating the event. While Grey stood to the side, Moore and Cornwallis had their health drunk three times three, each; then three more for Captains Hammond, Sutton, and Gore, and then three after that for all the brave men and officers concerned. Grey was lighting a pipe as the ball began—couples dancing together; pairs rather than squares or lines, as if it were Spain and not Gibraltar. Cornwallis himself—Billy Bachelor—began the affair by leading a dark-eyed Mediterranean beauty onto the floor; Grey wondered if she was Spanish; if she knew just what the ball was celebrating; if in a week's time, she would be able to cross the Spanish-Gibraltar border freely as she had likely done earlier in the day. Moore had brought the Spanish frigates in by the dark of the moon and tucked them deep in Gibraltar's harbor, where they wouldn't be seen by prying eyes looking from the other side of Algeciras Bay. Aside from the officers, who were being billeted under guard at a private mansion in town, the several hundred crewmen of the captured frigates were still aboard their ships, shortly to be taken to England and readied for the first prisoner exchange of a new Anglo-Spanish war. The English crews were all aboard their own ships, and their officers understood the need for discretion. For the moment, the word at the party was that Moore had won a tremendous action against four *French* frigates, and only a few dozen attendees knew—or had any reason to think—otherwise. Still, it was certain that before long word of the treasure fleet's failure to arrive at Cadiz would reach Madrid, and then the jig (or a waltz of some kind) would be up.

Familiar faces filled the room, and though Grey was as pleased as any of them, he didn't feel particularly inclined towards conversation. He was tired. Bone tired. Perhaps Sir Edward had been right; perhaps he did need a rest. Where would he be now if Fairbanks had had this assignment as planned? Probably going mad at his home in Kent. Perhaps walking with Mrs. Boothe. There was an interesting thought. He took a sip of a sweet Spanish wine that he didn't particularly like. He wondered how Fairbanks was doing; if the wounds incurred dueling over an insult to Grey had healed properly. If Fairbanks had lost any of the use of his hand, Grey would be damned sorry—and in all likelihood, damned guilty. Of course it was Grey who should have fought the duel. Fairbanks the sportsman had just been faster to issue a blow. And after that, it was in God's hands.

A hand clapped onto Grey's shoulder. He turned, expecting Moore—instead, it was O'Bannon, extending his hand.

"I give you joy of . . . something, Captain Grey," said O'Bannon. "The details elude me."

Grey happily returned the handshake. "O'Bannon—it's good to see you, brother. A drink with you?"

"It would be my pleasure, sir."

"Your glass is empty and mine's filled with something wicked. Let's see what else Billy Blue—Admiral Cornwallis, I mean—has on offer."

As the dancing got going in earnest, a table laid with refreshments grew rapidly less crowded; still, it was no simple task forging through the wallflowers—mostly junior officers—to the barman.

Failing to get the barman's attention, Grey rounded the table's edge and began examining the bottles beneath it, browsing cases of wine and champagne, looking for something dry enough to be drinkable.

There was a case of Château d'Aumont. Grey stared at it for a moment before pulling off the unnailed lid and extracting a bottle. A bottle of blanc de blancs. Grey circled back to the public side of the table and reached between a pair of midshipmen to retrieve a pair of glasses. As he did, a hand again touched him on the shoulder. He turned, expecting this time to see O'Bannon; seeing instead a young, beautiful Catalan lady of his acquaintance. One Mademoiselle Montcada.

O'Bannon was there too, over her shoulder. He winked at Grey, smiled, and then backed away, disappearing into the crowd.

"Mademoiselle Montcada. Or, as we're no longer in France, I should say, Senyoreta Montcada."

Grey had met her a year earlier, at a party in Paris; she had been on the arm of a Captain Aubert of the French navy. Grey had been posing as a disaffected Englishman looking to sell out his country for cash; Aubert had been one of the few Frenchmen who had doubted his sincerity. As Aubert poked at Grey's story, Grey had played for time by asking Mademoiselle Montcada for the honor of a dance—to give himself time to think, and also to irritate Aubert. They'd had part of a waltz and part of a quadrille before Aubert had cut in.

"Captain Grey—how surprised I am to see you here."

She had a lace fan, more for decoration than anything else, with which she blew away a bit of tobacco smoke from Grey's pipe that had clouded around her.

"Your pardon, senyoreta—I will put it out." He reached up to remove the pipe from his mouth—awkwardly, encumbered as he was by the bottle and two glasses.

"No, no, Captain Grey, not on my account, please."

"Well, perhaps the smoke would be less offensive if we withdrew to the garden."

"Am I not interposing between yourself and an engagement?" she said, using the fan to gesture to the bottle and two glasses.

"Oh no," said Grey, "I always carry a spare glass, when I attend festivities in the vicinity of Spain. That way, if there's a toast and I'm obliged to throw my glass into a fire, I can resume drinking with the shortest possible delay."

Senyoreta Montcada smiled. "Very well then."

The garden was warm and balmy; the Mediterranean breezes were staunched by the Rock, which loomed in the distance, somewhere beyond the garden's back wall. Senyoreta Montcada gazed up at it— an impressive sight—as Grey set the glasses down on a stone bench.

"Can I offer you a drink, senyoreta?"

"Yes," she said, turning towards him. "Shall we sit?"

"Certainly, senyoreta," said Grey, popping the cork from the champagne bottle.

Senyoreta Montcada sat as Grey poured two glasses, and then, handing the lady one, sat beside her—at a decorous remove.

"Captain Grey, you may call me Esperanza; I appreciate your manners, but under the circumstances, I think my Christian name is more appropriate."

"Very well, Esperanza. Do please call me Thomas."

"Thomas," she said, and took a sip of champagne. "Thomas, what are you doing here?"

"I could easily ask you the same question," said Grey.

"My aunt is a governess for some of the many foreign children on Gibraltar. I visit frequently because my brother is an instructor at the Guardiamarinas."

"Is he really? You know, there are naval academies in Britain now too, and though I have the highest respect for formal educa-tion, I have always wondered at the idea of learning seamanship by land. As a profession, it seems to make the quintessential demand of apprenticeship."

"My brother teaches cones and spheres," said Esperanza.

"You don't look old enough to have a brother who teaches cones and spheres."

"He's the oldest of six brothers. My mother was determined to have a daughter."

"Ah," said Grey, smiling. "Well, that's most interesting. I have something of a dilettante interest in geometry, having been many years at sea. Perhaps you will introduce me. Does he play chess?"

"You are avoiding my question, Thomas."

They were speaking Catalan, but Esperanza pronounced "Thomas" in a curiously unaccented way, rather than calling him "Tomás." It gave her question an accusatory dissonance.

"I'm here as a guest of the admiral."

"I wouldn't have thought the admiral entertained defectors to France."

"I'm sure he doesn't, as a rule. So I hope you will keep it to yourself."

"Oh," said Esperanza, "don't you think it would behoove you to have him know of your assassination of a senior French naval officer?"

Grey half smiled. "Where did you hear that?"

"From the lips of Julia d'Aumont."

Grey looked down at the champagne glass in his hands, then back up at Esperanza. No guilt read on his face—only a little sadness.

"How is she?"

"Better than you might expect," said Esperanza. "When I last saw her at her house in the country—some years ago now—she seemed oppressed by life. Since the death of her brother, she seems revitalized. By her intense hatred of you."

Grey nodded. "Well, I can't say I blame her."

"You needn't be contrite for my benefit, Thomas. I am now on no better terms with the circle of the French admiralty than you are."

"Oh?" said Grey.

"I believe the expression in English would be 'breach of promise.' "

"Ah," said Grey, nodding. "Would you like me to instruct you in assassination?"

Esperanza laughed, then sighed. "No, thank you, Thomas, it is all well. I no longer frequent Paris, and to preempt any damage to my reputation here, I have put about that I am a widow of a French cad who got what he deserved in the Haitian revolution."

Grey smiled. "Very sensible."

Grey took a sip of champagne. "If anyone you meet ever attempts to dispute that, please to refer the offending party to me. I will set him to rights."

Esperanza Montcada looked at Grey with an expression of earnest and slightly surprised gratitude. "I appreciate that, Thomas."

By this time Grey's pipe had gone out. He knocked it clean on the edge of the stone bench upon which he and Esperanza sat, slipped it into his pocket, and stood, extending a hand to Esperanza as he did.

"Might you favor me with a dance, senyoreta?"

As they waltzed to something new from Vienna, it occurred to Grey that he had left something quite important unsaid. Carried away by conversation, he had forgotten that he, but almost no one else, knew that Spain and Britain would soon be at war. At an interlude between songs, before releasing Esperanza to one of the many officers vying for her next dance—and careful to stay beyond their earshot—he asked her if he was correct in his recollection that she was Catalan. She found this peculiar, as they had been speaking Catalan to each other since meeting by the refreshments table. But all the same, she answered:

"Yes, Captain Grey—why do you ask?"

"If it is not too presumptuous of me to ask, might you satisfy my curiosity on one point? Do you consider yourself a daughter of Catalonia, or of Spain?"

It was not possible that she would fully grasp the meaning of the question—not until news of the taking of the treasure fleet became widely known; however, with the perpetual rumbling of independence from Catalonia, she would certainly grasp it in part.

In a discreet, conversational tone, she said, "I've never cared for Madrid, Captain Grey. Too far inland. Give me a capital by the sea."

Grey nodded, and escorted her to her next partner.

32

GREY DIDN'T FIND O'BANNON AGAIN, and just two nights later, after moonset and with only the sidelights of a harbor cutter to guide them, Grey was carried out of Gibraltar by Moore's convoy, again four frigates, now composed of *Indefatigable* and three new additions to His Majesty's navy: HMS *Iphigenia*, née *Medea*; HMS *Leocadia*, née *Santa Clara*, and—perhaps to emphasize that, though she had had to be captured twice, she had indeed been captured—or perhaps because Moore and Cornwallis had jointly been too overwrought, after the festivities, to come up with a third name—HMS *Fama*, née *Fama*.

Before dawn they had sunk the land behind them and begun a slow turn north designed to keep Cape St. Vincent beyond the horizon. Moore spent most of his time moving up and down the line of four ships, investigating their sailing qualities—how close they could lie to the wind, how much leeway they gave up, that sort of thing. Grey, meanwhile, spent most of his time recumbent on a cot in Moore's cabin, gently rocking back and forth, reading and, in almost equal measures, dozing. The only books available were from Moore's private collection, which—bizarrely—seemed to be, almost exclusively, instructional materials on the running of a modern farm. Grey asked Moore about this, only to learn that, despite having spent his entire life at sea, and despite fully intending to spend the rest of his life at sea, he harbored certain bucolic inclinations, and that he had resolved if he ever made a rich strike in prize money, he would purchase a farm somewhere between London and Portsmouth. Grey asked how much he intended to be there—

"As little as possible," said Moore, with a chuckle, "but one has to prepare himself for the grim possibility of peace breaking out. Which I daresay has become at least marginally more likely in the last few days. And as for prize money . . . I expect we shall all do very well. Well enough that any man aboard our little expedition of October the fifth won't ever go to sea again unless he wants to. How nice for a sailor to go to sea just for the sport of it, ey?"

Grey nodded.

"Have you seen our takings, incidentally?"

"Besides the bit that showered down on us, I have not. It's been under close guard since we returned to Gibraltar, and frankly, I couldn't muster the strength to go about the harbor hoping to find you or Coachee to let me in."

"Ah, lad, you've been denied a pleasure you're most eminently entitled to. Let's have a look now, shall we? Ali Baba's cave simply ain't in it."

It took only a few minutes aboard Moore's cutter to wear slowly through the wind and allow *Fama* to come up from the rear; a few minutes after that, Grey was following Moore down into her hold, past a four-man, well-armed marine guard. With the transatlantic stores *Fama* had carried from Montevideo almost entirely eaten up, the hold had enough space for the two men to walk about in it, atop large wooden chests and elaborately tied-down stacks of barrels. Moore got his bearings, chose a chest, and—with a hammer obtained from a carpenter's mate—pried open its lid. Moore stood back, taking a lantern from Grey and holding it up to light the chest's contents.

Inside the chest, stacked like so many building bricks, were bars of solid gold. They sparkled as Moore's lantern rocked slowly back and forth. Grey had never seen anything like it. The color was so pure and intense—really nothing at all like brass, he now realized. It was sui generis. He ran a finger over one of the bars, stopping to feel the arms of the Spanish House of Bourbon that were stamped into its top. He felt avarice run up his arm and into his shoulder and chest like a chill from a block of ice. He pulled his hand back and laughed.

"Gold does something to a man, doesn't it?" he said to Moore.

"Yes . . . it seems to carry a certain—how would you say it?—a certain iniquity to it. Camel's eye, thirty of silver, and all that."

"Yes," said Grey, standing, taking care not to knock his head against the crossbeams.

"And have a look at this one," said Moore, stooping to nail the first chest's lid back into place, then prying open a second.

This one was filled with an immense mess of Spanish gold dollars. Moore had been right: Ali Baba had nothing on this. Grey picked up a handful of the coins and let them trickle back into their case.

"The Spanish are going to be mad as hell," said Grey, with a chuckle and a shake of his head.

"I'd expect so," said Moore. "Damned funny thing to behold. I wonder what Adam Smith would make of all of it."

33

THE ENTRY OF THE FOUR FRIGATES into Portsmouth harbor was a quiet affair. News of the events of October 5th remained closely held, and in any case, it had run only a few days ahead of the frigates themselves. Portsmouth was crowded, as always, with bumboats of vendors and prostitutes selling to sailors, most of whom were confined in their ships to prevent their escape from involuntary sea duty. Once Moore had seen all four ships safely anchored, and the marine complements of the three carrying treasure doubled, he and Grey took his jolly boat to shore, where they found a chaise-and-six waiting to bring them to London—direct to the navy office at Somerset House for Moore; direct to the Old Admiralty Building for Grey. On the way, Moore pointed out the farm he hoped to buy—a great, empty, green and rolling place in Cobham, Surrey, that they could see a few hundred yards off the highway. At Admiralty House, Grey and Moore shared a handshake after Grey had climbed out, Moore promising to let Grey know if he were detained in London longer than it took to report the events— saying he was eager, of course, to return to sea, but was always happy for a hand of something at White's or Buttle's. As the coach rolled off, Grey wondered if it would be another five-odd years before they met again.

Inside the Old Admiralty Building, Grey was surrounded by an extraordinary flurry of activity as clerks ran back and forth with letters, letters to be writ fair, replies to those letters, reports, requests for appointments. Everyone in Whitehall seemed to be trying to get details of the Spanish situation—and, naturally, were looking for them in the lee of Sir Edward Banks. In Sir Edward's outer office, the broadsides of correspondence were enough for Grey's arrival to go unnoticed until—pushing through a knot of pimply-faced messenger boys and equally pimpled midshipmen—he rapped on the office door of the chief of staff. For a moment Sir Edward's coterie of secretaries looked up, to see if someone had committed the unpardonable sin of rapping on the ebony door of Sir Edward's private office; his sanctum sanctorum, but seeing it was Grey, and that he was presuming only to attempt a meeting with Mr. Willys, they returned to their work.

"Open it!" shouted Willys from the other side of his door.

Grey let himself in and found Willys dictating semi-duplicative letters to four different young gentlemen, who would be carrying them back to various admirals and Admiralty men seeking details of the action of October 5th.

"Ah, Thomas, stout fellow, come in, come in—I'll be with you in a trice."

Willys finished his dictation, "Your faithful servant, et cetera, Willys for Banks. Close letter. Now, nippers, out"—he waved away the young midshipmen, all of them between twelve and fifteen; barking "Cut along now" at one who dawdled—and then looked at Grey with a big, toothy smile.

"Tom, you old horse thief, hanged if I ever doubted you, but allow me to say: Damned fine work, brother, damned fine."

Willys dug through some of the papers that buried his desk and produced a small, bare wooden box.

"I was given these recently," he said, opening the box and extracting two cigars. "Been saving them for a suitable moment. They're Spanish, ha ha. Sit down, sit down."

Grey accepted a cigar, and a light, and a chair, and took a few deep puffs.

"My word, Aaron, but these are fine."

"Aren't they? Yes, they're from the Spaniards' half of Hispaniola. They were a gift from a matador friend of mine who has been on a tour of the home counties. Have you met him? Romero. Pedro Romero. Very interesting chap, and very friendly. Though I imagine he won't be so well disposed towards Englishmen a week from now. In any case—Sir Edward is under siege at the moment, answering *most terribly urgent* inquiries from most of the board and half of the cabinet—but then he'll want a full accounting, from the time you left his office till the time you returned to it, and though I daresay I'm myself anxious to hear the details firsthand, I won't make you tell it twice. So, in keeping ourselves, momentarily, to more trivial topics—I have here a précis of your dispatch detailing the total contents of the captured ships. For the purposes of prize money, you will be ranked as a nominal captain, which means your total share should be . . ."

Willys scratched some arithmetic in the margin of a discarded letter, wrote a final number, underlined it, and slipped the page to Grey. Grey looked at it, and his eyes opened wide.

"That's just an estimate, of course, but I feel fairly certain it's within a few percent of the final value. I'm sorry to say that being so long in my role here, I'm very practiced at this sort of pettifogging calculation."

" 'Pettifogging,' " said Grey.

"Well, normally, it's pettifogging. I suppose in this case grossofogging would be more appropriate."

"This can't possibly be right," said Grey.

"Well, I suppose it would be prudent not to count your eggs before they're in the pudding, but as I say, I know whereof I speak."

"Forty-five thousand pounds. That's appalling."

"Well, look at it this way—it's your regular Admiralty salary, for the next four hundred years."

Grey stared at the number a moment longer before dropping Willys's letter back onto his desk and shaking his head in stoic disbelief.

"Well, only two hundred years' salary."

"Oh? After this I wouldn't expect a pay increase anytime soon, Tom."

Grey chuckled. "No, I mean, I ought to give half of this—at least—to Fairbanks. If not for an unlucky stroke, it would have been his."

Willys frowned for a moment, took a slow pull on his cigar, glanced down at his desk and then back up at Grey.

"Fairbanks is dead, Tom. The cut across his face went sour. He's been dead more than two months now."

FOR THE NEXT SIX or so hours, Grey went through his story, start to finish, several times. Sir Edward was uncharacteristically demonstrative in congratulating Grey on this or that coup, but it made barely an impression. Grey was talking by instinct. The best part of his mind was lost in a fog of self-recrimination and impotent rage. When he was dismissed for the evening, he walked, glassy-eyed, through the Old Admiralty Building's courtyard. At the gate, he turned left, to walk to Buttle's. At the end of Whitehall, he turned left again, to walk to Spears.

It took him just over an hour to walk to Fairbanks's club. With every step, Grey saw the gratuitous cut—the backhand slice—that Gresham—Baronet Gresham—had made across Fairbanks's face, after Fairbanks had already been disarmed. Grey heard himself intruding into Gresham's odious remarks about his late friend Louis Antoine, Duc d'Enghien. He saw Fairbanks issuing a challenge that Grey should have been quick enough to issue himself. He thanked God Fairbanks had not been married. He would ask Willys if his parents were still alive, and make a penitent visit to them if they were.

In the foyer of Spears, the butler asked Grey if he was meeting someone; Grey shook his head and walked past, into the hall and towards the dining room. The place was noisy; it was late in the evening, and most of the residing members appeared to be on the premises, many of them at dinner. The butler Grey had flouted quickly caught up with him and put a hand on Grey's arm. Grey spun around and withered the man with a look. The butler retreated, doubtless to fetch one of the large footmen all such establishments have to deal with troublemakers. It didn't matter. Grey was now at the threshold of the dining room, and looking from face to face, searching for Gresham, whom he now saw at a round table near the room's center, talking loudly and eating with some four or five companions.

Weaving his way through a dozen or so tables, Grey approached. Gresham saw him coming, wiped his mouth with a napkin, and smiled modestly.

Grey walked round Gresham's table, stopped a few feet short of the man, and said:

"Stand up."

Gresham snorted a laugh and looked to his dinner party with feigned amused confusion. Some of the other diners laughed in response to his look.

"And why?" said Gresham, finally, looking up at Grey.

"I intend to give offense, swine, and you should be on your feet to receive it."

At the word "swine," Gresham stood.

"You will retract that word, sir, and make your apologies, or by God you'll be sorry."

Grey delivered a straight-armed, closed-fisted blow to Gresham's face, with the whole force of his torqued body behind it. Gresham tumbled backward, falling into a neighboring dinner table before sliding to the floor, dazed. The room fell utterly silent. Two large footmen were walking fast in Grey's direction. But Grey had time to pick a napkin off Gresham's table and toss it into the baronet's lap.

"There's your gauntlet. I await your response, Gresham."

Grey turned and began to exit the way he came. One of the footmen tried to grab him by the elbow; Grey grabbed the man's shirtfront and threw him to the floor. No one else interfered as he walked back out to the street, and then towards Buttle's.

34

GREY RECEIVED A CHALLENGE from Gresham the next day and asked Willys to second him. Willys agreed, solemnly and without hesitation, but upon a meeting with Gresham's second, Talbot, returned to tell Grey that Talbot had insisted on Willys's withdrawal. Talbot had cited the provision in the dueling code that seconds may, quote, "chance to become principals in the quarrel," and equality between them is therefore indispensable. Talbot said that he would not profess equality with any man who, like Willys, had refused a commission as unwilling, for reasons of religion, to take the oath of allegiance prescribed for officers of His Majesty's Royal Marines. Willys might have been willing to leave it at that, had Talbot not gone on to make a rather ugly remark about Willys's religion, whereupon Willys blew Talbot down with a right hand to the mouth. Grey agreed he would have to choose a different second, but hoped for the opportunity to second Willys, when the time came. Willys thanked him, but for his own part suspected Talbot would lack the intestinal fortitude to seek satisfaction. Even for a blow.

In the event, Grey's second was his friend and man of business Pater. The weapons were *épées de combat*; and the ground, the fencing hall of Spears where Gresham had fought Fairbanks. The two pairs of men arrived only minutes apart, early on a Saturday morning. Pater had not known Fairbanks but was a close friend of Willys's, and refused to shake Talbot's hand, saying he would give Talbot satisfaction of it if he liked. This lending an additional hotness to the proceedings, Grey and Gresham removed their jackets and met sword tip to sword tip in the center of the room. After asking each man if he was ready, Pater issued the command, *en garde*.

Either sensing or knowing that Grey was a swordsman of much more experience than Fairbanks—that Grey's aptitude for this sort of thing was more or less equivalent to his own—Gresham didn't, as he had with Fairbanks, wait for his opposite to make the first move. With his left hand on his hip, he took a lunging step towards Grey. Grey matched the lunge forward, and their sabers crossed blades, slid their lengths, and met at the hilt; Grey pushed hard and knocked Gresham back, followed him with a lunge towards his chest, which Gresham parried away. Taking another step backward to reposition his feet, Gresham resumed his hand-on-the-hip stance and began to fence Grey, making jabs and short slices at the chest, at the hips, at the arm, while Grey parried and did the same—each man was looking for the moment when the other would be too slow, and blood would be drawn.

It was Grey who first missed stays and was cut—a horizontal slice across his torso just below the rib cage. Gresham raised his sword and said, with biting contempt, that Grey might now beg pardon and the matter would be resolved. Grey shook his head, took a step back, removed a kerchief from his hip pocket and wiped away some of the blood.

"Fairbanks's soul is but a little way above our heads, Gresham—staying for yours to keep him company. Either you, or I, or both, will go with him."

Gresham then looked at Grey as if he were a bedlam lunatic, turned to the seconds, then back to Grey, and said:

"Is that Shakespeare?"

"Yes," said Grey, taking his stance. *"En garde."*

Gresham took a ready stance as well, and tapping Grey's blade with his own, resumed the duel. The fencing was short and tight, and entirely in the wrist and elbow; neither man moving his feet or his body for an eternity—near twenty seconds—before Gresham took a sharp step forward and thrust at Grey's shoulder. Grey dropped his shoulder slightly, leaning forward, letting the thrust go over it, and made a deep cut in Gresham's chest.

Gresham staggered back, and now it was Grey who lifted his sword.

"Now if you would like to beg pardon for the needless cut across Fairbanks's face, an act of no gentleman, which killed him, we may consider the matter closed."

"Come again, you shy bastard," said Gresham, with venom in his voice.

Pater, who was not disposed to treat serious moments seriously, now shouted, "Part them, Osric, they are incensed!"

Grey laughed and Gresham lunged at him again. Grey gave some ground, fencing Gresham in wider strokes, circling to Gresham's left, and then landing a long cut up the inside of Gresham's right forearm. Gresham involuntarily pulled the right arm away, twisting in pain, leaving himself open, and Grey made a second, deep cut across his chest.

Gresham stumbled back. Grey aimed a slice at Gresham's throat, meaning to kill him. At the last moment, already mid-swing— with the sword tip inches from Gresham's pulsing neck vein—Grey directed the tip of his blade a few inches higher and cut shallowly upward, slicing through Gresham's cheek. It was not mercy; rather, Grey saw at that last moment that the baronet was disabled and could no longer defend himself, which meant that Grey no longer had the moral right to kill him. The cut on the cheek was not meant to be a symbol of Fairbanks's death; in any case, it was much shorter and shallower and at a different angle. But Grey thought that Fairbanks would have found it amusing, game fellow that he was.

Grey took a step back as Gresham dropped his sword and fell to the floor. Grey took two unhurried steps towards the sword and kicked it away. It skittered across the flagstone.

"Now the matter is settled," said Grey.

He turned towards the door, and the seconds.

"Shall we?" he said to Pater.

Talbot was already walking quickly towards his wounded principal. Pater and Grey made their exit.

35

U NDER NORMAL CIRCUMSTANCES, Grey would have retold the story he'd told to Sir Edward and Willys—his accounting of the Spanish Treasure Affair—to innumerable admirals, officials, and ministers. Under the circumstances that prevailed, this duty was assumed by Willys. In the choppy wake of his duel with Gresham, Grey had been advised by Sir Edward to leave the metropolis for a few months. Gresham was a reasonably senior officer as well as a minor noble—it was conceivable there would be a scandal—it didn't take much—and it wouldn't do to have Grey exposed to any press.

Doing as he was told, Grey went to his home in Sheerness— Marsh Downs—on the coast of Kent where the Thames meets the North Sea. The first thing Grey did, after being welcomed home by his demonstrative Irish setter Fred, and his demonstrative housekeeper Mrs. Hubble, and his northern groundskeeper Canfield, and sleeping for nearly two days, was to write to Pater and ask him to locate any family that Fairbanks had. Fairbanks's only blood relation, Pater wrote back to say, was a younger half brother at Rugby School. Grey replied with a request that Pater set up a fund in the boy's name, and that he inform Rugby's headmaster of its existence, should the younger Fairbanks come into any financial need.

It was a month later when, after considerable legal dispute (to which Grey was neither party nor privy), it was determined that *Fama*, *Medea*, and *Santa Clara* were, in fact, *not* legal prizes. They were not droits of the Admiralty, but rather droits of the Crown, as they had been captured before Spain and Britain had been officially at war. This was widely viewed as unjust—not just by the men concerned, but by the Admiralty at large, and by the popular press, which liked the idea of spontaneous private fortunes. In the end—in middle November—a decision was made to issue grace and favor payments to some of the men involved. Grey, along with the captains of *Lively*, *Amphion*, and *Medusa*, would each receive fifteen thousand pounds. Grey was content with this outcome. He had no qualms about getting rich—in fact, prize money and Pater's canny investing had already made him somewhat wealthy—but forty-five thousand pounds in a stroke would have thrust him unwillingly into a higher strata of society, for which, at this moment, he had no energy.

In the meantime, with nothing in particular to do, he wrote to Lord Elgin with various questions about the Parthenon, Athena Nike, the Propylaea and Erechtheum. He did some shooting, with Canfield and Fred. He repaired the mechanism of his large hall clock and wondered if he would be able, with the right instruments, to do the same with a pocket watch. He sent away to Breguet for a new watch, his most recent one having been lost either in the waters off Cape St. Roque or to the pocket of a pirate. He swam in the increasingly cold water of the Thames Estuary, and took increasingly long rides through Kent. These rides ended up, as often as not, at The Try Pot, the seaman's inn and public house owned by Mrs. Hubble's father, and managed, in large part, by her sister, Angela Boothe. Grey would water his horse (the young, energetic creature named Casca) and then water himself, with porter or cider or sometimes the Try Pot's four-water grog. Though ostensibly in the professions—Grey's pretended employment was with the Foreign Office—his frequent arrivals caked in riding mud, and his willingness to swap sea stories, had won him acceptance by the Pot's regulars. On occasion he would even yield to a request to sit at Mr. Hubble's piano and pick out some of the old chanteys. And on occasion, he would accompany Mrs. Boothe to pick her daughters up from the minister's house, where the minister's wife taught history, orthography, and French.

During these walks, the conversation ranged quite widely. Grey was interested to hear about Mrs. Boothe's childhood, which had been an unusual combination of the gentle society of a London grammar school or wealthy merchants in the whale or candle trades, and of the rougher but no less pleasant society of her father's old shipmates and the men from both sides of the mast who gave custom to her father's inn. They spoke of London, to which Mrs. Boothe periodically traveled to see acquaintances from her school days; friends who sometimes returned her to gentle society, took her to pay calls or to concerts or the theater, or even to balls. Grey speculated (to himself) that some of her friends were trying to find her a husband, though Mrs. Boothe came nowhere near implying this. Grey simply drew this conclusion from the number of somewhat older, well-off gentlemen to whom Mrs. Boothe seemed to have been introduced— some with very interesting anecdotes of business or past naval service; all of them (Grey speculated, again, to himself) widowers in need of a young and pretty second wife. For reasons he refused to delve into too deeply, he found this very irritating.

"Mr. Grey, are you acquainted with Mr. John Soane?" Mrs. Boothe was saying.

Grey refocused himself on the conversation.

"The architect of the Bank of London? I have not had that pleasure."

"I met him only very briefly, at his house, accompanying a school friend and her father. Her father had some business with Mr. Soane. After he introduced himself, he suggested that, while he and my friend's father spoke, his secretary might give us a tour of the house. I believe you would have found it very much after your own tastes, Mr. Grey. It is simply the most remarkable house."

"In what way remarkable, Mrs. Boothe? Was it very grand?"

"Oh no, Mr. Grey—in fact it is very close; in a way it reminded me of a time my father showed me the lower decks of a whaling ship. It is a labyrinth, a very large one—the size cannot be suspected from the outside—Mr. Soane, you see, has bought the two adjoining properties and combined them into a single house, though you cannot tell from the street. The hallways—which sometimes cut into open spaces three or four stories high, open from the ceiling to the basement—are lined with his collection. This stone from Egypt, that glass from Rome, this pot from Canton. This drawing from the collection of Mr. Christopher Wren, or that painting from Venice. Mr. Canalo?"

"Canaletto, perhaps?"

"Yes, I believe that sounds correct. And models of buildings— did you know there was a proposal for the Bank of England to be designed as a sort of Greek or Roman ruin? With vaults and offices tucked among bare arches and columns intended to look as if they'd survived a thousand years' weather."

What an idiotic design that would have been, thought Grey. "Fascinating," he said.

"I tell you, Mr. Grey, I believe I could have spent days there and not passed my eyes over the same object twice. And I am certain, had it not been for our guide, I would never have found my way back to Mr. Soane's entry hall. Truly it was a maze."

"I trust there was no Minotaur there, Mrs. Boothe," said Grey.

"'Minotaur,' Mr. Grey?"

"Oh, well—there is a Greek legend about a man who was half bull, who was trapped at the center of a labyrinth to keep him from running amok."

"Why a labyrinth, Mr. Grey, and not simply a locked room?"

Grey had never considered that.

"I don't know," said Grey. "That would certainly have been a simpler solution. Perhaps because it would have been less dramatic. Like the Bank of England compared to a ruined Bank of England. But it is puzzling, Mrs. Boothe."

"Well, a good puzzle is its own justification, I have often thought."

"Indeed," said Grey.

For a moment they walked on in a pleasant silence.

"Let me pose this to you, Mrs. Boothe, if I may. Why does a mirror reverse an image left to right but not top to bottom?"

Mrs. Boothe took a moment to answer. "Well, Mr. Grey," she said, "it does not reverse things at all, does it? In a mirror, the left side of your face is still on the left side of the mirror. It is reversed only if you imagine yourself in the place of the mirror-you—that is, facing the other direction. The mirror-you has your right hand for his left hand, which seems backwards. But in fact, the mirror is simply showing things where they are—your left hand on the left side of the mirror, and your head at the top."

For another moment they walked on in silence.

"You are a remarkable woman, Mrs. Boothe," said Grey at last.

ONCE MRS. BOOTHE'S CHILDREN had been returned from the minister's wife, Grey would sometimes remain at The Try Pot into the evening, when Mrs. Boothe would be busy with her work, and Mr. Hubble would, in partial consequence, become anxious to make Grey feel at home. Often, over drinks for which Grey was never permitted to pay, they would discuss music or sailing and— with distressing regularity—play backgammon. Hubble was a voracious, if rather haphazard, collector of skills, and was a great hand at backgammon, which Grey had previously considered a game of chance. Hubble took, perhaps, nine games out of ten, and occasionally they would switch to chess to allow Grey to recover some of his own. It was during one of these chess games that a boy of about ten arrived at The Try Pot, red-faced and out of breath, saying Mrs. Hubble had sent him to say that he was needed at home immediately. An important man with important business was there waiting for him. Grey asked the boy who the man was, but the boy didn't know. Grey asked if Mrs. Hubble knew him, and the boy said he didn't know.

Resigning the game and making his apologies to Mr. Hubble, he gave the boy sixpence for the message and six more for dinner, retrieved Casca from the stables and rode hurriedly home. Who was his visitor? Grey hoped it was one of Sir Edward's men recalling him to London for a new assignment. Much as he was enjoying his time with Mrs. Boothe et al., he felt as if he were moldering out in the country and yearned for more active employment.

Canfield was waiting for him at his front door, taking Casca's halter while Grey stamped some mud off his boots and walked inside. Mrs. Hubble was standing in the foyer, waiting; she apologized for having summoned him, as if it were her place; Grey silenced her apologies as unnecessary, and Mrs. Hubble gestured to the sitting room, where a man was standing in front of the fireplace, looking absently into the flames.

It was Philo Parker. The long, matted hair and beard were gone now, leaving in their place short, neatly trimmed hair and a mustache.

"Parker, dear fellow, what in God's name brings you here?" said Grey, walking quickly up to him with his hand out.

Parker shook it and mustered a weary smile.

"It's good to see you, Grey," said Parker. "I wish I were here on happier business."

"Please to have a seat and tell me what the matter is."

The two men sat opposite each other in wingbacks aimed diagonally at the fire.

"I arrived in Gibraltar a week or two, I believe, after you left it. I was sailing with *Congress* and *Constellation*, on their way to relieve the Mediterranean squadron. Changing of the pirate guards."

Grey nodded.

"Inquiring at considerable length, I was unable to locate Corporal O'Bannon. I found the room where he was staying, and spoke to your admiral Cornwallis, who assured me I should find him about the town. By the time the squadron moved on, sailing for Malta, I had become certain that he had been pressed into service on one of your navy's ships."

Grey's face tightened. Cornwallis had assured him that O'Bannon would be protected from the press gangs . . . but Grey was fully aware that the gangs were laws onto themselves. Once a man is on a boat for Canton, he can't very well report you to the powers that be. An American pressed illegally had only one recourse—to write to the Admiralty court pleading his case. The correspondence was liable to take years—and as often as not, the petition was rejected on the basis that the American could not *prove* he was American. With Britain's survival dependent on her navy, and her navy dependent on finding enough men to hand, reef, and steer her ships, the gangs were given every latitude. And while he waited for his appeal to be heard, the pressed American received no pay, despite being forced to work as if he were a regular member of a ship's company. If he were injured during the period of his appeal, he would simply be put ashore—no stipend, no fee for a seaman's hospital. His only alternative was to enter his name in the ship's books, which was the tacit acceptance of his status as a subject of the British Crown. From that point on, he forfeited his right to plead his case—and if he then tried to escape, he would be labeled a deserter, condemned to be hanged by any ship of the Royal Navy that he might subsequently encounter. It was an impossible choice, and a disgrace to Britain—often debated, and often defended as a legitimate response to American merchantmen "stealing" British sailors with offers of higher pay.

Grey was silent for some time before answering Parker.

"Have you spoken to your ambassador here?"

"Yes," said Parker. "And to various men at your admiralty. Admiral Cornwallis was kind enough to give me a letter of introduction. I am assured by any number of these men that they will assiduously look into the matter; that of course there can be no question of impressing American marines; that they will take every possible course to finding the corporal, or a satisfactory explanation. One vice admiral I spoke to had the almighty gall to suggest he might have enlisted in the Royal Navy voluntarily. I provided them with a list of all the British ships I know to have touched at Gibraltar during the time O'Bannon was there—but the roads are so thickly packed, it is impossible to know if I discovered them all."

Grey set his jaw. "I'm very sorry, Parker."

"I don't doubt it, Grey. The reason I'm here—and I hope you won't take this amiss—is that I don't trust your government or your admiralty. But I trust you."

Grey nodded. "Have you the list of the ships?"

"Yes," said Parker, pulling a folded leaf from his pocket and handing it over.

"I'll see that he's found," said Grey. "Let it sit with me."

Parker nodded. "Thank you."

He stood. "I won't take up any more of your time, Grey, and I must be going. I've an appointment in Paris."

"In Paris?" said Grey, following Parker to his feet.

"Yes," said Parker, with a hint of an ironic smile, "Paris. As I said, Grey, I trust you, and if I could say more, I would. In a month or two you'll read of it in the papers, I'd guess."

Grey nodded. "Are you certain I can't put you up for the night? Give you a hot meal and fresh horse for the morning?"

"No," said Parker. "I wish I could accept the invitation, but I'm bespoke. Your Mrs. Hubble has fed me already, I should say, and very well; my horse is more than fresh enough and I have miles to go before I sleep."

They walked together to Grey's threshold and shook hands.

"When I've found O'Bannon, whom should I tell?"

"Our man at the Court of St. James's. James Monroe."

"Very well, Parker. God speed you."

"And you," said Parker, turning and walking into the night, towards Grey's stable—then stopping and turning back. "I almost forgot: I was favored with a meeting with your Mr. Aaron Willys. I told him you were my next port of call, and he gave me this, asked me to deliver it to you."

Parker produced a small, sealed letter from his pocket and handed it over.

"Thank you," said Grey.

Parker nodded and resumed his walk to the stable. Grey opened the folded letter.

Tom— A quick note to find you by Mr. Parker—you sent me a letter to forward to Lord Elgin, if I could suss out his location. I have. He had the misfortune of being in France when the Amiens peace broke, and Bones had him arrested. Perhaps he wants the marbles in exchange for the Rosetta Stone; perhaps he's just being bloody-minded. Elgin is in the prison of Lourdes, in the Pyrenees, and at present, incommunicado. Lady Elgin is detained in Paris. Will let you know if I learn anything further. Yours, etc. —Willys

Grey leaned a moment on the doorjamb and hung his head. What an insufferable world.

36

BEFORE NOON THE FOLLOWING DAY, Grey was back in London, sitting in Sir Edward's office, asking about O'Bannon.

"Independent of the actions of the Admiralty Board," Sir Edward was saying, "I will be sending letters in my own name in search of those ships, as well as letters to the commanders of each of our naval stations emphasizing the importance of Corporal O'Bannon being located and released to an American vessel with all possible speed. The clerks are making reams of fair copies now."

"Thank you, sir."

"Well, I daresay it's the least we can do after the service he did us in getting you back to Gibraltar."

"Speaking of which, sir—I would like your permission to go back to Gibraltar."

Sir Edward exhaled a puff of smoke and removed his pipe from his mouth.

"Why? To look for O'Bannon yourself? You certainly won't be able to do any more than Mr. Parker has done."

"I believe our officers will be more candid with me than with an American. Certainly on this particular subject."

"You may be right, Thomas, but I don't like the idea of another excursion so soon. I had wanted you to take a leave of six months, six months ago."

"Yes, sir. I appreciate that fact. But I'm honor bound to do this."

"Will you give me your word to keep the journey as brief and as . . . civil as is possible?"

"I will give my word to try, sir."

Sir Edward took a long draw on his pipe.

"Very well, Tom. Travel on your own account, but have Willys give you a protection to carry."

"Thank you, sir."

Grey stood up, but was stopped by Sir Edward with a wave of his pipestem.

"Another moment, Thomas. Gibraltar, as you may have heard, is not far from the Pyrenees. I trust you won't attempt to involve yourself with Lord Elgin. I enjoy a Greek pediment as much as the next man, but this matter is entirely beyond your remit. And it will stay there. In any case, I've received this letter from Lord Hawkesbury, who is acting as secretary in this manner. A duplicate of the response he's just sent to Lady Elgin in Paris. It reads:

"'Madam, I have received the honor of your ladyship's letter, which I lost no time in laying before His Majesty. It would have given His Majesty the most sincere satisfaction to have contributed to the release of Lord Elgin by allowing his exchange for General Boyer— but a sense of duty renders it impossible for him in any way to admit or sanction the principle of exchanging persons made prisoners according to the laws of war, against any of his own subjects who have been detained in France in violation of the law of nations and of the pledged faith of the French government.

"'The account of the imprisonment of General Boyer was wholly without foundation. That officer has never been in confinement, but has been considered merely as a prisoner of war on parole, and is at present residing at Chesterfield in the enjoyment of as much liberty as is ever accorded to persons in similar situations.

"'I can assure your ladyship that it is with very deep regret that I find myself unable to render you the assistance you desire. I should have felt the greatest pleasure in contributing by any practicable means to Lord Elgin's release and to the deliverance of your ladyship and him from the very unpleasant situation in which you have been placed by the arbitrary proceeding of the French government.

" 'I have the honor to be, Hawkesbury.' "

Grey was standing before Sir Edward's desk. "So no one is going to do anything?"

"That's what I said to Hawkesbury when he gave me this. No, in fact, the key is in the reference to General Boyer—there is apparently a rumor, much believed in Paris, that we have imprisoned a French general in some sort of English Bastille. General Boyer is currently being persuaded to correct that impression with a true account to the contrary. Hawkesbury believes that will effect Elgin's release. But he doesn't wish the boat to be rocked in advance of that. Do you understand?"

"Yes, sir," said Grey.

"Very well," said Sir Edward, replacing the letter on his desk and picking up another, beginning to read it to himself, resuming his work. "That's all, Grey."

"Thank you, sir."

A FEW HOURS LATER Grey was back at his house, packing light and, as he always did, leaving a few letters—powers of attorney, disposal of some property, and so on—for the event in which he didn't return. There was one other important thing he had to do. For this, he went to speak to Mrs. Hubble in her kitchen.

"Mr. Grey, sir," she said as he came in, and quickly wiped her hands on her apron; they had been covered in flour—she was baking. "Can I get you something?"

"No, Mrs. Hubble, in fact, I wondered if I might speak to you a moment."

"Why of course, sir," she said with the hint of a smile. "What a thing to say. Please to tell me the matter."

"Well, Mrs. Hubble, I wanted to say—well, I wanted to ask—well, you are aware, I believe, that I have been seen walking about with your sister Mrs. Boothe."

With an expression of curiosity on her face, she nodded. "Yes, Mr. Grey, I have."

"I wanted to know . . . well, as you know, Mrs. Hubble, there are scarce people of whom I think more highly than you, and scarce things more important to me than to have your good opinion."

Mrs. Hubble smiled, maternally.

"I wanted to know, Mrs. Hubble, if my attentions to your sister are a source of . . . embarrassment, in any way, for you. And to say that I hope you would tell me, in perfect candor, if they are."

"Bless your heart, Mr. Grey—no, they are not. I understand your concern, but this is the nineteenth century, sir, and she is a widow with young children. And in whose judgment should I have more faith than in yours, sir? No, I appreciate your concern, but please to do as . . . you and she think best. As for the other questions, we may cross those bridges as they appear."

Grey nodded sheepishly, and delayed his withdrawal from the kitchen long enough for Mrs. Hubble to embrace him, and make him promise to take care of himself while he was away, particularly as regarded warm meals and dry clothes, two things she felt Grey had a strong tendency to discount. He went through a more restrained parting from Canfield, the groundskeeper, who wanted to thank Grey for the loan of Josephus (since Grey had given him *Julius Caesar* to read, he had become quite preoccupied with the Roman Empire).

And then Grey was on his horse Casca (whom Canfield had named) and riding towards the final call he had to make before finding a ship bound for Gibraltar. He arrived at The Try Pot about an hour later. Mr. Hubble was sitting with his back to the piano, talking; Grey shared a quiet word with him, after which Mr. Hubble nodded and pointed to the storage room behind the bar.

That was where Grey found Angela Boothe, tallying a shipment of something or other, in casks.

"Mrs. Boothe, I'm sorry to intrude . . . May I have a moment of your time?"

She turned to him, somewhat surprised both by his appearance in the storeroom and by his vaguely nervous manner.

"Why of course, Mr. Grey. Is there something I can do for you?"

"Well," said Grey; he paused, and continued. "You see, I am bound for Portsmouth and Gibraltar. I don't know when I'll return."

Mrs. Boothe looked sorry to hear it, but nodded and said, "No doubt it will be an interesting voyage."

Grey hesitated, again feeling slightly sheepish; then said, "Mrs. Boothe—I wonder if, while I'm away, I might have the privilege of writing to you."

She smiled.

"I would be very glad if you did, Mr. Grey."

The End

Epilogue

LIKE SIR EDWARD BANKS, Henry Dearborn hated wigs; unlike Sir
Edward Banks, he was an American, and therefore never had to
wear them. While some men in Washington did, the style of dressing was, by 1804, already notoriously informal—so much so that
a not-entirely-trivial diplomatic incident had occurred when the
newly delegated British ambassador, Anthony Merry, arrived at the
White House, escorted by Secretary of State James Madison, to be
introduced to President Thomas Jefferson. Merry was dressed in a
dark blue, gold-trimmed velvet coat, silk breeches and stockings,
polished buckle shoes and a ceremonial sword—and a wig—and he
was greeted at the door by no one. There were no servants, no butler, just Madison, who—looking around and seeing no one in the
public rooms at the front of the building—led Merry back to Jefferson's private study, where the Envoy Extraordinary and Minister
Plenipotentiary from the Court of St. James's was greeted by the
President of the United States, who was wearing bedroom slippers.
Merry wrote of the incident to Lord Hawkesbury, saying that "Mr.
Jefferson" was "actually standing in slippers down at the heels, and
his pantaloons, coat and underclothes indicative of utter slovenliness
and indifference to appearances, and in a state of negligence actually
studied." So, that Secretary of War Dearborn eschewed wigs drew
comment from no one.

There were other similarities between Sir Edward and Henry Dearborn; also some considerable differences. Sir Edward had one job—leading His Majesty's secret intelligence service, beneath the umbrella of His Royal Navy. Hundreds of men reported directly to Sir Edward. Secretary Dearborn, on the other hand, was in charge of the entire American military establishment—which had no standing army and a tiny navy. The entire staff of the Washington war office was fewer than a dozen men.

George Washington had been a great proponent of military intelligence, but with little military to gather it, American spying had essentially ended with the disbanding of the revolutionary army. Thomas Jefferson, though a determined opponent of a standing army, had revived the practice. Intending this new service to keep the United States out of wars, he decided it would not be a military organization, but for simplicity's sake, it was formed under the umbrella of the War Department. It carried the innocuous name Department of Topographic Engineers. That is to say, surveyors, of the landscape and whatever happened to be on that landscape. The first "Topogs," as they came to be called, were Philo Parker and his friend Meriwether Lewis; the group was soon expanded to include, among others, Parker and Lewis's mutual friend William Clark. Lewis and, in time, Clark formed the core of an intelligence group dedicated to America's West, nicknamed the Corps of Discovery. Parker, meanwhile, was detailed to the powers of the old world, prompting him to nickname his own group the Corps of Rediscovery, though he kept the name out of official papers.

In any case, Parker had been sent to Paris because Dearborn trusted him, and because Dearborn did not trust America's ambassador to France. He was John Armstrong Jr., a very capable man, and a very capable soldier. During the revolution, Armstrong and Dearborn had served on General Horatio Gates's staff together, until Dearborn had been requisitioned by General Washington. Dearborn knew, though he had been sworn to secrecy by Washington himself, that Armstrong had been the author of a letter to Washington proposing a military coup, to seize power from the Continental

Congress in retaliation for the Congress having repeatedly reneged on commitments to the men of the Continental Army. Washington, though expressing sympathy with the plight of the men for whom Armstrong had been chosen to speak, crushed the idea in no uncertain terms, telling Armstrong et al.,

> *in the name of our common country, as you value your own sacred honor, as you respect the rights of humanity, and as you regard the military and national character of America, to express your utmost horror and detestation of the man who wishes, under any specious pretenses, to overturn the liberties of our country, and who wickedly attempts to open the flood gates of civil discord, and deluge our rising empire in blood.*
>
> *By thus determining, and thus acting, you will pursue the plain and direct road to the attainment of your wishes; you will defeat the insidious designs of our enemies, who are compelled to resort from open force to secret artifice. You will give one more distinguished proof of unexampled patriotism and patient virtue, rising superior to the pressure of the most complicated sufferings: and you will, by the dignity of your conduct, afford occasion for posterity to say, when speaking of the glorious example you have exhibited to mankind—"Had this day been wanting, the world had never seen the last stage of perfection to which human nature is capable of attaining."*

Armstrong and the others took his advice, and Washington let the matter drop. And the Congress eventually made good on its obligations. That had been twenty years ago. Dearborn had not forgotten. As the matter in hand *now* involved exactly what Armstrong had once proposed for the United States—a military takeover of the democratic process—Dearborn was unwilling to rely on any account or analysis Armstrong might provide. So, by a letter that was delivered when the fleet arrived at Isla Cangrejo, Dearborn had detailed Parker to give him a second opinion of the event. The event which was just now beginning.

Where in the crowd of five thousand Armstrong stood, Parker

did not know. He had not made his presence known to the ambassador. For the moment, he was just another spectator, following a procession. It was led by a bishop on a mule, holding the papal crucifix; behind it walked the pope himself—Pius VII—and a substantial Vatican coterie. Parker joined the part of the crowd that now went ahead of the pope, to take their places in the cathedral of Notre-Dame de Paris. The choir began to sing the Palestrina choral *Tu es Petrus*, and the pope entered, through the western portal, and walked slowly to a throne set beside the altar. A moment later a cannon fired outside—apparently a signal cannon, informing the second precession that it was time to depart the palace at the Tuileries. It was perhaps an hour before this second procession arrived. It was announced by the intense cheering of the crowds on Notre-Dame's steps. And then, in gold-trimmed white satin, wearing a laurel wreath like a Caesar, First Consul for Life Napoleon Bonaparte appeared in the entrance to the nave. Josephine entered next and stood beside him, in a matching dress. Following the path of the pope, they approached the crossing. Napoleon's throne was set not beside the altar, but directly before it; Josephine's somewhat more modest throne sat to Napoleon's left. Once they were seated, the pope began the ceremony, mostly in Latin. Gigantic ermine-trimmed robes, each requiring four men to carry them, were brought forth, blessed by the pope, and then placed, in turn, on the shoulders of Napoleon and Josephine. Then came livery collars, scepters, crucifixes—all the regal symbols of office, blessed by the pope, in pairs of two, with each of Napoleon's accoutrements being accompanied by a feminine version for Josephine.

Parker noted that Napoleon twice stifled a yawn, which struck him as peculiar—surely this was the culmination of everything Napoleon had worked for—was he somehow indifferent to the proceedings? Was he bored? Perhaps he had had a sleepless night.

The pope anointed Napoleon with the triple unction on the head and both hands, and Napoleon suppressed a momentary reflex to wipe his hands clean. Now the pope anointed Josephine in the same way and switched to French, for the benefit of the spectators, saying,

"Diffuse, O Lord, by my hands, the treasures of your grace and benediction on your servant, Napoleon, whom, in spite of our personal unworthiness, we this day anoint emperor, in your name." Napoleon removed his crown of laurels and the pope picked up the so-called Crown of Charlemagne from the altar. He approached Napoleon to crown him, but Napoleon stopped him with a raised hand. The pope looked at Napoleon blankly; Napoleon stepped forward, took the crown from the pope, and placed it on his head himself.

Notre-Dame had been under intense repair in preparation for this day. It had nearly been demolished at the hands of the aggressively atheistic Jacobins, and now, during the ceremony, several bits of the part-crumbling cathedral fell from the walls and ceiling, into the crowd. At the moment Napoleon crowned himself, a walnut-sized chunk of stone fell from the ceiling and hit his shoulder. He continued as if he hadn't felt it, though Parker was sure it would leave a tremendous welt—and that if Napoleon had not been wearing his fancy, ermine-lined outfit, it would have broken bone.

This done, Napoleon removed the Crown of Charlemagne and accepted a smaller, simpler crown, with only a crucifix on it. He waved Josephine forward, and as she knelt before him, he removed this crown from his head and, declaring her Empress Josephine, placed it daintily on her head. Then he shifted it a little, lifted it up, shifted it around again, arranged it *just so*, with a light, airy smile on his face—drawing laughter and applause from the crowd. Two sounds, Parker imagined, not generally heard in Notre-Dame. The man certainly knew how to endear himself to his people.

A gigantic orchestra in the choir played celebratory, royal music, interspersed with hymns, and then the pope led mass. At its conclusion, he added a prayer for the Virgin Mother, the patron saint of the cathedral, and—in French, speaking to Napoleon—"May God confirm you on this throne, and may Christ give you to rule with him in his eternal kingdom"; then—in Latin, to the crowd, "May the emperor live forever!" Then he withdrew to a chapel, before the commencement of a civil ceremony, of which he perhaps did not approve.

The president of the Senate, the president of the Legislature, and the president of the Council of State were now called forward. One of them—Parker didn't know which was which—held a Bible on which Napoleon placed his hand, while the other two held a parchment for him to read off. It was the first time Parker had heard the voice of the most powerful man in the world. It carried well but had an unpleasant rasp to it, and—noticeable even to Parker—a distinct Corsican accent.

"I swear to maintain the integrity of the territory of the Republic," recited Napoleon, "to respect and enforce respect for the Concordat and freedom of religion, equality of rights, political and civil liberty, the irrevocability of the sale of national lands, not to raise any tax except in virtue of the law, to maintain the institution of the Legion of Honor, and to govern in the sole interest of the happiness and glory of the French people."

Someone—Parker couldn't see who—shouted, "The thrice glorious and thrice august Emperor Napoleon is crowned and enthroned. Long live the emperor!" The choir began to sing an unfamiliar hymn, with the Latin lyric "God save our emperor Napoleon," and Napoleon, with Josephine beside him, walked slowly back up the nave, and out the cathedral's west end. As he exited, the crowd that had followed him from the Tuileries, mostly unable to fit inside, exploded in shouts of adulation.

Around Parker, the interior crowd began to break up and make its way towards the various passages out of Notre-Dame. Parker moved along with them, thinking that the world was a very different place than it had been that morning.

"Emperor Napoleon the First." This ceremony was the official seal on the proclamation that the first test of democracy in Europe had failed. And Parker had no idea what would happen next.

Coda

In Vienna, Ferdinand Ries walked into Beethoven's study, where Beethoven was sitting at his piano, deep in thought and plucking notes. G, G, G, E-flat. G, G, G, E-flat. Ries hesitated ever to interrupt Beethoven at his work, but Beethoven had told him to be quick in returning the original manuscript of the *Sinfonia Bonaparte*, which Ries had been copying. Ries was, in fact, returning from his delivery of his fair-writ copy of the symphony to Beethoven's publisher.

He also had news to deliver.

For a few moments he stood silently in the doorway, hoping Beethoven would notice him, saving him the embarrassment of having to announce himself during the maestro's work. After a minute or so, Beethoven glanced back over his shoulder and said:

"Ries. What?"

"Your original, sir," said Ries, loudly.

Beethoven's hearing had grown substantially worse over the last few years, the symptom of an illness that had begun when an incompetent singer sent him into a explosive rage.

"Put it on the table and go," said Beethoven, who spoke in a normal conversational tone, either still able to hear himself or not needing to.

"Yes, sir. I have also some news."

"Yes? What is it?"

"Napoleon has declared himself emperor."

Beethoven stood and approached Ries.

"Say that again, and very clearly."

"Napoleon has declared himself an emperor."

"So," said Beethoven.

He nodded, to no one. Then he picked up a tabletop music stand and hurled it into the wall, smashing it apart and chipping the plaster.

"So!" said Beethoven, now shouting. "So he is no more than a common mortal! Now he too will tread underfoot the rights of Man! And indulge only his ambition! Now he will think himself superior to all other men, and become a tyrant."

Beethoven swiped at the top of the score of the *Sinfonia Bonaparte*, sending pages flying, grabbing the title page and tearing it in half, throwing it to the floor. He grabbed a clean leaf of paper and began to write, speaking aloud to Ries as he did.

"Ries, you will carry this at once to the publisher, and be certain that this is the name under which the score will be printed. *Composta per festeggiare il sovvenire di un grand' uomo*—composed to celebrate the *memory* of a great man—the *Eroica* Symphony."

Historical Note

NEXT TO THE FIRST TWO BOOKS in the Thomas Grey series, *The Montevideo Brief* may seem a little theatrical at times; pirates always do. But everything that happens in the story—even the pirate stuff—is pretty well anchored in historical fact. Starting with the Tripolitan War: aside from the addition of Philo Parker, everything described in the prologue is, though abridged, exactly as it happened.

Isla Cangrejo is not a real island but rather a composite island based on several real places. Pirate islands, and pirate colonies—despite seeming like they were invented for Hollywood—are a historical fact, and for most of the age of sail, could be found all over the place. There are some particularly famous ones like Tortuga, off the coast of Hispaniola, and Nassau, now the capital of the Bahamas, or—several hundred years before the events of this novel—Port Royal, in Jamaica. What is now the country Belize was founded by pirates. Jean Lafitte—a very interesting character, who would go on to be an American war hero defending New Orleans from the British during the War of 1812—really did have a sort of pirate empire. In fact, several of his personal pirate islands are now within the United States, including Grand Isle and Grand Terre, off the south coast of Louisiana, and Galveston Island in Texas. These were the models for Isla Cangrejo, both for its markets and its heavy defenses.

The story of the wreck of the *Desaix* (originally christened *Tyran-nicide*), is also true, though, so far as I know, her cannon are still underwater.

Geologically speaking, Caldera Islands can be found all over the world; the most famous, I suppose, is either Krakatoa or San-torini, or possibly Deception Island off Antarctica. Or, if it counts (it's a borderline case), Isabela, the largest of the Galápagos Islands. They're most common in the most tectonically active parts of the world, but there are actually quite a few volcanoes in Latin America. The southern half of the Caribbean island of Montserrat is still an uninhabitable "exclusion zone" of volcanic dangerousness. Its Sou-frière Hills volcano erupted in 1995, burying the island's capital city of Plymouth under forty feet of ash and mud.

Isla Cangrejo also owes a little of its composition to the Brazilian island Ilha da Queimada Grande. Though none of Latin America is suffering a snake shortage, Queimada Grande takes its snake situa-tion to a bizarre, almost comical level; I've always wanted to write about it, but the opportunity has never presented itself. It's a tiny island, of roughly 430,000 square yards, with an estimated popu-lation of 430,000 golden lancehead vipers on it. I.e., one extremely venomous, ill-tempered snake per square yard. No one lives there and no one is allowed to go there, but someday it will be the setting of the most ambitious reality TV show of all time. But I digress.

The American navy really did launch an enormous campaign to root out these Caribbean pirate colonies—a sort of sequel to the Barbary Wars—and USS *Congress* really was one of the flagships. However, most of that took place after, rather than before, the War of 1812.

And, incidentally, the story of Black Bart raising his Jolly Roger in Trepassey harbor, in Newfoundland, in 1720—so terrifying the crews of every single ship in the harbor that they instantly surren-dered and escaped to shore—is also (apparently) a true story.

Leaving pirates behind: the story of Manuel Godoy, of the secret treaty and the treasure fleet, is all real. Some of the minor characters and minor details are fictional, but the details of the treaty, and all the details of the treasure fleet itself, as well as the battle between the two sets of four frigates, are factual. Like the *Philadelphia*'s magazine, the magazine of the *Mercedes* did explode and totally destroy the ship. The two men being killed by her figurehead is actually from the semihistorical account of the incident written by my particular literary hero, Patrick O'Brian, in his novel *Post Captain*. I haven't been able to work out if that detail was fact or his creation, but in deference to him, I included it.

I want to include this, too, though it's not strictly relevant: The destruction of the *Mercedes* has a sad epilogue, playing out two hundred years after its explosion. A group called Odyssey Marine Exploration discovered the wreck in the early 2000s and went on to recover seventeen tons of artifacts and treasure from it, worth something like half a billion dollars. Despite the wreck being in international waters, and the Spanish government not having lifted a finger to recover the *Mercedes* itself, the Spanish government sued, and after five years of legal nonsense, the United States Supreme Court forced Odyssey to give the treasure to Spain, along with a million dollars' cash compensation.

As to whether Spain was in the right, I express no opinion. (Peru, where the treasure was mined, is now, I believe, suing Spain to re-recover it.) But there's a larger, sadder point. For treasure hunters, half a billion dollars is an utterly life-changing discovery. For a national government—let alone the thirteenth- or fourteenth-wealthiest country in the world, which Spain is—it's nearly nothing. If my math is right, the value of the treasure is equal to one-third of one-tenth of one percent of Spain's annual gross domestic product. So the money question means nothing to Spain and everything to treasure hunters—not just these treasure hunters, but all treasure hunters—and we—people interested in maritime history, and more broadly, everyone—are much the poorer for it. Treasure hunters—private adventurers and private investors—have discovered an enormous number of wrecks and generated an incalculable quantity of historical knowledge at no cost to anyone other than themselves. The explorers mostly do it for the adventure; the investors, though no doubt interested in the adventure angle, expect a return on their investment. Neither they nor the explorers expect (or should expect) to spend five years in court only to lose all their work, all their investment, and pay a million-dollar fine to boot. What incentive will investors have, in the future, to foot the bill for finding wrecks like the *Mercedes*? The adventurers may want to go anyway, but, to quote *The Right Stuff*, no bucks, no Buck Rogers. So who will discover these wrecks and recover their artifacts? National governments? The ship was a few dozen miles from Spain for two hundred years and they didn't go out and find it.

The Spanish government could have taken the windfall of having their history discovered without having to risk any money on the attempt, purchased the treasure instead of suing for it, and everyone would have come out happy. Instead, they helped drive a lot of romance and adventure out of the world, and will help keep a lot of history buried. That's how I see it, anyway. (Assuming the version of the story I've heard is accurate; it's possible Madrid remembers things differently.)

In any case—back to our story:

The Department of Topographic Engineers and the Corps of Discovery were real. Though it wasn't officially chartered until 1838, the Department of Topographic Engineers is considered to have had its genesis in the Lewis & Clark expedition—whose beginning, for point of reference, was January 18th, 1803, when Jefferson formally (though secretly) put the idea for it to Congress. Training and preparation began on March 15th, 1803, and the expedition got underway on August 31st, 1803. Lewis carried with him a Girandoni repeating air rifle.

Real tennis, as it is generally called, or court tennis, was, of course, a real game, and the progenitor of modern lawn tennis, now generally called just tennis, and often not even played on lawns. (For shame.) Despite the archaic complexity of the rules, there is still a world championship, contested every two years. It is, evidently, the oldest sports world championship that still exists. It dates back to 1740 and the championship of Clergé de Elder. There are lots of interesting details that I couldn't logically work into the book—the asymmetrical shape of the rackets, or the fact that, even today, real tennis balls are not manufactured, but handmade by every individual real tennis club, of which there are about five dozen in the world. The balls, therefore, vary (as, incidentally, do the specific size and layout of the universal court features), and though superficially the balls seem similar to modern tennis balls, they are much harder and less bouncy, and have doubtless killed some players over the last quarter millennium.

The recounting of Napoleon's coronation—aside from having been cut for time—is precisely accurate. Much of the description comes from the memoirs of Laure Junot, Duchesse d'Abrantès, a famous wit and beauty with whom Napoleon was close friends for most of his life. She is the source for the stone hitting Napoleon's shoulder, as well as his inclination to wipe the anointing oil off his hands, and his playfulness in crowning Josephine, as well as the better-known details (his outfit, the order or service, etc.).

BEETHOVEN NOTE

The description Ries gives Grey of Beethoven and Haydn's friendship is correct—they were simultaneously very close and prone to feuds. Most of the grudge-holding was on Beethoven's side; Beethoven was always temperamental, and Haydn was famously likable. In fact, perhaps the only unkind remark an acquaintance ever made about him was Beethoven's saying "I never learned anything from Haydn." The two men first met when Haydn was on his way to England for the first of his highly successful tours there (it was a trip that Mozart, incidentally, advised Haydn not to make, pointing out that Haydn didn't speak the language. Haydn's famous response was, "My language is understood everywhere"). Haydn stopped at Bonn and Beethoven was presented to him; Haydn was fifty-eight and Beethoven was twenty. They met again on Haydn's return trip, after which Count Ferdinand von Waldstein arranged for Beethoven to follow Haydn to Vienna and study with him. Waldstein, who would be immortalized by Beethoven's *Waldstein* Sonata, wrote to Beethoven that he would "receive Mozart's spirit from Haydn's hands." Ultimately, though, Beethoven didn't care for Haydn's somewhat careless approach to teaching, or for Haydn's preoccupation with his own compositions rather than Beethoven's. They fell out; Beethoven had begun to study with other composers (one of them Salieri), and Haydn returned to England for another Haydn-mania concert tour. In later life, they fell in and out again several times. Haydn's affectionate nickname for Beethoven was "*der große Mogul*": the big shot. In 1795, Beethoven debuted three piano trios in a small concert to which he invited Haydn as guest of honor. Afterwards, Beethoven solicited Haydn's opinion. Haydn suggested some revision to the third of the three trios. This prompted both another feud and Beethoven's remark that he'd never learned anything from Haydn. However, shortly before Haydn's death in 1809, at a concert celebrating his life's work, *der große Mogul* Beethoven approached Haydn, kissed his forehead, then knelt and kissed his hands.

Regarding Beethoven's Third Symphony: the change of titles from "Bonaparte" to "Eroica" is entirely historical and comes straight from the memoirs of Ferdinand Ries. The account of the first private performance of the piece is more or less historical—some of it is speculative, and some of it (the audience's reaction, for instance) is taken from the first public performance, which received several reviews, all of them either negative or confused; they all say it was much too long, too new, too radical, and too bizarre, and one notes Beethoven's evident rudeness in not adequately acknowledging the audience at its conclusion. Several mention, with sadness, the departure from Beethoven's much-heralded earlier work, which was more in line with his great predecessors Haydn and Mozart.

Nowadays, of course, it is universally known to be among the greatest, and most important, pieces of music ever written: the piece which ended the "classical" age of music and began the "romantic." Interestingly, this view was already being reached by 1807 and 1808, and sometimes in the same publications that had panned the symphony to begin with. (These details come, incidentally, from *The Critical Reception of Beethoven's Compositions by His German Contempo-*

raries, volume 2, published by the University of Nebraska Press; collected, translated, and analyzed by Wayne Senner, Robin Wallace, and William Meredith.)

The ballroom which hosted that first private performance of Beethoven's Third Symphony, in the Palais Lobkowitz in Vienna, has, for the last two hundred years, been known as "Eroica Hall."

One final interesting note from Ferdinand Ries, about the *Eroica* Symphony. The mistake Grey makes in thinking one of the horns entered too early with a recapitulation of the theme was a common one, made by any number of people upon hearing the symphony for the first time. Ries writes in his memoir (translated by Frederick Noonan), "The hornist did, in fact, come in on cue. I was standing next to Beethoven and, believing that he had made a wrong entrance, I said, 'That damned hornist! Can't he count? It sounds frightfully wrong.' I believe I was in danger of getting my ears boxed. Beethoven did not forgive me for a long time."

Acknowledgments

I'D LIKE TO START by thanking the editors whom I've definitely annoyed by adding these acknowledgments after the book had already been typeset. . . . Sorry about that. Really thought I'd sent them in already! You guys are the best.

I'd like to thank the marvelous Star Lawrence, my editor, and the marvelous Nneoma Amadi-Obi, Star's assistant and my liaison with my marvelous publisher, W. W. Norton. Being edited by Star and published by Norton are two of the great thrills of my life. I am deeply grateful.

I'd like to thank Rebecca Homiski and Amy Robbins, my splendid copyeditors, whom I torment with appallingly messy manuscripts. I am grateful not only for their great editing, but for their decision not to take out a contract on me.

I'd like to thank the rest of the Norton guys that have taken this book from text file to finished product—Elisabeth Kerr, Kyle Radler, Steve Colca, Meredith McGuiness, Anna Oler, and Ingsu Liu. Champions all.

I'd like to thank my superb agent, Warren Frazier, for getting this whole thing going in the first place.

I'd like to thank my father for teaching me how to write and my mother and brother for proofreading the first draft of this book (and a bunch of other books).

I'd like to thank my parents also for never having discouraged my inchoate writing career by saying things like "learn some practical skills" or "get a real job, loser," or anything of that nature. I'm sure there were times when the temptation must have been strong.

I'd like to thank some friends who've helped out my writing over the years, catching typos and giving notes—Anthony Nicolaysen, Allison Holcomb, Beth Christenberry, Sarah Hubschman, Nimisha Jain, Angela Vasquez, Steve Socha, Kate Shapiro, Monica Mierzejewski, Chris Tasso, and John Kleinheinz.

I'd like to thank Steve Cohen for buying the New York Mets.

And finally, I'd like to condemn Major League Baseball for forcing that National League to adopt the designated hitter. Idiots.